Aunt Dimity:
Vampire Hunter

AUNT DIMITY: VAMPIRE HUNTER

NANCY ATHERTON

THORNDIKE
CHIVERS

This Large Print edition is published by Thorndike Press, Waterville, Maine, USA and by BBC Audiobooks Ltd, Bath, England.
Thorndike Press, a part of Gale, Cengage Learning.

The text of this Large Print edition is unabridged.
Other aspects of the book may vary from the original edition.
Set in 16 pt. Plantin.
Printed on permanent paper.

LIBRARY OF CONGRESS CATALOGING-IN-PUBLICATION DATA

Atherton, Nancy.
  Aunt Dimity, vampire hunter / by Nancy Atherton.
    p. cm. — (Thorndike Press large print mystery)
  ISBN-13: 978-1-4104-0655-2 (hardcover : alk. paper)
  ISBN-10: 1-4104-0655-5 (hardcover : alk. paper)
  1. Dimity, Aunt (Fictitious character) — Fiction. 2. Women detectives — England — Cotswold Hills — Fiction. 3. Cotswold Hills (England) — Fiction. 4. Vampires — Fiction. 5. Large type books. I. Title.
PS3551.T426A9349 2008b
813'.54—dc22   2008008453

BRITISH LIBRARY CATALOGUING-IN-PUBLICATION DATA AVAILABLE

Published in 2008 in the U.S. by arrangement with Viking, a member of Penguin Group (USA) Inc.
Published in 2008 in the U.K. by arrangement with the author.
U.K. Hardcover: 978 1 408 41167 4 (Chivers Large Print)
U.K. Softcover: 978 1 408 41168 1 (Camden Large Print)

Printed in the United States of America
1 2 3 4 5 6 7 12 11 10 09 08

For
Dr. Craig Thornally,
chiropractor,
and
Sarah Marron,
licensed massage therapist,
without whom this book
would never have been finished

ONE

Kit Smith hadn't eloped with Nell Harris, which was a good thing, because it meant that I wouldn't have to push my best friend, Emma Harris, off a cliff.

Before I'd left England for a summerlong vacation in the Rocky Mountains, I'd given Emma strict instructions: While I was away, she was to do everything in her power to keep her stepdaughter, Nell, from marrying her stable master, Kit Smith. If she had to send Nell to a convent and lock Kit in the tack room for a couple of months, so be it. Emma was to prevent anything of a matrimonial nature from taking place between the two in my absence, or face dire consequences upon my return.

It wasn't that I opposed the marriage. To the contrary, I was rooting for it to happen. I'd been rooting for it for so long, in fact, that it would have killed me — and possibly Emma — if it had happened while I was three thousand miles away. Luckily for Emma, it hadn't.

"I told you they wouldn't elope," she said serenely.

It was a raw and murky Tuesday afternoon in mid-October. My husband, Bill, was at work; our sons, Will and Rob, were at school; and their inestimable nanny, Annelise Sciaparelli, was in the dining room, humming softly to herself while she beaded the left sleeve of her exquisite, hand-sewn wedding dress. The wedding was still eight months away, but Annelise wasn't the sort of person who left things until the last minute.

Stanley, our black cat, had been banned from the dining room because of his unhealthy habit of pouncing on moving needles. I wasn't sure where he'd gone, but I suspected that he'd retreated to Bill's favorite armchair in the living room. Stanley had decided long ago that he was Bill's cat.

Emma Harris and I were seated at the kitchen table, sharing a pot of Earl Grey tea, a plate of fresh-baked macaroons, and the latest gossip. Although bullets of cold rain pelted the windows overlooking my waterlogged back garden, the warm oven kept the kitchen cozy.

It had been ages since Emma and I had sat down together for a good old-fashioned natter, because Emma's busy schedule usually kept her from sitting down at all. When she wasn't giving lessons to aspiring equestrians at the Anscombe Riding Center, she was tending to her large vegetable garden, or bottling the fruits thereof, or designing Web sites for demanding clients, or supervising endless repairs and improvements at Anscombe Manor, the venerable home she shared with her husband, Derek.

I'd been utterly delighted when the rotten weather and a burning desire to get away from her endless chores had driven her to my cottage for a cup of tea and a bucket of gossip. Talk of Annelise's wedding had led naturally to speculation about Kit and Nell's. The latter was, unfortunately, a very familiar topic, one we'd hashed and rehashed many times before.

"I *know* you told me that they wouldn't elope," I said. "What I can't figure out is *why*. Why hasn't Kit proposed? Why hasn't he thrown Nell over his saddle and run away with her? He and Nell are a match made in heaven. Everyone knows it, including Kit. What's holding him back?"

"He *says* it's the age thing," said Emma.

"What's age got to do with it?" I demanded impatiently. "Okay, so Kit's a little older than Nell —"

"Kit's twice as old as Nell," Emma interjected. "Nell's eighteen and Kit's thirty-six."

"So what?" I retorted. "You know as well as I do that Nell's always been old for her age. The important thing is that she loves Kit and she'll never love anyone but Kit. *Princes* proposed to her when she was at the Sorbonne, but she turned them down because they weren't Kit. You'd think he'd get the message."

"I think it's none of our business," Emma said quietly.

I clucked my tongue disdainfully and wondered, not for the first time, how two such disparate personalities could get along so well. Where Emma was calm and analytical, I was hotheaded and intuitive. Her reserved approach to matters of the heart was as alien to me as my passionate approach was to her, but it never seemed to matter. Ours was a classic case of opposites attracting.

"Of *course* it's our business," I protested. "Kit's one of our dearest friends. He'll be miserable for the rest of his life if he doesn't marry Nell, and we can't allow a friend to make himself miserable." I thumped a fist on the kitchen table, rattling the teacups.

"It's up to us to see to it that he makes the right decision."

"No, Lori, it's not up to us," Emma said evenly. "It's up to Kit."

I was about to accuse her — in a friendly way — of being cold-blooded, cowardly, and disgracefully rational when the telephone rang. I threw Emma a disgusted look as I got up to answer it, but all thoughts of her perfidy were driven from my mind when I heard the terrible voice on the other end.

"Yes," I said into the phone. "Yes, I understand. . . . Ten o'clock tomorrow morning? . . . Yes, we'll both be there. Good-bye."

My hand trembled as I hung up the telephone, but a wave of protectiveness steadied me as I glanced at a framed photograph on the kitchen wall. It was a photograph of my sons.

Will and Rob were identical twins, blessed with their father's velvety dark brown eyes as well as his sweet nature. When asked their age, they proudly replied that they were "five-and-a-half-nearly-six," but they were so tall and strong that most strangers thought they were older. To me they were still babes in arms, far too young to face the rigors of the cold, uncaring world beyond the cottage.

11

We never should have let them start school, I thought bitterly, scowling at my reflection in the photograph. We should have tutored them at home.

Home was a honey-colored stone cottage near the tiny village of Finch, in the Cotswolds, a region of rolling hills and patchwork fields in England's West Midlands. Although Bill and I were Americans, we'd lived in England long enough to feel like honorary natives. Bill ran the European branch of his family's illustrious law firm from a high-tech office in Finch, I played an active role in village affairs, and we both believed firmly that we'd found the perfect place to raise our children. Finch was small, safe, and familiar. I couldn't for the life of me remember why we'd sent the twins farther afield, but I knew exactly how to rectify our mistake.

"Lori?" said Emma, looking up at me with concern. "What is it?"

I brushed my fingertips across the photograph, returned to my seat at the kitchen table, and announced solemnly, "It's the twins. Bill and I have to withdraw them from Morningside."

Emma didn't seem to be shaken by the news. She paused to sip her tea before asking, "Why do you have to withdraw the boys

12

from Morningside?"

"Because I can't allow our sons to attend a school run by such a creepy woman," I replied.

"Miss Archer isn't creepy," Emma said.

"Yes, she is," I insisted. "The pale skin, the slick red hair, the way she stares at you over those half-glasses . . . She looks as though she rolls out of her coffin every morning, looking for fresh blood to drink. She's *scary*."

Emma nibbled delicately at the edge of a macaroon. "Remind me, Lori," she said. "Why did you and Bill enroll your five-year-old sons in a school run by a creepy, scary woman who looks like she drinks blood and sleeps in a coffin?"

"Because we were distracted," I answered firmly. "We were so impressed by Morningside's friendly teachers and cheerful classrooms that we forgot about its creepy headmistress." I drummed my fingers nervously on the table. "I bet she comes from Transylvania."

"Of course she does," Emma said dryly. "Penelope Elizabeth Archer is clearly an old Transylvanian name."

"She could have changed her name," I pointed out.

"As well as everything else in her CV?"

Emma's nostrils flared — a sure sign that she was losing patience — but her voice remained calm. "I give riding lessons to a half dozen Morningside students, Lori. Their parents talk about Miss Archer all the time. She was born in Warwickshire, she has multiple degrees from Oxford, and everyone agrees that she's a marvelous headmistress — a highly intelligent woman who's devoted her life to children."

"Yeah," I muttered. "The children of the night."

"Oh, for pity's sake," Emma said, her patience snapping. "Will you please stop tapping the table? I can't talk to you when you're fidgeting."

I folded my arms and eyed her pugnaciously.

"You've been trying to withdraw the boys from Morningside ever since you and Bill enrolled them there," she went on. "First you were afraid that they'd catch the flu from their classmates, then the measles, then head lice, then fleas. Last week you were worried about them running out of the school yard and being hit by a car. The week before that, you were afraid that a train carrying chlorine gas would derail in Upper Deeping and *poison* all the children. Now you tell me that your sons' headmistress is a bloodsucking fiend! What's next? Aliens? Leprosy? Unprovoked rhinoceros attacks?"

"Is it wrong for a mother to worry about her children?" I asked.

"You're not worried," said Emma. "You're hysterical. You're so obsessed with worst-case scenarios that you're neglecting your volunteer activities. You haven't been to the hospital in Oxford once since the boys started school. Why?"

"It's too far away," I said. "If something happened at the school —"

"You see?" said Emma. "You're out of control. You're also missing a very important point: The boys are *flourishing* at Morningside. They love their teacher and their classmates and all their little projects. They love going to school almost as much as they love spending time at the stables."

"I know," I acknowledged gloomily.

"Then why are you constantly looking for excuses to keep them at home?" Emma demanded. "I could understand it if you'd packed the twins off to boarding school, but you haven't. They attend afternoon sessions for a few hours a day, five days a week, and they're as happy as I've ever seen them. Why can't you be happy for them?"

"Will and Rob may be happy with the

15

school," I replied bleakly, "but evidently the school isn't happy with them."

Emma squinted at me uncomprehendingly.

"The telephone call was from Miss Archer," I explained. "She wants me and Bill to meet with her at the school tomorrow morning at ten o'clock. Why would she summon us to her office on a Wednesday morning if everything's hunky-dory?"

"To tell you how wonderful your sons are?" Emma ventured. "How well liked they are? What a credit they are to the school?"

"She could have done that on parents' day," I said.

"Maybe she doesn't want to make the other parents jealous," Emma suggested.

"Maybe she can't handle Will and Rob," I countered. "You know how energetic they are, Emma. They've probably broken every rule in the book out of sheer exuberance." I hunched forward and chewed a thumbnail anxiously. "Miss Archer probably wants to lecture us on the boys' home life because she thinks we've spawned a pair of unteachable delinquents."

"Your sons are neither unteachable nor delinquent," Emma said. "Rob and Will may be high-spirited, but they're perfectly well behaved. Heaven knows you've worked hard

16

enough to teach them good manners."

I snorted derisively. "Have you forgotten the incident at the village shop? When the boys read those racy tabloid headlines *out loud* to the visiting bishop? I thought the poor man would never stop blushing."

"Will and Rob were barely four years old at the time," Emma reminded me. "The bishop was impressed by their reading skills."

"I'll bet he's *still* blushing," I muttered.

"In any case," Emma continued, disregarding my comment, "I doubt that they leave tabloids lying around at Morningside for the children to read."

"All right," I conceded, "but maybe the boys have been using the naughty language they learned when we were in Colorado last summer. Bill and I talked to them about it, but they could have slipped up." I buried my face in my hands. "Miss Archer probably thinks Bill and I swear our heads off at home."

"Which you don't," said Emma. "You set a good example for the twins. They learned the naughty language by accident, and if they slip up once in a while, I'm sure their teacher can handle it without going to the headmistress." She reached over to pull my hands away from my face and peered at me encouragingly. "You'll see, Lori. Everything will be fine."

"Will it?" I asked hopelessly.

"Of course it will," Emma soothed. "I'm sure Miss Archer simply wants to give you a personal update on the boys' progress, or ask you to volunteer for a committee, or explain how badly her school needs private donations. She's just doing her job, Lori, and her job *does not* involve getting hysterical over a few swear words any more than it involves drinking her students' blood."

I wanted Emma to be right. I wanted to believe that Miss Archer had called me and Bill in for a routine meeting about committees and donations, but I couldn't shake the feeling of dread that had filled me ever since I'd spoken with her on the telephone.

"You didn't take the call," I said, shuddering. "You didn't hear Miss Archer's voice. She sounded . . . terrifying."

"Terrifying?" Emma studied me in mystified silence for a moment, then sat back, nodded, and said knowingly, "Oh. I get it."

I regarded her warily. "What do you get?"

"I get why you're afraid of Miss Archer," said Emma.

"I'm not afraid of Miss Archer," I lied.

"Yes, you are," said Emma. "You're so afraid of her that you'd rather yank the boys out of school than go to a meeting with her. And I know why." A smug grin spread over my best friend's face. "It's because of your mother."

"What about my mother?" I asked, taken aback.

"Your mother wasn't just your mother," she replied, with an air of triumph. "Your mother was also a *schoolteacher.* Even though she's been dead and gone for nearly ten years — God rest her soul — you're *still* afraid of what she'll do when she finds out that *you've* been called to the *principal's office.*"

In an instant I was transported back through time to the nightmarish afternoon when my eleven-year-old self had perched forlornly on the hard wooden chair in Mr. Shackleford's office while my mother listened gravely to the list of charges he'd drawn up against me: running in the hallway, passing notes during class, and, worst of all, talking back to a teacher. The journey home afterward had been one of the longest in recorded history. My mother hadn't shouted. She hadn't scolded. She hadn't said a single word until we were inside our apartment, when she'd said, quietly and crisply, "I don't ever want to see you in Mr. Shackleford's office again."

She never did.

"Am I right?" Emma asked.

Her question jerked me back to the present. I looked down at the table and nodded.

"I only went to the principal's office once," I confessed shamefacedly, "but it was worse than going to the dentist's."

"Did your principal have red hair and half-glasses?" Emma inquired.

"No," I said, picturing Mr. Shackleford. "He had wavy black hair and he didn't wear glasses."

"But he was terrifying?" said Emma.

"He was the *principal,* for Pete's sake," I snapped. "Isn't that terrifying enough?"

"To a child perhaps," Emma said sternly. "But you're not a child, Lori. You're a grown woman with children of your own. You should be over your fear of principals — and headmistresses — by now."

"I guess I should," I mumbled, avoiding Emma's eyes.

"Your fear will infect the boys if you're not careful," she warned. "In fact, if I were you, I wouldn't even mention the meeting to Will or Rob. After all, it may have nothing to do with them."

"I wish I had your confidence," I said, slumping back in my chair, "but I still think the twins are in trouble."

The sound of someone opening the front door came to us from the hallway, followed by a rush of cold air and my husband's voice calling, "Lori? I hope you have the kettle boiling, because I'm chilled to the bone."

"One pot of piping hot tea, coming up!" I called back, and looked at Emma in amazement. "Will wonders never cease? He must have decided to knock off work early for a change."

"The furnace broke down at the office!" Bill hollered. "Mr. Barlow will fix it, but until he does, I'm working from home."

"I should have known," I said to Emma, with a sigh. "Bill *never* knocks off work early."

"Speaking of work," she said, standing, "I'd better get back to mine. Thanks for the tea break, though. I needed it. And don't tie yourself in knots about tomorrow. I'm sure everything will be fine."

I shrugged noncommittally and busied myself with making a fresh pot of tea for my chilled husband. Emma paused to chat with him in the front hall while she put on her rain jacket and he divested himself of his. I couldn't quite catch what they were saying, but I heard a short burst of muffled laughter before Emma let herself out the front door.

A moment later Bill strode into the kitchen, rubbing his hands together. The brisk wind had reddened his handsome face, and raindrops glistened in his dark brown hair. As he took a seat at the kitchen table, he gazed at me so lovingly that I couldn't bring myself to break the bad news to him right away.

"Your tea will be ready in a minute," I told him. "Have a macaroon while you're waiting."

"Don't mind if I do," he said. He helped himself to a handful of macaroons, turned his soulful eyes toward me, and said, with the merest hint of a smirk, "I don't know why you're worried about the meeting tomorrow, Lori. I'm sure Miss Archer won't make you stay after school."

I felt myself blush crimson as the reason for the muffled laughter dawned on me.

"I'll kill Emma," I growled.

"Or clean the blackboards," Bill went on, snorting with laughter. "Or write a hundred times, 'I must not accuse my headmistress of sinking her fangs into my classmates' necks.'"

I gave him such a scathing look that he suspended his comic monologue, but he continued to chortle merrily to himself

22

through the rest of the afternoon and on into the evening. Although he agreed not to mention the meeting to the boys, he was still having fits of the giggles when we climbed into bed. By then I was ready to throttle him.

"I'm warning you," I said crossly, sitting up in bed and shaking a fist at him. "If you say one word to Miss Archer about vampires, you're toast."

"Your vish is my command, dahlink." With a fiendish laugh, Bill seized my fist and covered it with kisses.

I fell back on my pillows and groaned. If Miss Archer wasn't concerned about the boys' home life already, I told myself, she would be after she met Count Bill.

Two

Bill dropped his faux-Transylvanian accent before he left the bedroom the following morning, but he picked it up again as soon as Annelise had taken Will and Rob to Anscombe Manor for their riding lessons. After they'd gone, I spent a gruesome hour in the kitchen, listening to Bill deliver such gems as, "I vant to drink your . . . tea" and "I vill have my bacon . . . rare" before fleeing back upstairs to dress.

I was afraid Count Bill would never go away, but my husband knew better than to push a joke too far. He slipped into his suave, international-lawyer persona the minute we got into his Mercedes and didn't utter a single "vill" or "vant" all the way to Upper Deeping, the busy market town in which Morningside School was located.

The rain had tapered off during the night, but a chill mist clung to Upper Deeping's sidewalks, and the sky was as gray and leaden as my mood. My husband's apparent willingness to take the situation seriously should have heartened me, but I was beyond heartening. I'd spent half the night imagining the myriad ways in which a pair of energetic and intelligent five-year-olds could aggravate a humorless headmistress. By the time Bill parked the car in the school's small parking lot, I was a nervous wreck.

"Cheer up," he said as we got out of the car. "It's not as if you're going to the dentist's."

"The dentist is looking real good to me right now," I muttered dismally.

We made our way to the school's front entrance, where Ted, the security guard, checked our IDs before handing us off to Mrs. Findle, Miss Archer's stout, gray-haired personal assistant. Mrs. Findle never discussed her boss's business with a parent, so she and Bill exchanged innocuous remarks about the weather while she relieved us of our raincoats and escorted us down the long, echoing corridor to the forbidding double doors at the far end.

I was too jittery to join in the conversation. Although I'd dressed with particular care — in cashmere, Harris tweed, and classic pearls — the closer we got to those

25

double doors, the more I felt like a guilt-ridden eleven-year-old with scraggly braids, scabby knees, and dirty elbows. Half of my brain remembered that I was a responsible adult, but the other half was wishing that I hadn't blown all those spitballs at Corky Campbell in the fifth grade. My legs were actually shaking when Mrs. Findle opened the double doors and ushered us into Miss Archer's office.

As far as I was concerned, Miss Archer's office was as creepy as she was. Whereas the rest of Morningside was decorated in gay primary colors, the headmistress's inner sanctum reflected the somber taste of the school's Victorian founder. In my opinion, the funereal furnishings and heavy drapes served only to accentuate the unhealthy pallor of the present headmistress's complexion and the unnatural glossiness of her tightly bound cherry-red hair.

After greeting us perfunctorily and motioning us to a pair of disturbingly familiar hard wooden chairs, Miss Archer resumed her seat behind her mahogany desk, smoothed her gray wool skirt, and began leafing through the pages in a file folder that lay open before her.

While she leafed, Bill sat back in his chair, relaxed and politely attentive. I, on the other hand, perched rigidly on the edge of mine, braced for a scolding. Old habits die hard.

An eternity seemed to pass before Miss Archer closed the folder, placed her hands on top of it, and fixed us with a penetrating stare over her black-framed half-glasses.

"I apologize for asking you to see me at such short notice, and on a workday," she began, "but a situation has arisen that requires your immediate attention." She removed her glasses, laid them on the desk, and folded her hands. "I believe you are acquainted with Louisa Lawrence."

Bill nodded. "We met Mrs. Lawrence and her husband last month, at parents' day. Their little girl, Matilda, is in our sons' class."

"Indeed, she is," Miss Archer said gravely.

I shrank back in my chair, wondering what on earth the twins had done to little Matilda Lawrence.

"I received a rather disturbing telephone call from Mrs. Lawrence yesterday," Miss Archer continued. "She informed me that Matilda has been having nightmares ever since she started school. It wasn't until the small hours of Tuesday morning that Mrs. Lawrence was able to ascertain the cause of Matilda's most recent nightmare."

"And the cause is . . . ?" Bill prompted.

27

"Your sons," Miss Archer replied succinctly.

"Will and Rob have been giving a little girl nightmares?" I said, aghast. "How?"

Miss Archer pursed her lips. "Before I answer, let me say first that no one appreciates creativity more than I. The curriculum at Morningside School is designed, in part, to nurture the creativity inherent in every child. There comes a time, however, when the creative imagination must be reined in."

"I see," said Bill, cleverly refusing to agree or disagree with Miss Archer until he'd heard specific details. My husband was a good lawyer.

"I am also cognizant of the fact that certain children have difficulty adjusting to school," Miss Archer went on. "The new setting, the new playmates, and the new routine can create a sense of disorientation that can lead particular children to act out in troublesome ways."

I wrung my hands nervously, wishing Miss Archer would come to the point. I didn't want to hear a speech about child psychology. I wanted to know exactly what my sons had done to join the ranks of Morningside's maladjusted troublemakers. Bill evidently felt the same way.

"I don't mean to rush you, Miss Archer,"

he said, crossing his legs nonchalantly, "but I'd appreciate it if you'd answer my wife's question. In what way are Rob and Will responsible for Matilda Lawrence's nightmares?"

"Matilda Lawrence is not their only victim," Miss Archer informed us, tapping the file folder with a rigid index finger. "I spoke with your sons' teacher yesterday. Miss Brightman confirmed that Will and Rob have frightened several of their fellow pupils."

"How?" I reiterated.

"Your sons have concocted a number of stories that can only be described as lurid," Miss Archer answered at last, her lip curling in distaste. "They have shared these stories with their fellow pupils, some of whom are quite impressionable. When challenged by Miss Brightman, your sons have insisted that the stories are true." Miss Archer tilted her head to one side. "While I do, to a certain extent, admire your sons' inventiveness, I am as dismayed by their inability to tell fact from fiction as I am by their willingness to repeatedly terrorize their classmates."

My nervousness fell away as my hackles rose. I would have held my tongue if Miss Archer had accused Will and Rob of disorderly conduct, but no one — not even a well-respected headmistress who scared the bejesus out of me — could accuse my sons of lying and get away with it. My boys were *always* truthful.

I squared my shoulders and gave her a look that should have made her duck for cover. "Are you suggesting that my sons are liars?"

"I'm not merely suggesting it," she responded. "I'm stating it plainly."

Bill must have realized that Miss Archer was treading on thin ice, because he put a restraining hand on my arm.

"An interesting statement, Miss Archer," he said quickly. "Do you have evidence to support it? Perhaps you can give us an example of the sort of story Will and Rob have been telling their classmates."

"I fully intend to," said Miss Archer. "Thanks to Miss Brightman, I can recount the stories quite accurately." She put on her glasses and opened the file folder. After referring to her notes, she regarded us skeptically. "In one tale a so-called bad man drags your sons from a castle on a faraway island and attempts to throw them into the sea during a tumultuous thunderstorm." She shook her head disapprovingly. "Now, *really* —"

"Ha," I interrupted, with icy disdain. "Will and Rob didn't invent *that* story. It's absolutely true. It happened less than a year ago, up in Scotland, and there was nothing 'so-called' about the bad man. The lunatic shot me in the shoulder at point-blank range." I leaned toward her. "Would you like to see the scar?"

Miss Archer peered at me over her half-glasses. "I . . . I beg your pardon?"

"We had a run-in with a stalker last April," Bill explained, adding helpfully, "It was written up in the *Times*."

"Yet you didn't see fit to mention it to me when we discussed your sons' home life?" Miss Archer said, gazing at us in disbelief.

"It wasn't part of their home life," I said defensively. "It's not the sort of thing that happens every day."

"I should hope not." Miss Archer blinked owlishly at us, then looked down at her notes and soldiered on. "Your sons also claim that an invisible man taught them how to curse."

"Also true," I confirmed. "The man wasn't really invisible, of course, but Will and Rob couldn't see him because he was tunneling underneath their floorboards. They could hear his voice, though, and he was a foul-mouthed old coot."

"A . . . a foul-mouthed old coot was tunneling beneath your sons' floorboards?" Miss Archer said, her eyes widening.

"Actually, he was using a tunnel that was already there," I told her brightly. "It happened in an old mining district in Colorado, where we spent the summer, so he had a lot of mine shafts to choose from."

"Naturally." Miss Archer clasped her hands and tapped the tips of her thumbs together. "I can only presume that since the tunneling incident happened overseas, you didn't consider *it* worth noting either when we discussed the boys' home life."

"Correct," I acknowledged. "Besides, you didn't ask us about our summer vacation."

"Rest assured, I shall do so from now on." Miss Archer cleared her throat and turned a page in the file folder. "And the story about the mountain exploding in the dead of night? Is it true as well?"

"It is," I assured her. "There are court records to prove it, though you'd have to go to Colorado to find them."

"My word," Miss Archer said. "What colorful lives you lead." She looked from me to Bill, then said, almost pleadingly, "But the story about the vampire can't possibly be true." She hesitated. "Can it?"

"V-vampire?" I stammered, brought up

short. "The boys told a story about a *vampire?* How could they? We've never met one."

"I can't tell you how relieved I am to hear it," said Miss Archer, raising a limp hand to her brow. "Most experts agree that vampires are imaginary creatures, but with your . . . er, dramatic history, it seemed almost possible . . ." Her words trailed off into silence.

I stared in puzzlement at a point just above Miss Archer's left shoulder until a sudden flash of insight told me who must have put the idea of vampires into the twins' heads. I shot an accusatory glance in Bill's direction — only to find *him* glaring accusingly at *me.* It was transparently clear that he suspected me of telling the boys about bloodsucking headmistresses, just as I suspected him of practicing his Count Bill routine in front of them. He raised an eyebrow to signal that we'd discuss our mutual suspicions later, then turned a look of innocent perplexity on Miss Archer.

"I'm afraid we're unfamiliar with the vampire tale," he said. "What have our sons been saying?"

"They claim to have seen one," Miss Archer replied.

"Where?" I asked. "When?"

Miss Archer glanced down at her notes.

33

"They explained to Miss Brightman that a vampire appeared to them while they were riding their ponies at the Anscombe Riding Center. They didn't mention a specific time or date." She flipped a page over, then looked at us. "According to Mrs. Lawrence, however, Matilda suffered her first vampire nightmare on Monday night, so I assume that the story is a relatively new one."

"We'll look into it," Bill told Miss Archer. "As for the other stories —"

"We won't ask the boys to lie," I declared adamantly. "Our sons can't help it if they've faced more scary situations than the average child. Believe me, we wish they hadn't."

"Surely it's good for them to talk about it," Bill chimed in.

To my surprise, Miss Archer nodded.

"I concur," she said. "Will and Rob must be allowed to process their traumatic experiences in whatever way suits them best."

"Would you like us to keep them home from school this afternoon?" Bill inquired.

"Not at all," said Miss Archer. "I don't wish to upset their routine. I will, however, ensure that Miss Brightman curtails any storytelling in which they might engage today." She removed her glasses and gazed thoughtfully into the middle distance. "It would be helpful if you would discuss the *true* stories

— that is, the stories that *do not* involve vampires — with Miss Brightman at some point in the near future. She would then be able to discuss them with the class as a whole, in a way that might alleviate the other children's fears." She bent her head toward Bill. "May Miss Brightman contact you?"

"I look forward to her call," said Bill. "In the meantime please extend our sincere apologies to Mrs. Lawrence. Tell her that our sons never meant to give Matilda or any other child nightmares."

"I will," said Miss Archer. "Once I've described your sons' . . . er, unusual experiences to her, I'm sure she'll understand. I hope that you, in turn, will accept *my* apology for making assumptions I had no right to make. In light of what you've told me today, your sons are astonishingly well adjusted."

"They're good boys," I agreed.

"We'll have a serious talk with them tonight," Bill promised. "And we'll keep you and Miss Brightman informed on the vampire situation."

"Thank you," said Miss Archer.

She pressed a buzzer on her desk, and Mrs. Findle entered the office, carrying our raincoats. We took them from her, said good-bye to Miss Archer, and headed for the door, but before we reached it, the headmistress spoke again.

"As a matter of curiosity," she said, "what do your sons want to be when they grow up?"

I grinned. "At the moment, they want to be horses."

"Oh, no." Miss Archer shook her head. "With so much good material to choose from, they're bound to be bestselling novelists."

A glimmer of amusement lit Miss Archer's creepy eyes as she closed the file folder. I shuddered and escaped into the corridor.

THREE

"I wonder where our sons heard about vampires?" I mused aloud as we drove back to the cottage.

"Don't look at me," said Bill. "I've never mentioned the *v*-word in their presence." He gave me a sidelong glance. "What about you?"

"Not so much as a syllable," I replied, and when he pursed his lips doubtfully, I protested. "Credit me with some sense, Bill. I've never criticized Miss Archer in front of them. I certainly haven't told them that she reminds me of a bloodsucking fiend. Are you sure you haven't been entertaining them with your cheesy Dracula act?"

"Vhy vould I?" said Bill. "It is for your ears only, my dahlink."

"Hilarious," I said grimly.

"Come on, Lori," Bill cajoled, "you have to admit that it's at least a little bit funny. Our sons, the fearless vampire hunters." He shook his head, chuckling. "I'm with Miss Archer. I admire their inventiveness."

"I will, too, once I'm sure they made it all up," I said.

"Well, *of course* they made it up," said Bill. "They ran out of true stories to tell, so they manufactured a thrilling tale to impress their friends."

"Is that what you think of our sons?" I asked, scandalized. "That they're a pair of lying show-offs?"

"I think our sons are perfectly normal little boys who are learning how to get along with other children," Bill said calmly. "They're bound to make mistakes now and them. How else will they learn what's right?"

"We'll tell them," I said resolutely. "There won't be time for a proper talk after lunch, so we'll sit them down after dinner, when we have their full attention. Agreed?"

"Agreed," said Bill.

"I just hope Miss Brightman can keep them from spooking their classmates this afternoon," I said. "You may think the whole thing's a big joke, but I don't want any more Matilda Lawrences on my conscience."

"Nor do I," said Bill, patting my knee.

I reviewed the situation in silence for a

moment, then burst out plaintively, "Why haven't the twins told *us* about the vampire?"

"Maybe they didn't want to scare us," Bill reasoned. "Or maybe they've gotten so used to strange things happening that they didn't think a vampire sighting was worth mentioning."

"Oh, Bill," I moaned. "Our poor babies. What have we done to them?"

"We haven't done anything to them," Bill stated firmly. "Except make them strong enough to cope with situations that give other children nightmares."

I took some consolation from his words, but as we cruised through the mist-shrouded countryside, I couldn't help wishing that Will and Rob didn't have to be quite so strong.

The rest of the day passed in a typical blur of activity. After lunch, Annelise whisked the boys off to school, I attended a Guy Fawkes Day committee meeting at the village hall, and Bill juggled paperwork, phone calls, and e-mail at the cottage while Mr. Barlow, the local handyman, attempted to repair the malfunctioning furnace at the office in Finch.

Due to a lengthy debate as to whether the

Guy Fawkes Day bonfire should be moved from its traditional location on the village green to a new spot nearer the church — a debate that was entirely pointless, because Finch's traditionalists *always* won — I returned to the cottage much later than I'd expected. By the time I got there, the twins were already home from school and playing with their train set in the solarium.

After calling a quick hello to Bill, who was sharing desk space in the study with a deeply contented Stanley, I put a roast into the oven, set the kitchen table for dinner, and went looking for Annelise. I found her upstairs, in the boys' room, folding clean laundry and putting it away. While she sorted socks, I filled her in on our meeting with Miss Archer.

Annelise usually knew everything that was going on in the twins' lives, but the vampire story came as a complete surprise to her.

"I've never discussed vampires with them," she assured me, "or werewolves or banshees, for that matter. But childhood's filled with terrors," she went on matter-of-factly. "The bogeyman under the bed, the goblin in the garden . . . The boys were bound to hear about vampires sooner or later. Very popular these days, vampires."

"Not in this house," I declared. "I don't

want Will and Rob filling their heads with ghoulish nonsense."

"I don't know if you can stop them," said Annelise. "They're out in the world now, Lori. They're going to hear all sorts of things they don't hear at home. The best we can do is help them to sort out the truth from the nonsense."

"That's exactly what we're going to do after dinner," I said. "And by 'we' I mean all of us. I want you to be there, too. We have to present a united front on this issue."

"You can count on me," said Annelise.

"I always do," I said, and returned to the kitchen to cut up vegetables to put in with the roast.

After dinner, Annelise took the twins upstairs for their baths, then settled them in the living room with crayons and drawing paper. Bill and I spent their bath time in the kitchen, clearing the table and devising a game plan for the big talk. We decided that I would start the ball rolling and Bill would follow my lead.

We entered the living room to find Will and Rob kneeling at the coffee table, drawing pictures of their favorite subjects — their gray ponies, Thunder and Storm. Annelise

41

sat quietly by the fire, reading a novel, but she closed the book and set it aside when we came in.

Bill had to evict Stanley from his armchair before he could take possession of it. As usual, Stanley waited until Bill was seated comfortably, then leapt gracefully into his lap, where he curled into a purring black ball. I sat on the chintz sofa, facing the boys across the coffee table.

"Daddy and I were at your school this morning," I said to them. "We had a little chat with Miss Archer. She told us that you've been telling stories to the other children at school."

"Uh-huh," Will agreed, adding strands to Thunder's tail.

"Daddy and I know that *most* of your stories are true," I said, "but we wanted to ask you about one of them."

"Okay," Rob said equably.

"Did you . . ." I looked uncertainly at Bill, who gave me a supportive thumbs-up, and then I got down to the business at hand. "Have you been telling your school friends that you saw a vampire at Anscombe Manor?"

"Yes," said Will as he filled out Thunder's mane. "We saw Rendor, the Destroyer of Souls."

42

I don't know if Bill's jaw dropped, but mine did, almost to my knees.

"You saw *who?*" I asked, sitting bolt upright.

" 'Whom,' " Bill corrected automatically.

"Oh, Lord," said Annelise with a tired sigh. "I should have guessed."

I turned to her, round-eyed, wondering *what* she should have guessed.

"It's a comic book," she explained, reading the question in my eyes. "Or a graphic novel, as they're called nowadays. *Rendor, the Destroyer of Souls*. I've seen it at the bookstore in Upper Deeping. It's not meant for young children." She turned her attention to the twins. "Did someone bring a comic book to school, Rob?"

"Uh-huh." He looked over his shoulder at her. "Clive Pickle did, but it's Nigel's comic."

"Who's Nigel?" I asked.

"Clive Pickle's big brother," Rob replied, sitting back on his heels. "He's at university. Clive goes into his room and takes his things when he's away."

I made a mental note to telephone Mrs. Pickle in the morning and ask her to put Nigel's belongings under lock and key, then began the painstaking task of piecing the boys' story together.

According to them, Clive Pickle had sneaked his older brother's comic book out of the house and brought it to school several times over the past few weeks. He'd shown it freely to his pals, but he'd been clever enough to conceal it from Miss Brightman and every other adult at Morningside.

Rob and Will had regarded the comic as just another kind of storybook until they'd seen the Destroyer of Souls with their own eyes. They insisted that they'd seen Rendor in the flesh, lurking in the woods above Anscombe Manor, during their most recent trail ride.

"That would have been on Sunday," Annelise deduced. "Kit took them on a trail ride after church."

Kit Smith, the stable master at Anscombe Manor, was the boys' riding instructor as well as their trail guide.

"Clive Pickle said we didn't see Rendor," Will told us darkly, "but we did."

Further questioning revealed that Clive had made his accusation on Monday and that the twins had argued the point with him in the presence of several other children, including the highly impressionable Matilda Lawrence, who, Bill and I knew, had relayed the boys' eyewitness report to her mother after awakening from a nightmare in the wee hours of Tuesday morning.

"Did you tell Uncle Kit that you'd seen Rendor?" Bill asked.

"Uh-huh." Rob shrugged. "He didn't believe us."

"He said we saw a tree," Will clarified.

"But it was Rendor," Rob concluded placidly. "He *swooped.*"

"Swooped?" Bill said.

"Like this." Rob pulled an afghan from the sofa, wrapped it around his shoulders, and twirled in a half circle toward Annelise. The afghan swirled around him.

"Then he turned into a lot of little bats and flew away." Rob let the afghan fall to the floor and returned to the coffee table.

I gazed in fascination from his face to Will's. "Weren't you afraid?"

"No," answered Will nonchalantly. "We were on Thunder and Storm."

"They're faster than bats," Rob explained.

Bill stroked Stanley's sleek black fur for a moment, then asked, "What did Rendor look like, boys? Can you draw a picture of him?"

Will obligingly pulled a clean sheet of drawing paper from the pile on the coffee table and picked up a black crayon. Five minutes and several crayons later, he presented us with a portrait that had, I suspected, been strongly influenced by the illustrations he'd seen in Clive Pickle's comic book.

The bone-thin figure had bloodred lips and canines like stalactites. Its face was deathly pale, and it wore a voluminous black cloak with a crimson lining. A cloud of tiny bats hovered around its grotesque head, and a lightning bolt split the sky above it. Although the drawing was primitive, it was powerful enough to give *me* nightmares.

A moment of silence ensued while the grown-ups in the room pondered their next move.

Finally Bill dislodged Stanley from his lap and motioned for the boys to come to him. After they'd climbed into his lap, he put his arms around them and explained gently but firmly that Rendor wasn't real, that he was a make-believe character in a very silly book, and that Uncle Kit had been right to tell them that they'd mistaken a shadow for a vampire because *vampires did not exist.* Bill repeated the last point several times, to emphasize its importance.

He concluded his fatherly lecture by asking, "Do you both understand what I've told you?"

"Yes," said Will, nodding.

"Vampires are make-believe," Rob confirmed.

"But we saw one," added Will.

Bill sighed but responded patiently, "You saw something that *looked like* a vampire, boys. If you see *something else* that looks like a vampire, I want you to tell Mummy and Annelise and me about it. I *don't* want you to tell the kids at school."

Will frowned slightly. "But, Daddy, we —"

Bill cut him off. "Listen to me, sons. Some of your new friends are afraid of make-believe monsters. It's not nice to frighten people. You don't want to scare your friends, do you?"

"No, Daddy," the boys chorused.

"I want you to promise me you won't tell anyone at school that you saw a vampire," Bill said gravely. "Not even Clive Pickle."

The twins hesitated, as though the thought of letting Clive Pickle have the last word on vampires weighed heavily on them, but finally gave in.

"Okay, Daddy," said Rob. "We promise."

"And you'll tell one of us" — Bill touched his chest, then gestured to me and Annelise — "the next time you see someone that *looks like* Rendor?"

"Okay, Daddy," said Will.

"Good boys." Bill pulled Will and Rob

into hugs, then set them on their feet. "Time for bed, cowpokes. I can't come up with you because I have a few telephone calls to make, but I'll see you in the morning."

"G'night, Daddy," the twins said, and trotted toward the stairs.

While Annelise folded the afghan and tidied away the drawing materials on the coffee table, Bill headed for the study and I went up to tuck the boys in bed. Much to my relief, they expressed no interest whatsoever in discussing vampires, preferring instead to hear a chapter from *Brighty of the Grand Canyon* as a bedtime story. I'd have read the whole book to them if they'd asked. To my mind, Brighty, the brave and kindly mule, was the perfect antidote to Rendor, the Destroyer of Souls.

On my way downstairs, I ran into Annelise, who was on her way up to her room.

"What did you do with the drawing Will made?" I asked her quietly. "The drawing of Rendor."

"I was going to toss it on the fire," she said, "but I thought you might want another look at it, so I put it in the drawer in the kitchen."

I nodded, bade her good night, and continued down the stairs.

There were many drawers in the kitchen, but only one was universally referred to as "the" drawer. I went straight to it and extricated Will's drawing from a miscellany of chopsticks, birthday-candle holders, tea strainers, mushroom brushes, bottle openers, toy cars, toothpicks, and small plastic dinosaurs. The homeliness of the drawer's contents made the portrait of Rendor seem even more unsettling than it had when I'd first seen it.

After a brief struggle with an unruly chopstick, I closed the drawer, laid the drawing on the kitchen counter, and studied it intently. I was still gazing down at it when Bill emerged from the study, caught sight of me from the hallway, and joined me in the kitchen.

"Mr. Barlow says it'll take a week to ten days to get the parts he needs to fix the furnace," he announced. He glanced down at the drawing, then leaned back against the counter and folded his arms. "I can't work from home, Lori, not for more than one or two days. There are too many distractions, and the study isn't a fully equipped office. I need more than a laptop and a telephone to do my job properly."

"You're not thinking of going to London, are you?" I said, stunned. "For *ten days?*"

"I have to," Bill replied. "We're in the middle of sorting out the Shuttleworth bequest, which, owing to Mrs. Shuttleworth's deep and abiding love for her many, many cats, is insanely complicated. It's all hands on deck at the London office, and I have to be there to make sure the paperwork flows smoothly. We mustn't confuse Miss Muffin's trust fund with Mr. Muddy-Buddy's."

"You'd put a cat's welfare before your sons'?" I said, appalled. "Don't you understand? The boys could be in *danger*."

Bill sighed. "If I thought for one moment that the boys were in any kind of danger, I'd stay home."

I waved Will's drawing under his nose. "What about Rendor?"

"There is no Rendor, Lori," Bill reminded me.

"I *know* there's no Rendor," I said, exasperated. "But the boys saw *someone*. I'll bet there's a creepy pervert lurking in the woods above Anscombe Manor."

"You'd lose the bet," Bill said complacently. "I just finished speaking with Kit. He checked out the place where Rendor allegedly appeared to the boys, and he didn't find anything to indicate that anyone had been there — no footprints, no broken branches, no bat droppings. But there *is* a gnarly old tree that, on a misty October day, could be mistaken for a lot of things. He's convinced that the boys mistook the tree for a vampire. That's why he didn't report it to us. He thought it was too trivial to merit a phone call."

"What about the bats?" I demanded, pointing to the picture.

"Dead leaves blowing in the wind." Bill took me by the shoulders and regarded me steadily. "Kit loves Will and Rob as if they were his own sons. He's responsible for every child who sets foot in the stables. Do you really think he'd stand by and do nothing if he thought a creepy pervert was lurking anywhere near Anscombe Manor?"

"No," I answered reluctantly, "but maybe he wasn't looking in the right place."

"I spoke with Emma as well," Bill said, "and she —"

"Why didn't *she* tell me about the vampire?" I interrupted. "She was here yesterday. She could have told me then, but she didn't say a word."

"She didn't say anything because she knew you'd overreact, just as you overreacted to the telephone call from Miss Archer." Bill raised a quizzical eyebrow.

"Hmmm . . . I wonder if she was right?"

"But Kit might have missed something," I insisted.

"I don't think he did," said Bill. "Emma told me that there were nearly forty people at the manor on Sunday — children, adults, stable hands, scattered all over the property. *No one* reported seeing a stranger in the woods, no one except Will and Rob, who had vampires on the brain because of that stupid comic book. They're young, they're suggestible. They mistook a tree for a vampire." He tugged Will's drawing from my hand, crumpled it into a ball, and deposited it in the wastebasket under the sink. "End of story."

With some difficulty I swallowed my frustration and gave a short nod. "I suppose you're right."

"Have I ever been anything else?" he said, grinning. "I'll stay at the Flamborough while I'm in London."

"Naturally," I said. Bill always stayed at the Flamborough Hotel when he was in London.

"If Miss Brightman or Miss Archer wishes to speak with me," he went on, "they can reach me there or on my cell phone."

"Right," I said, trying not to look in the direction of the wastebasket.

Bill pulled me into his arms. "Coming to bed?"

"I'll be up in a little while," I told him, resting my cheek against his chest. "I have to go through my notes from the Guy Fawkes Day meeting. Peggy Taxman is chairing the next meeting, and I want to be prepared."

"You'd better be," he said, shuddering. Peggy Taxman was one of Finch's more forceful personalities. She had the same effect on Bill that Miss Archer had on me. "Peggy will have your guts for garters if you don't do your homework." He stood back and peered down at me. "No more worrying about Rendor?"

"No more worrying about Rendor," I promised, and gave him a gentle push toward the hallway. "Go to bed, Bill. If you want to beat the rush to London, you're going to need an early start."

"Too true," he acknowledged. "Good night, love."

Bill kissed me on the top of the head and went upstairs, with Stanley padding happily in his wake. I listened carefully, until I heard the sound of our bedroom door closing, then darted over to retrieve Will's drawing from the wastebasket.

"I'm not worried about Rendor, Bill," I

53

said under my breath. "I'm worried about someone much scarier."

I spread the crumpled sheet of paper on the countertop, smoothed it flat with the edge of my hand, and took it with me as I headed for the study. I hadn't lied to my husband, I told myself. I *would* go through my Guy Fawkes Day notes — tomorrow. I had something far more important to do tonight.

I needed to speak with Aunt Dimity.

FOUR

I frequently poured my troubles into Aunt Dimity's willing ears, which might strike some people as odd, since I'd never actually seen Aunt Dimity's ears — or her nose or her knees or any other part of her anatomy. Although she was always around when I needed her, Aunt Dimity wasn't, in the strictest sense of the term, alive. She wasn't even my aunt.

Aunt Dimity was an Englishwoman named Dimity Westwood. She and my late mother had met in London while serving their respective countries during the Second World War. When the war ended and my mother returned to the States, the two friends kept in touch by sending hundreds of letters back and forth over the Atlantic. Although they never saw each other again, their friendship became stronger and more vibrant after the war than it had been while they were dodging doodlebugs in London.

My mother's postwar life hadn't been an easy one. After my father's early death, she'd raised me on her own while working full-time as an underpaid, overburdened teacher. There must have been days when she longed to run away with the circus, but she never let me know about them. Whenever she got fed up with her pinched paycheck, her crowded classroom, and/or her rambunctious daughter, she turned to Dimity.

The letters my mother exchanged with her old friend became a refuge for her, a private place where she could go to regain her sense of humor and enjoy a moment's peace. She kept her refuge a closely guarded secret, even from her only child. When I was growing up, I knew Dimity Westwood only as Aunt Dimity, the redoubtable heroine of a series of bedtime stories invented by my mother. I didn't know that Aunt Dimity was a real person until after both she and my mother had died.

It was then that Dimity Westwood bequeathed to me a comfortable fortune, the honey-colored cottage in which she'd grown up, the hoard of letters she and my mother had written to each other, and a remarkable journal bound in dark blue leather.

It was through the blue journal that I

came to know Dimity Westwood. Whenever I spoke to its blank pages, her handwriting would appear, an old-fashioned copperplate taught in the village school at a time when fine penmanship was still awarded prizes. Miss Archer would have called for a psychiatrist if I'd told her I could communicate with the dead, but I would never have dreamed of telling her. Aunt Dimity was *my* refuge, *my* closely guarded secret. Apart from myself, only three people — Bill, Emma, and Kit — knew about the blue journal.

I had no idea how Aunt Dimity managed to bridge the gap between here and the hereafter, and she wasn't too clear about it either, but I didn't need a technical explanation. The important bit, the only bit that mattered to me, was that she was as good a friend to me as she'd been to my mother.

I entered the study quietly, closed the door behind me, and switched on the mantelshelf lights. The book-lined room was unusually tidy, considering that Bill had spent the day working there. His laptop and his briefcase were stacked on the old oak desk that faced the ivy-covered, diamond-paned window, and the fire in the hearth had been neatly banked.

Before I reached for the blue journal, I

placed a log atop the glowing embers in the hearth and stirred them with the poker until the fire was crackling again. I also paused to say hello to another friend, a much-loved companion who spent most of his time perched in a special niche on the study's bookshelves.

Reginald was a small, powder-pink flannel rabbit who'd been at my side almost from the moment of my birth. I'd started confiding in him as soon as I'd learned to talk, and I'd never found a good reason to stop. Although I was now in my midthirties, I still regarded Reginald as my oldest and most trusted confidant. It would have been unthinkably rude of me to enter the study without saying hello to him.

"Hey, Reg," I said, touching the faded grape-juice stain on his snout. "Seen any vampires lately?"

Reginald's hand-sewn whiskers seemed to quiver in the firelight, but his black button eyes remained neutral. He was clearly unwilling to commit himself until he'd heard more.

"The boys have seen one," I informed him. "His name is Rendor, and he looks like this."

As I held up Will's wrinkled drawing, I could have sworn that Reginald shrank away from it. I knew that his apparent reaction was nothing more than an illusion of shifting shadows created by the dancing flames, but an involuntary shiver passed through me nonetheless as I took the blue journal down from its place on the bookshelves and settled into one of the tall leather armchairs that faced the hearth.

"Dimity?" I said, opening the journal. "Do you think Reginald believes in vampires?"

There was a long pause before the curving lines of royal-blue ink began to scroll gracefully across the page.

Good evening, Lori. I'm afraid that I don't quite know how to answer you. You have addressed many curious questions to me over the years, but I cannot recall one as strikingly peculiar as the one you've just asked. Do I think that a small rabbit made of pink flannel believes in vampires? Are you entirely sober, my dear?

I grinned sheepishly. I could always rely on Aunt Dimity to tame my wilder flights of fancy.

"Yes, I'm sober," I told her. "But I'm also . . . rattled. Bill and I had a private conference with Miss Archer this morning."

Aunt Dimity's handwriting sped across the page before I could say another word. *Oh, for pity's sake, Lori. You're not going on about Miss Archer again, are you? How many times must I tell you that she is NOT a vampire?*

"I'm not talking about Miss Archer," I said indignantly. "I'm talking about Rendor, the Destroyer of Souls."

I see. No, on second thought, I do not see. Who on earth, or elsewhere, is Rendor, the Destroyer of Souls?

"He's a character in a comic book," I replied, and launched into a summary of the day's many conversations, beginning with Miss Archer's accusations and ending with Bill's confident dismissal of the boys' claims.

"Bill's convinced that there's nothing to worry about," I concluded, "but I'm not so sure."

I must say that I agree with you, Lori. Bill is quite wrong to dismiss the boys' story out of hand.

A wave of gratitude welled up in me. "Then you believe Rob and Will?"

Why shouldn't I? I've never known them to lie.

"That's what I told Miss Archer," I said eagerly. "I mean, the boys make up stories about their ponies and they pretend to be dinosaurs, but they've never told an outright whopper."

I don't think they're doing so now. I believe they're telling the truth. Furthermore, I disagree with Kit's assumption that the twins mistook an old tree for a vampirelike figure. Rob said that the figure swooped, didn't he? I've never known a tree to swoop.

"Me neither," I said, wondering how I'd missed such an obvious flaw in Kit's argument.

The tree in question may, in fact, have blocked the figure from everyone's view but the boys'. The cloaked figure — shall we call him Rendor, for simplicity's sake?

"Sure," I said, straining to keep up. I'd hoped that Aunt Dimity would take my part, but I hadn't expected her to take it quite so vigorously. She was coming up with ideas that hadn't even occurred to me.

Rendor, then, may have chosen to stand in that particular spot because he wanted only the twins to see him. Perhaps he hoped to lure them farther into the woods.

"But what about Kit's search?" I asked. "Kit checked out the place where Rendor had been standing. He didn't find any evidence to suggest that anyone had been there."

I'm not at all surprised to hear that Kit's search for evidence proved fruitless. When the boys identified the figure as Rendor, they lost credibility with Kit. Since he believes that vampires are imaginary creatures, I suspect that he failed to search the area as thoroughly as he should have.

"In other words," I said, nodding wisely, "Kit found nothing because he *expected* to find nothing."

Precisely.

I glanced at the portrait of Rendor and became momentarily fixated on his absurdly long canines. Will had colored the tips of the pointy teeth in a lurid shade of crimson. A chill crept down my spine as I tore my gaze away from the picture and turned back to the journal.

"Dimity?" I said. "What do you know about vampires?"

If you think I'm an expert on the subject because of my . . . affinity with the undead, you are sadly mistaken, Lori. I doubt if I know any more about vampires than you do.

"But you might," I coaxed. "Please, Dimity, tell me what you know."

Very well, if you insist, I'll dredge up what I can from distant memory. Let us start with the basics, shall we? A vampire is a reanimated dead person. It rises from the grave and feeds on the blood of the living. It is averse to garlic, crucifixes, holy water, sunlight

"Sunlight?" I cut in. "Then we can't be

dealing with a vampire, Dimity. The twins saw . . . whatever they saw during the day."

Rendor was wearing a long, hooded cloak, was he not? Such a cloak would shield him from the sun. I would also point out that the English sky, in October, is not famous for its abundance of bright sunshine.

"The sun was in and out of the clouds on Sunday," I acknowledged. "So I suppose the boys could have seen a —" I broke off abruptly, gave myself a mental shake, and went on. "I interrupted you, Dimity. Please, continue. Tell me more about vampires."

A vampire casts no shadow, has no reflection in a mirror, and cannot be photographed. It can turn into a bat or a cloud of mist. It can be immensely charming when it wishes to be, which is usually when it's attempting to seduce a potential victim. It possesses great strength and heightened senses. It is virtually immortal, but it can be killed if a wooden stake is driven through its heart. Decapitation after the staking is advisable, as is the burning of the corpse. And there you have it, my dear, the sum total of my knowledge of vampires.

"Thanks." I glanced at Will's drawing again, then asked hesitantly, "Do you believe in vampires?"

The concept of vampirism has been embed-

ded in the folklore of many cultures for thou-sands of years, Lori. Although some dismiss it as mere superstition — a naive misreading of easily explained natural phenomena — learned scholars have written dissertations and treatises supporting it. People all over the world believe in vampires.

"People all over the world believe in a lot of things that aren't true," I pointed out. "As do a few allegedly learned scholars."

Let us say, then, that I prefer to keep an open mind on the subject. After all, there are those who would tell you that I don't exist.

"But you do," I said thoughtfully.

Strange as it may seem to some, I do. But it doesn't really matter whether vampires exist or not, does it? Will and Rob saw a queer figure lurking in the woods where they ride Thunder and Storm. I, for one, would like to know who — or what — they saw.

"So would I," I said firmly. "And I intend to find out. I went into hiding when Abaddon came after my sons in Scotland, but I'm not going to hide this time. I'm going to Anscombe Manor tomorrow, to do a little vampire hunting of my own."

I would expect nothing less of you. It would, however, be foolhardy to pursue Rendor by yourself, Lori. He — or it — might resent your interference. If challenged, he might become

*dangerous. Cornered animals often do, you
know.*

I gulped nervously and brought a hand up
to cover my neck. "I take your point, but
who's going to come with me? Bill will be
in London, Emma's always busy, and I need
Annelise to take care of the boys while I'm
looking for Rendor."

*Might I suggest enlisting Kit's help? As you
know, he's intimately familiar with every corner
of the Anscombe estate.*

"Ask Kit to help me find Rendor?" I said
skeptically. "He'll think it's a waste of time."

*I'm sure you'll find a way to change his mind.
Just think of how satisfying it will be when you
prove him wrong.*

"It'll be satisfying to prove that Will and
Rob are telling the truth," I said virtuously.

*A noble goal, my dear, but you won't prove
anything if you run into a situation you can't
handle on your own.*

"All right," I said, shrugging. "I'll ask Kit
to come along with me, but if he refuses,
I'm going after Rendor without him."

*You'd best get a good night's sleep, then.
You'll need your wits about you in the morning.*

"I'll need more than that," I muttered
distractedly, then added, in a normal tone
of voice, "A good night's sleep is the next

thing on my agenda, Dimity. I'll let you know what I find at Anscombe Manor."

I expect to be kept fully informed on your progress. Good night, Lori. And be careful.

"I will," I promised. "Good night."

I waited until the lines of royal-blue ink had faded from the page, then closed the journal, leaned back in the chair, and gazed at the fire, stroking my neck absentmindedly and wondering, for the first time in my life, if *I* believed in vampires.

I would have scoffed at the notion a day ago, but after speaking with Aunt Dimity, I no longer felt like scoffing. Vampires might be imaginary creatures born of superstition and kept alive by dark imaginations, but then again they might be as real as Aunt Dimity. As I sat and watched the dancing flames, I decided that I, too, would keep an open mind on the subject. There just might be more things in heaven and earth than were dreamt of in Bill's philosophy.

Although I was still undecided about vampires, I was fully aware of how dangerous humans could be. I'd been shot and nearly killed in Scotland by a maniac who'd dragged the twins from their beds and tried to hurl them into the sea. It wasn't the sort of thing I'd soon forget.

I touched the star-shaped scar below my

left collarbone and made a silent vow. If another sicko was stalking Will and Rob, I'd do everything in my power to track him down and put him away for good. If he turned out to be a vampire, I'd drive a stake through his heart with my own hands.

I would allow no one, living or dead, to harm my sons.

FIVE

After considering the situation from many angles, I decided that it would be irresponsible of me to tell my husband about my plan to track down Rendor. Bill would do nothing but worry if I informed him of my intention to comb the woods for a potentially dangerous pervert, and worrying would do nothing but distract him from the important work awaiting him in London. Heaven alone knew what would happen to the firm if Bill confused Miss Muffin's trust fund with Mr. Muddy-Buddy's. The consequences were too terrible to contemplate, so I resolved to keep mum about my mission, for Bill's sake as well as the firm's.

It was with a clear conscience, therefore, that I saw my husband off the following morning without mentioning my plan. After he'd gone, I made a quick run into the village for some needed supplies, returning to the cottage in plenty of time to prepare a hearty breakfast for the twins while Anne-lise helped them dress for their nine o'clock riding lesson. All three were surprised when I joined them in our canary-yellow Range Rover for the short drive to the stables.

As Annelise backed the Rover out of our graveled drive and onto the narrow county lane that ran past the cottage, she cast an appraising look over my hiking boots, rain jacket, and day pack.

"Going for a ramble?" she ventured.

"I thought I'd stretch my legs," I informed her airily. Since Annelise was as big a worrywart as Bill, I'd decided to conceal my true intentions from her as well. "I'm tired of being confined to barracks by the lousy weather."

"Why drive to Anscombe Manor to stretch your legs?" Annelise glanced doubtfully at the cloud-covered sky. "It's just as wet there as it is here."

"I thought I'd watch the boys ride before I head out," I explained. "It's been a long time since I attended one of their lessons."

"That's because you don't like horses," Rob observed sagely from the backseat.

"You're *afraid* of horses," Will chimed in.

"You won't even feed Toby carrots, and he doesn't hardly have any teeth," Rob went on, relentlessly.

"Yes, all right, boys," I said, giving them a quelling look over my shoulder. "I may not be as comfortable around horses as you are, but I still want to see you ride."

"From the fence," Rob said, giggling.

"From *behind* the fence," Will added wickedly.

I faced forward and maintained a dignified silence. It was pointless to ask for sympathy from my horse-crazy sons or from anyone else in the riding world. Horse people expected everyone to be as fearless as they were. They couldn't understand how a person could love horses *from a safe distance,* as I did. When I refused to risk life and limb by climbing aboard a huge, muscular creature that could kick, rear, buck, bite, step on, and run away with me, they simply shook their heads and wondered how on earth I'd given birth to Will and Rob.

It took us only ten minutes to reach the entrance to the long, curving drive that led to Emma and Derek Harris's house, though to call Anscombe Manor a house was to grossly understate its quirky grandeur. It was a partly fourteenth-century manor house, the fourteenth-century bit being the foundation upon which a succession of owners had, over some five hundred years, built a succession of manor houses.

Anscombe Manor had entered the twenty-first century with, among other things, fifteen interior staircases — one of which stopped unexpectedly at a bricked-in doorway beyond which there was nothing but fresh air and an abrupt drop onto Emma's cucumber frames — a timber-roofed great hall, a pair of mismatched towers, a cobbled courtyard, odd stretches of crenellated wall, and a collection of outbuildings that included a beautiful nineteenth-century stable constructed of mellow Cotswold stone.

Emma and Derek had made their own mark on the estate, first by refurbishing the manor house from top to bottom, then by adding three open-air riding rings, a modest indoor riding arena, a modern stable block for boarding horses, an assortment of storage sheds, and, last but not least, a cement-lined manure pit. I was particularly fond of the manure pit. On hot summer days, its odor seemed authentically medieval.

The Anscombe Riding Center, as Emma and Derek called their creation, had proved to be a great success, in part because of its fine facilities and splendid rural setting but to a much greater degree because of the skill and talent of its stellar stable master, Kit Smith.

Kit had an uncanny way with horses, and

71

he was pretty good at teaching humans, too. He knew when to be patient and when to crack the whip — at the humans, that is, not the horses. I'd never seen Kit scold a horse, let alone use a whip on one. Even the most ill-mannered mounts seemed to obey him, not out of fear but because they didn't want to disappoint him.

Clients came from far and wide to board their horses at the ARC and to take lessons from Kit. Most of the clients were wealthy — riding is an expensive hobby — so I was accustomed to seeing an array of pricey cars parked on the gravel apron at the end of the long drive. I was not, however, accustomed to seeing cars that looked as though they'd popped off the pages of a racing magazine.

"What's with all the sports cars?" I asked as the manor house came into view.

"Didn't Emma tell you about the cars when she came over the other day?" Annelise asked.

"She never got around to it," I said. "Our conversation was interrupted by the telephone call from Miss Archer."

"After which you went to pieces," Annelise said, nodding.

"I became . . . distracted," I admitted.

"Right, then," said Annelise. "I'll fill you in. The sports cars belong to the new stable hands. Emma's hired quite a few since Nell came back from France. None of them need to work for a living, but they're queuing up for jobs all the same."

I put the words "Nell," "stable hands," and "sports cars" together and came to the obvious conclusion. "The new stable hands wouldn't happen to be rich but pathetically lovesick young men, would they?"

"They would," said Annelise. "Lucca's not too happy about it."

"Poor kid," I murmured.

Lucca was one of Annelise's many brothers. He'd had a major crush on Nell Harris for years. Most girls would have welcomed Lucca's attentions — he was as sweet-natured as he was gorgeous — but, sadly for Lucca, Nell wasn't most girls.

"Poor fool, you mean," said Annelise, with an older sister's casual ruthlessness. "Let's face it, Lori, Lucca's kidding himself if he thinks the new arrivals will hurt his chances with Nell, because he never had a chance. Nor have the new boys, come to that. No one's ever had a chance with Nell but Kit, and the sooner Lucca realizes it, the sooner he'll be able to get on with his life. I've told him time and again that Nell's not the only girl in the world."

"Maybe not," I said quietly, "but she's the

73

only Nell."

Annelise gave me a rueful glance and nodded her agreement, then parked the Rover between a fire-engine-red Ferrari and a gleaming silver Porsche. We climbed out of the Rover, helped the twins down from their booster seats, and walked sedately after them as they made their usual mad dash for the stables.

"Who owns the Porsche?" I asked, hitching my day pack's straps onto my shoulders.

"Friedrich," Annelise replied. "He's from Berlin. He met Nell at the Sorbonne and followed her home."

I had to smile. Annelise made it sound as if Friedrich were a stray dog.

"Nell takes no notice of him," Annelise went on. "Friedrich drives here from Oxford every day, and all he gets for his trouble is heartache and a pair of smelly wellies."

"Good grief," I said.

"He's not the only one," said Annelise. "There's Mario from Milan and Rafael from Barcelona and a handful of French boys with names I can't pronounce. Honestly, Lori, I think the Sorbonne lost half its male undergrads to Oxford when Nell came home from Paris, and half of *them* are skiving off classes to work *here*. How they'll ever get their degrees, I don't know."

"It depends on what they're studying, I suppose," I said.

"I know what they're studying," Annelise said portentously, "and they don't give degrees for it at Oxford."

We were ten feet or so from the stable yard's open gate when I caught sight of the blossom that had attracted so many ardent bees to Anscombe Manor. It always took me a moment to catch my breath when I saw Nell Harris. She was quite simply the loveliest young woman I'd ever seen. When I tried to describe her to those who'd never encountered her, I always ended up mumbling feebly, "Have you ever seen Botticelli's Venus? Nell's like that, only more so."

Eleanor Harris was tall and willowy, with a halo of golden curls framing a flawless oval face adorned with features so pristine and delicate that they might have been carved out of marble. Her dark-blue eyes were as fathomless as the night sky and as brilliant as the stars sprinkled across it. She was as graceful as a nymph, as regal as a queen, and as beautiful as Botticelli's Venus — only more so.

It didn't matter that she was wearing a nondescript navy-blue nylon jacket, a fairly ratty pair of fawn-colored riding breeches, wrinkled leather work gloves, and black

Wellington boots splashed with unspeakable horsey filth. It didn't matter that she was wheeling a barrowful of disgusting muck out of the stables. Nell made old clothes and horse manure seem . . . ethereal.

I was about to call out to her when Annelise seized my arm and dragged me behind the stable-yard wall.

"There's an interesting tableau going on in there," she said softly. "Take a peek."

I leaned forward cautiously and saw a tall, broad-shouldered youth with flaxen hair sweeping the cobbles near a water butt on the far side of the yard. His sky-blue eyes were so firmly fixed on Nell that he seemed unaware of the fact that he, too, was being watched — by Kit Smith.

Kit stood half hidden in the barrel-vaulted passageway that connected the manor's rear courtyard to the stable yard. As I looked on, his gaze moved slowly from the flaxen-haired boy to Nell. Then he ducked his head abruptly and turned back toward the courtyard, as if he didn't want to intrude upon the scene.

Beside me, Annelise was shaking her head.

"If Kit's jealous of Friedrich," she whispered, "then he's as big a fool as Lucca. Doesn't he know Nell's his for the asking?"

"He knows," I whispered back, "but he

doesn't want her to be. I imagine he wants her to fall for Friedrich, or for any of the young stable hands. He thinks he's too old for her."

"He's mad," Annelise declared.

I nodded. "I couldn't agree with you more."

We peered into the stable yard again, but the interesting tableau had dissolved. Nell was wheeling her barrow around the corner of the stables, on her way to the manure pit, and Friedrich was trailing after her as faithfully as Ham, her ancient black Labrador retriever. Annelise rolled her eyes, as if to say, "*All* men are mad," and went into the stables to find the twins.

I headed for the courtyard, to find Kit.

When I'd first met Kit Smith, he'd been unshaven, unshorn, homeless, half starved, and dressed in rags, but none of it had mattered. Kit's breathtaking physical beauty, like Nell's, transcended circumstance, but there was more to it than that. When I'd first looked into his violet eyes, I'd seen the soul of a saint.

Kit had changed a lot since then. He was gainfully employed, for one thing, and Anscombe Manor was his home as well as his workplace. He'd gotten rid of his scraggly beard, clipped his prematurely gray hair short, and added flesh and muscle to his lean frame. His face — his heart-stoppingly beautiful face — which had once been so gaunt and pale, was now radiant with good health. The only things that hadn't changed about him were his eyes. When I looked into them, I still saw the soul of a saint.

He was a tortured saint, to be sure, but his suffering was entirely self-imposed. I knew in my bones that it would come to an end once he allowed himself to acknowledge his love for Nell. All he needed was a nudge — or a good hard kick — in the right direction.

"I don't care what Emma says," I muttered as I crossed the stable yard. "Friends don't let friends suffer."

By the time I entered the barrel-vaulted passage, I'd made a small but important addition to my original plan. I'd use the vampire hunt to find Rendor, of course, but I'd also use it as an opportunity to talk some sense into Kit. The more I thought about it, the better I liked my revised mission statement. No one could resist me when my heart was set on something, and my heart was set on helping Kit live happily ever after. If I could spread the hunt out over several days, I had no doubt whatsoever that I would be able to cure him of his age-gap phobia, convince him that he was making a dreadful mistake by rejecting Nell, and persuade him to ask for her hand in marriage.

Emma might be willing to stand by and do nothing while Kit ruined his life, but my boots were made for kicking — and I intended to use them. I was sure that Aunt Dimity would approve.

There was a bounce in my step and a determined gleam in my eye when I strode into the courtyard, but when I caught sight of Kit, I stopped short.

Why was Anscombe Manor's stellar stable master sitting idly on a damp wooden bench? I asked myself. Why was he wearing hiking boots instead of riding boots, wool trousers instead of breeches, and a rain jacket instead of his customary barn coat? Had he relinquished his role to one of Nell's many suitors? Had the new herd of young studs driven him from the stables?

"Hey, Kit," I called, hurrying over to sit beside him on the bench. "Why aren't you dressed for work? Are you ill?"

"No, I'm not ill." He heaved a mournful sigh. "I'm on holiday."

My eyebrows rose. To my knowledge Kit had never taken a single day off of work, much less a whole vacation.

"Since when do you take holidays?" I asked.

"Since Emma ordered me to," he replied. "She thinks we should take advantage of the extra help while we can."

I glanced toward the stable yard. "Can the extra help manage without you?"

"Oh, yes," Kit answered dully. "Most of them were raised around stables much grander than ours. They don't need me to tell them what to do."

"What about your lessons?" I asked.

He shrugged apathetically. "Emma and Nell are covering for me. They're both excellent instructors."

His shoulders sagged, and he shuffled his feet aimlessly on the cobbles, as if he were bored to tears. I, on the other hand, had to restrain myself from jumping for joy. It would be ten times easier to persuade Kit to come with me, now that he had nothing else to do. He wouldn't even have to change his clothes.

"Are you planning to spend your entire holiday sitting here?" I teased.

Kit extended his long legs and leaned against the wall behind the bench.

"I was going to go for a walk," he said, "but I ran out of energy."

"Then you can borrow some of mine," I

said, beaming at him. "I have a favor to ask of you, Kit."

"Do you?" he said lazily. "What sort of favor?"

"I want you to help me to find Rendor." I held up a hand to forestall interruption. "I know all about the gnarled tree and the missing footprints, but Will drew a detailed picture of Rendor, so I'm convinced that he and Rob saw *someone.* I don't know who it was, but I'm going to find out, and I want you to come with me because . . ." I paused for a breath, then went on in a rush. "Because he might turn out to be another violent psycho and I don't want to run the risk of ending up in the hospital again — or worse." I paused again before adding craftily, "And seeing as you're at loose ends . . ."

Kit continued to lounge against the wall for a minute or so. Then he sat up and turned to face me. "All right," he said. "I'll come with you. On one condition."

"Name it," I said, smiling brightly.

"Once we've proved to your satisfaction that the woods are safe," he said, "you'll take riding lessons."

My smile vanished. "I'll . . . *what? Me? Ride? A horse?"*

"Yes," Kit said gravely. "You. Ride. A horse."

"I don't think so," I said, waving my hands to ward off the insane suggestion. "Not in *this* lifetime at any rate. You *know* how I feel about horses."

"I do," he said, "and it's high time you got over it. Wouldn't it be fun to go for a hack with Emma every now and then?"

"Sure," I said. "If you leave out the part where I take a nosedive into the nearest hedgerow."

"Listen to me, Lori." Kit folded his arms and regarded me severely. "You can't go on standing on the far side of the fence. If you do, Will and Rob will always see you as an outsider looking in. You'll never earn their respect, you'll never fully bond with them, you'll never truly understand your sons until you overcome your fear of horses."

"Ouch," I said, wincing. "You really know how to hit a mom where it hurts."

"I'm not telling you anything you don't already know." He smiled sweetly, unfolded his arms, and gave my shoulder an encouraging squeeze. "You know I'd never do anything to hurt you, Lori. We'll take it very slowly, one step at a time. I'll put you on Toby. He's small, gentle, patient —"

"And toothless," I finished for him. "Yes, I know Toby. I petted him once."

"You see? You're halfway there." Kit stuck

out his hand. "Do we have a deal?"

I whimpered piteously but shook his hand to seal the deal.

"You won't regret it." Kit sprang to his feet, as if energized by my surrender, and said cheerfully, "Wait here. I'll be right back."

He disappeared into the manor house and returned a moment later, sliding the straps of a bulging day pack over his shoulders.

"That was quick," I commented.

"I like to keep a pack handy, for long trail rides," he explained. He nodded toward the tree-covered hills behind the manor house. "Shall we?"

I got up and trudged after him, feeling a bit shell-shocked. I'd never expected Kit Smith, of all people, to drive such a hard bargain. To my way of thinking, there wasn't much difference between doing battle with a vampiric psycho pervert and riding a horse.

But Kit would have to keep his part of the bargain, too, I reminded myself. Before I risked life and limb by climbing into a saddle, he'd have to prove to me that neither man nor monster haunted the woods above Anscombe Manor.

Six

We were nearing the fringe of trees at the base of the hill behind the manor house when Kit wheeled around to face me.

"Before we go any farther," he said, "I'd like to get one thing straight. You're not expecting to find a vampire in the woods, are you, Lori?"

"Of course not," I said, avoiding his eyes. "What kind of an idiot do you think I am, Kit? I don't believe in vampires."

"Just checking," said Kit. "You said you wanted to find Rendor, who, according to Rob and Will, is a soul-eating king of vampires, so I thought you might —"

"I used the name for convenience's sake," I interrupted. "I don't care what we call the creep who was spying on the boys. If it'll make you more comfortable, we can call him Mr. X."

"I don't mind calling him Rendor," said Kit, smiling, "as long as you don't expect me to string garlic around my neck and add a wooden stake to my emergency gear."

I chuckled appreciatively, though I shifted my pack uneasily on my shoulders and continued to look anywhere but at Kit.

"Don't be silly," I said. "I'm looking for a *real* monster — a voyeur or a child molester — not a make-believe one. And I'd like to start in the exact spot where Rendor appeared to the boys on Sunday."

"The spot where Rendor *allegedly* appeared," Kit corrected. "I knew you'd want to start there, so that's where I'm taking you. It's about three-quarters of the way up Emma's Hill."

Emma's Hill was one link in a continuous chain of hills that stretched north and south for twenty miles or so, rising like a knobbly spinal cord between two fertile river valleys and shielding Anscombe Manor, Aunt Dimity's cottage, and the village of Finch, among many other places, from the harsh winter winds that blew in from the east. Since cartographers had never named the hill directly behind Anscombe Manor, Derek Harris had taken the liberty — time-honored by all great explorers — of naming it after his wife.

I'd climbed Emma's Hill more times than I could count. I knew the trails that led to my cottage, the ones that led to the hump-backed bridge in Finch, and the ones to avoid during rambling season, when tranquil byways became superhighways crammed with day hikers, bird-watchers, and long-distance backpackers. I knew the best picnic spots, the best overlooks, and the best places to ford the spring-fed stream that tumbled downhill on its way to join the river that ran through Finch. I thought I knew everything there was to know about Emma's Hill.

Kit, however, had grown up at Anscombe Manor — his family had once owned the estate — which gave him a slight advantage over me when it came to local knowledge. The path he selected for our assault on Emma's Hill was entirely unfamiliar to me. It was, by the looks of it, known only to Kit and a host of small wild animals, and its entrance was concealed by encroaching hawthorn bushes that hadn't yet shed their leaves.

"We could follow the bridle path," Kit informed me, pushing the hawthorns aside, "but I thought we'd take a shortcut. The sooner we reach the old tree, the sooner you'll learn to ride."

"You're awfully sure of yourself," I observed, ducking to avoid a whipping, dripping branch.

"Yes, I am," he said, and left it at that.

The shortcut was steep, rough, narrow, and so annoyingly slippery that I began to suspect that Kit had chosen it in order to discourage me from carrying out my search. I seemed to slide down one step for every two I took up, and I collected so much mud on the soles of my boots that I felt as if I were wearing ankle weights, but I was up to the challenge. Nothing brought out my stubborn streak like an attempt to discourage me.

All the same, I was relieved when Kit ended the punishing climb by turning onto a long and fairly level shelf that ran parallel to the hill's ridgeline. I clumped after him through the sopping underbrush, silently blessing the inventor of water-resistant hiking gear. Had I worn my customary blue jeans and sneakers, I would have been soaked to the skin within seconds of leaving the path.

After ten minutes of steady walking, Kit stepped over a decaying log, entered a tiny clearing, and placed his right hand on the trunk of an ancient apple tree that had seeded itself a long way from the nearest orchard.

"Here we are," he announced. "The twins and I were down below, on the bridle path, when they saw Rendor. They told me that he was standing right here, looking down at us. When I came up later, to take a look around, I realized instantly that they'd mistaken my old friend here" — he patted the tree's trunk affectionately — "for a man."

I paused at the log to scrape the mud from my boots, then subjected the tree to a critical examination, circling it slowly in order to see it from all sides.

"Are you sure you have the right tree?" I asked, coming to a halt in front of Kit. "I don't think it looks like a man."

"You would if you saw it from the bridle path on a misty day," said Kit.

"I'd have to be *hallucinating* to mistake your old friend for a man," I said flatly. "Look at it, Kit. The branches are bunched too closely together to be mistaken for arms, and I don't see anything remotely resembling legs or a head. If you leave out the arms, legs, and head, there's not much left to look manlike, is there?"

"Your sons have very active imaginations," Kit reminded me.

"They also have very good eyesight," I countered.

"We can argue about the tree for as long as you like," said Kit, sounding slightly offended, "but you can't argue with the fact that I didn't find any footprints up here."

"I most certainly can," I retorted. "Watch this."

I walked deliberately across the thick carpet of dead leaves that covered the floor of the small clearing, then turned to peer intently at the ground. The indentations made by my hiking boots were barely visible.

"So much for your tracking skills," I said. "The leaves are so wet and spongy that a guy would have to weigh three hundred pounds before he'd make a lasting impression in them. In Will's drawing, Rendor is as thin as a rail. He would have had to hop up and down to leave footprints here."

"Let me try," said Kit, stepping forward.

When his experiment produced the same results, I planted my hands on my hips and tut-tutted at him like a disapproving schoolmarm.

"Shame on you, Kit," I said. "You assumed that the twins were making up a story, so you didn't bother to check it out properly. No wonder you didn't find any clues."

"I may have overlooked one or two details," Kit acknowledged grumpily.

"Only one or two?" I said, raising an

eyebrow. "I just hope the rain hasn't already washed away the clues you must have missed."

Kit leaned against the apple tree, looking faintly bored, while I prowled the edge of the clearing, searching the surrounding undergrowth for a piece of hard evidence that would support the boys' story. When I saw the crushed toadstool, my heart skipped a beat, and when I dropped to my knees for a closer look, a tingle of excitement mixed with dread curled up my spine. For there, in a small patch of mud just beyond the crushed toadstool, was a V-shaped mark that might have been left by the pointed toe of a grown man's boot.

"Kit?" I called unsteadily. "I think I found some clues."

I sat back on my heels while Kit bent low to examine my discoveries. When he straightened, I expected him to shout "Eureka!" and apologize profusely for ever doubting my sons, but he did nothing of the sort.

"Interesting," he said, with a noncommittal shrug. "But I wouldn't call them clues. Toadstools collapse for any number of natural reasons, and the mark isn't distinct enough to count as a footprint."

I stared at him in prickly silence, then got

to my feet.

"It's distinct enough for me," I said coldly. "And I'm going to see where it leads."

I brushed past him imperiously and followed the point of the V-shaped mark into the woods. I should have crept along at a snail's pace, scanning the wet ground for more footprints, but I was too busy fuming to think clearly. How dare Kit cast aspersions on my splendid clues? Why couldn't he just admit that he'd made a mistake? It wasn't like him to be defensive, self-righteous, or grouchy, yet he'd been all three in quick succession under the apple tree. Perhaps, I thought, the sight of Nell's many suitors was getting to him.

Whatever the case, I wasn't about to let his doubts deter me from discovering the truth. When I heard him coming after me, I didn't slow down to wait for him but quickened my pace, crashing recklessly through the undergrowth until a wild rosebush caught me by the ankle and sent me tumbling headlong into another, much larger clearing.

I landed with a damp splat on a small mound of earth covered with long, rain-speckled grasses. I lay there for a moment, feeling foolish as well as vexed, but when I finally lifted my head clear of the grasses, I felt nothing but skin-crawling horror. The tip of my nose was less than a foot away from the decaying face of a weathered tombstone. The small mound upon which I'd fallen was a grave.

I let out a shriek that should have awakened the dead and scrambled to my feet, backpedaling so fast that I ran straight into a sycamore tree. I stood with my spine pressed to the tree's mottled bark, breathing hard and looking wildly around the clearing. No one had ever told me that there was a graveyard on Emma's Hill, but the clearing was dotted with headstones, all of them tilted at crazy angles, as if the ground had shifted beneath them — or as if someone had been pushing up on them from below. My heart nearly burst from my chest when I saw that one of the graves had been ripped open.

"Lori!" Kit's shout rang out as he burst into the clearing. He swung around, caught sight of me, and dashed over to peer down at me anxiously. "What happened? Why did you scream?"

My knees were so weak that if the sycamore hadn't been holding me up, I would have fallen into Kit's arms.

"The b-boys *did* see a v-vampire," I sputtered. I grabbed his wrist and spun him around until he was facing the open grave. "He came from *there*."

Kit stood stock-still for a moment, then bowed his head and pressed a hand to his mouth. When he turned back to me, he looked as if he were trying hard not to laugh.

"If he came from one of *these* graves," he said tremulously, "he must be a very *dainty* vampire."

"What are you talking about?" I demanded.

"Calm down," he soothed, "and come with me."

He pulled me away from the sycamore, put an arm around my shoulders, and walked me to the nearest headstone. As the adrenaline rush subsided, I began to notice a number of odd things about the grave. The marker was considerably smaller than the ones in the churchyard in Finch, and the mound, too, seemed abnormally tiny. Stranger still was the name that had been inscribed upon the headstone — it wasn't one usually bestowed upon a child.

"Snuffy?" I read the inscription aloud, in some confusion.

"A noble parakeet," Kit said somberly. He then guided me from one headstone to the next, narrating as he went. "And here we have Pom-Pom the Pomeranian, Leslie the

Labrador, Alex the Angora cat, Buckles the basset hound, Little Jim the turtle —"

"Animals?" I broke in, blinking stupidly. "Is this a *pet* cemetery?"

"I'm afraid so." He turned to gaze at the grave that had been dug up, then sighed heavily. "A badger must have unearthed poor Diane."

"Dachshund?" I guessed.

"Iguana," he replied.

"Oh, *man*," I groaned, burying my face in my hands. "I am *such* an idiot."

Kit was too kind to agree with me out loud. When I risked glancing up at him, I could tell by the twitching corners of his lips that he was royally amused, but he gallantly refrained from hooting like a hyena as he strolled to the easternmost edge of the cemetery and pulled a tangle of shriveled blackberry branches from a hitherto-hidden stone bench. It was the size and shape of a small love seat, with a weatherworn pattern of intertwined grapevines carved on the arms and the back.

"Sit down, Lori," Kit called. "You've had a shock, and I have the perfect remedy."

I shuffled sheepishly to the stone bench and sat huddled in silent humiliation while Kit placed his day pack on the ground and withdrew an insulated flask from its main compartment. He opened the flask and filled its cuplike cap with a steaming brew.

"Hot tea," he said, handing the cup to me. "With lots of sugar."

"You brought hot tea with you?" I said, astounded.

"Naturally." He sat beside me and nodded toward his pack. "I brought everything we'd need for a daylong expedition — sandwiches, snacks, hot tea, and spare socks, as well as the usual supplies and equipment." He eyed my day pack curiously. "What did you bring, Lori?"

"Some . . . things," I muttered, refusing to look at him.

"What things?" Kit asked.

I gave a forlorn little sigh, handed the cup of tea back to him, took off my day pack, opened it, and exposed its contents to his inquisitive gaze.

"I see that you brought spare socks, too," he said. "Along with two strings of garlic, a mallet, a wooden stake, a silver crucifix, a rosary, and let's see . . . one, two, three glass bottles filled with" — he glanced up at me for confirmation — "holy water? Does the vicar know that you raided his church?"

"The crucifix is mine," I said quickly. "It was my mother's. So was the rosary. The mallet's mine, too, and I made the stake from an old broom handle." I sighed dismally. "But the holy water is from St. George's. I went there after Bill left this morning. I wanted to be prepared."

"For what?" Kit asked. "You don't believe in vampires."

"I don't," I said, "but some people do, crazy people who dress up in capes and have their teeth sharpened and sleep in coffins. Some of them do it because they think it's cool, but some are true believers." I took my lower lip between my teeth and chewed it worriedly. "What if Will and Rob saw someone who *thinks* he's a vampire? If a man *acted* like a vampire, wouldn't the end results be just as . . . infernal?"

"Yes," Kit said thoughtfully. "I suppose they would."

"And if we run into someone like that," I went on, gaining confidence, "we might have to play along with his delusion, right? We might need the crucifix, the holy water, and the garlic to . . . to subdue him."

"What about the mallet and the stake?" Kit asked quietly.

"I don't know about you, but if someone waved a hammer and a sharpened stick at me, I'd back down in a hurry," I replied. "They're just props to you and me, Kit, but they'll mean something to Rendor. They may be our only hope of persuading him to come along peacefully."

Kit gave me a piercing look, as though he knew that the stake was more to me than a mere prop. Then he turned his face to the overcast sky and leaned back on the bench.

"Let's say you're right," he proposed. "Let's say that Rendor exists and that he's some sort of pseudovampire. Why would he appear to the boys during the day? If *you* know that vampires are allergic to sunlight, I think it's safe to assume that *he* would. Wouldn't he spend the hours from dawn to dusk safely tucked up in a pseudocoffin?"

"He might believe that his cloak protects him from the sun," I said, recalling Aunt Dimity's comment.

"What cloak?" Kit asked.

"The cloak he was wearing when the boys saw him," I explained. "Didn't they tell you? Rendor *swooped.*"

I flung out an arm to imitate Rob's impersonation of Rendor and flinched as the blackberry's prickly branches raked the back of my hand. I yelped in pain, turned to take stock of my scratches, and saw, impaled on the blackberry's thorns, a ragged strip of crimson fabric.

I stared at the fluttering wisp, transfixed, then reached out to disentangle it from the thorns. Fascinated, I rubbed the red scrap between my fingers, draped it across my palm, and turned to show it to Kit.

"Look," I whispered. "It's *silk.*"

"So it is," he said, stroking the cloth with a fingertip.

"It was stuck on the blackberry bush," I said. "But the rain hasn't rotted it and the sun hasn't bleached it, so it can't have been hanging there for very long."

"It looks like a fresh tear as well." Kit ran his finger along the scrap's frayed edge, frowning pensively. "It's not the sort of thing I'd expect hikers or horseback riders to wear."

"No, it's not," I agreed, my voice quivering with the thrill of discovery. "But in Will's drawing, Rendor's cloak has a *crimson lining.* He must have caught it on the thorns when he passed this way." I looked up at Kit. "And I'll bet you anything that he passed this way a short time after he stood beneath your old friend, the apple tree, watching you, Rob, and Will on the bridle path." I shivered at the thought and turned to look at the decaying headstones. "He must have felt right at home here."

Kit, too, turned to look at the headstones. Then he took the wisp of crimson silk from my hand and held it dangling at eye level.

"Lori," he declared. "I do believe you've finally found a clue."

SEVEN

Kit tucked the ragged scrap of silk into his breast pocket and passed the cup of tea back to me.

"I don't suppose there's the slightest chance of persuading you to call in the police," he said resignedly.

"Not the slightest," I assured him. "I've had a hard enough time getting *you* to believe me. Can you imagine what a desk sergeant would say if I told him that a pseudovampire was stalking my sons?"

"You're wasting police time, madam," Kit intoned in a ponderous rumble.

"Something like that," I said. "Then he'd remember the newspaper stories about Abaddon shooting me in Scotland, and he'd treat me like a crazy woman who sees stalkers hiding around every corner. He'd probably send me off to see a shrink." I shook my head. "Sorry, Kit, but it's up to us to find Rendor — if you're still willing to help me, that is."

"Do you really think I'd back out now?" Kit asked, reverting to his natural voice. "It's my fault he's still at large, Lori. I was careless on Sunday. I should have been more thorough when I checked out the boys' story, but I've been . . . distracted lately."

I thought I knew what was distracting Kit, but I decided to make sure.

"It can't be easy for you," I said casually, "having so many new employees to manage."

"They're hard workers," he allowed, "which is surprising when you consider their backgrounds. They all come from well-to-do families, you know. None of them need to work."

"Even rich boys will get their hands dirty when they have the right motivation." I swirled the tea gently in the cup. "Annelise seems to think they're trying to impress Nell."

"Yes, well . . . It's understandable, isn't it? Nell is . . ." Kit's gaze turned inward as his voice trailed off. He stared hollow-eyed at nothing for a few seconds, then shook his head as if to clear it and got to his feet. "Don't move, Lori. Stay here with the packs and finish your tea. I'm going to prove to you that my tracking skills aren't as rusty as you think."

I could almost see Nell's image dissolve mistily in midair as Kit tore his mind away from her and focused it on the task of tracking Rendor. It's a start, I told myself contentedly. Next time I'll mention how good-looking and well built the new stable hands are. Then I'll wonder aloud why so many strong, handsome, hardworking, filthy-rich, and utterly besotted young men have failed to make so much as an inch of headway with Nell. That would give Kit something to think about.

While I was busy sipping tea and scheming, Kit was searching the cemetery for more clues. Now that his heart was in it, he was as single-minded as a bloodhound. He began at the stone bench and worked his way outward in ever-widening circles, bending frequently to touch a blade of grass or a vagrant twig. He seemed to take a great deal of interest in a clump of wild geraniums at the clearing's northern edge. After crouching over it for some time, he called out that he would be right back and disappeared into the woods.

I was about to call Annelise, to tell her not to put lunch on hold for me, when my cell phone rang. I pulled it from my breast pocket, saw my husband's name and number on the little screen, and reminded myself that he'd be much better off not knowing about my vampire hunt.

"Hi, Bill," I said cheerily. "How's the work on the Shuttleworth bequest coming along?"

"It's like herding cats," he said dismally. "Every time we lasso one clause, another three start yowling for attention."

"I hope you're not going to take out your frustrations on Stanley when you get home," I said. "He worships you."

"Stanley worships his food bowl," Bill stated flatly. "As far as he's concerned, I'm just a warm lap."

"But you're *his* warm lap," I said, laughing.

Bill managed a weak chuckle, then said, "Enough about me. What are you up to?"

"I'm relieving Kit of his boredom," I replied. "Emma ordered him to take a few days off, and he didn't know what to do with himself, so I've taken him out for a hike."

"In this weather?" said Bill. "How charitable of you."

"Not entirely," I admitted. "I have an ulterior motive."

"I thought you might." Bill sighed. "Go

ahead, tell me the worst."

Bill hadn't heard about the situation at the stables, so I told him about Nell's herd of young stallions, then outlined my campaign to show Kit the error of his ways and help him achieve his heart's desire.

"I wish you luck," said Bill when I'd finished. "Kit's dug his heels in pretty deeply when it comes to Nell, but if anyone can budge him, you can. Where is he, by the way? He can't be within earshot, or you wouldn't be talking about him so freely."

"He's . . . hunting for wild mushrooms," I said, because, I told myself, it *could* be true — Kit *might* find a mushroom or two trodden underfoot by Rendor — but I felt a stab of guilt nonetheless and hurriedly changed the subject. "Did you know that there's a pet cemetery on Emma's Hill?"

"I did not," said Bill.

"I'm sitting in it right now," I told him. "It looks as though it's been here for ages. Some of the headstones are so old you can hardly read the inscriptions."

"A problem foreseen by Mrs. Shuttleworth," Bill said dryly. "She left instructions for us to set up a special fund to pay for the construction of a cat mausoleum. I won't be surprised if it's air-conditioned. Listen, Lori, I've got to go. I just wanted to touch base. I'm glad to hear that you're having a better day than I am."

"It's just about *purr*-fect," I agreed.

Bill groaned, promised to call again in the evening, and rang off, but I kept the cell phone out to call Annelise.

"You're missing the boys' lesson," she informed me.

I clapped a hand to my forehead. I'd completely forgotten to attend the boys' riding class as part of my cover story.

"Whoops," I said. "Are they very disappointed?"

"Not at all," said Annelise. "They think you're hiding in the manor house because you're afraid —"

"Of horses, yes, I know what they think," I broke in, bridling. "Well, I'm not hiding in the manor house. I'm up on Emma's Hill, hiking with Kit. I'm helping him to enjoy his time off."

"If I had a day off, I'd spend it near a roaring fire instead of tramping through the woods," said Annelise, "but I expect Kit wanted to get away from the stables."

"I expect so," I said. If Annelise was inclined to believe that Kit had come with me because he couldn't stand watching the new stable hands drool over Nell, I wasn't going to argue with her. "At any rate, don't

105

wait for me after the boys' lessons. Just give them lunch and take them to school as usual. If it looks as though I'll miss dinner, I'll let you know."

"How will you get home?" she asked.

"I'll cadge a lift from Kit or Emma," I said.

"Good," said Annelise. "I'm going to do some shopping after I drop the boys off at Morningside, so I'll stay in town until they're ready to come home."

"Have a good time," I told her, and rang off.

I slipped the cell phone into my pocket and finished drinking the tea. I'd just returned the insulated flask to Kit's pack when he strode into the clearing, looking both pleased and rather ashamed of himself.

"I should never have doubted you or the twins, Lori," he called as he crossed to the stone bench. "Someone *has* passed this way. Come along — I've lots to show you."

We donned our packs and headed into the woods, walking away from Anscombe Manor and toward the cleft between Emma's Hill and the unnamed hill to the north, still following the level shelf we'd been following since we'd left the apple tree. We hadn't gone far when I spotted a neon-orange plastic ribbon tied to a short length of stiff wire protruding from the ground beneath a fountain of damp brown bracken.

I pointed to the eye-catching ribbon. "Rendor didn't leave a calling card for us to find, did he?"

"It's mine," Kit informed me. "I always carry a pocketful of flags with me. I use them to mark protected species of wildflowers, so Emma can find and photograph them when she has the time. Fortunately, they work just as well for footprints."

When we reached the neon-orange flag, Kit pushed the withered bracken aside to reveal the unmistakable print of a long, narrow, pointy-toed boot.

"The bracken kept the print from being washed away by the rain," he explained. "You can still see where Rendor bent a few fronds in passing."

I gave a low whistle. "So I was right. I *did* find a footprint back at the apple tree."

"You certainly did. And it was made by the same boot that made the print you see here. The toe marks are identical." Kit plucked the flag from the ground and put it in his pocket.

"Good idea," I said. "If Rendor comes back this way, we don't want him to know we're trailing him."

Kit glanced over his shoulder, toward the pet cemetery, then let his gaze roam up and down the hill, as if he were taking stock of the terrain.

"This is the route I'd take," he said, "if I wanted to move quickly without being seen. It's not an established trail, so I'd run little risk of meeting anyone. The footing's not bad, and there's plenty of cover. I'd be far less exposed here than I would be along the ridgeline."

"So I was right about that, too," I said happily. "Rendor *was* sneaking around in the woods."

"He was certainly behaving in a suspicious manner," Kit conceded, and took off again. "Come along. I found more traces up ahead. I may be mistaken, of course, but I think I know where Rendor was going."

We moved on, pausing every few yards to examine the telltale signs Kit had marked with his flags — a broken branch, a crushed plant, a partial boot print. If he wanted to impress me with his tracking skills, he succeeded. It would have taken me a month to find half the clues he'd discovered in just over an hour.

Gradually the shelf began to curve around the shoulder of Emma's Hill, becoming narrower and narrower until it petered out completely on a ledge that overlooked the river valley to the east.

"I stopped here to go back and fetch you," Kit explained, bending to pull the last flag from the ground. "If I'd continued to follow Rendor's tracks, I'm almost certain that I would have ended up down there."

He drew a wavering line through the air to indicate a sketchy trail that wound downward from the ledge and vanished in a dense grove of trees extending from the bottom of the hill outward into the valley.

"What's down there?" I asked.

"Aldercot Hall," he replied. "You can't see it from here, but it's nestled in among those plane trees."

"Aldercot Hall?" I said, peering curiously at the stand of trees he'd indicated. "I thought I knew our neighborhood pretty well, but I've never heard of Aldercot Hall. Who lives there?"

"The DuCaral family," said Kit.

"I thought I knew my neighbors pretty well, too," I said, chagrined. "Why haven't I heard of the DuCarals?"

"They live in the wrong valley," said Kit, smiling. "You're familiar with the families on the other side of the hill, the families in and around Finch, and they tend to be a bit parochial. As far as they're concerned, Aldercot Hall might as well be on the dark side of the moon. Apart from that, the Du-

Carals like their privacy. They don't go out of their way to mix with their neighbors."

"If Rendor's gone there, the family might be in trouble," I said. "He might be holding them hostage or . . . worse."

"I doubt it," said Kit. "From what I've heard —" He broke off suddenly, turned away from the valley, and sniffed the air.

"What's up?" I asked.

"Look," he said, jutting his chin toward the forest. "Smoke."

I followed his gaze and saw a thin column of smoke rising above the canopy of trees.

"Good grief," I said, astonished. "How could anything burn in this weather?"

"I don't think it's a wildfire," said Kit. "It looks to me as though someone's camping in Gypsy Hollow. Perhaps I read the tracks incorrectly, Lori."

I gazed up at him, wide-eyed. "Do you think it might be Rendor?"

"It might be," said Kit, "but leave your stake in your pack for now. We have some rough going ahead of us. I don't want you impaling yourself — or me — if you stumble."

I grinned ruefully, but my pulse was racing as we began our descent into Gypsy Hollow.

EIGHT

Kit's description of our descent as "rough going" was appallingly accurate. He walked back around the shoulder of the hill for a short distance, then simply stepped off the edge of the shelf and plunged downward with the carefree air of a suicidal mountain goat. I gulped apprehensively but plunged after him, clinging to trees, grabbing at bushes, and wedging my boots behind rocks to keep myself from cartwheeling down the slippery slope. I'd hoped to creep up on Rendor as stealthily as a panther, but I ended up slithering uncontrollably downhill and sliding into Gypsy Hollow on my bottom.

Kit was already there, upright and with a dry bottom. I eyed him reproachfully, then scrambled to my feet and scanned the hollow for a pale, bone-thin lunatic in a silk-lined cloak.

Instead, I saw a deeply tanned, barrel-chested middle-aged man standing in the doorway of a small, mud-spattered, and very dilapidated motor home. He wore a dark brown, oiled-cotton rain jacket over a frayed and baggy blue sweater, and he'd tucked the legs of his brown corduroy trousers into a pair of round-toed Wellington boots. One glance at his footwear was enough to tell me that he wasn't responsible for the prints we'd found up on the shelf.

Whoever he was, he'd clearly made himself at home in the hollow. A patched nylon awning on four telescoping poles provided a simple rain shelter for a bicycle, a rickety-looking canvas camp chair, and a folding table. Beyond the awning, a cast-iron stock-pot hung from a tripod over a campfire ringed with large rocks. An old-fashioned teakettle sat on a flat rock near the fire, inside the ring of stones.

The folding table had been set for a solitary meal by someone who couldn't afford fancy travel gear. I noted a tin cup, a plastic plate, cheap silverware, a bottle of milk from the local dairy, a plastic carton filled with sugar, and a tin teapot covered with a shocking pink knitted tea cozy. A dented ladle rested on a plastic saucer beside the teapot, stained, presumably, with whatever was simmering in the cast-iron pot.

Unruly tufts of grizzled hair framed the man's creased and weathered face, and a glimmer of amusement lit his bright blue eyes as he walked down the steps of the motor home and ambled toward us.

"G'day," he said, grinning broadly. "You certainly know how to make a grand entrance, little lady. Haven't seen anything like it since my old boss trod on a fresh cowpat and went arse-over-teakettle into the water trough." He came to a halt before us and stuck out his hand. "Name's Leo."

"I'm Kit," said Kit, shaking Leo's hand. "And this is my friend, Lori. I work at Anscombe Manor."

"Right," said Leo, nodding wisely. "You'll be wanting to know why I haven't been round to ask your boss if I can stay on his land. Truth is, I just rolled in a couple of hours ago, and it took me a while to set up camp. I planned to pay a call on the manor after I'd had some tucker."

He inclined his head toward the cast-iron stockpot. The mouthwatering aromas emanating from it reminded me forcefully that I hadn't had a bite to eat since breakfast.

"I won't be here for long," Leo continued. "No more than a week at the most. Do you think you could square it with your boss for me, Kit? It'd spare me the bother of traipsing over there, and it'd spare *him* the bother of mopping up after me and my boots."

Kit looked from the rusting motor home to the white hair framing Leo's wrinkled face and said, "I'm sure the landowners won't mind, as long as you leave the site as you found it."

"No worries, mate." Leo's broad grin returned, and he thrust a thumb over his shoulder to indicate the folding table. "You're welcome to join me. There's plenty to go round."

"We've got sandwiches," I said hastily, not wanting to take anything from someone who seemed to have so little.

"What good are sandwiches on a rotten old day like today?" Leo demanded. "You need something hot to take the chill off." He leaned closer to me, cupped a hand around his mouth, and added in a stage whisper, "And between you and me, little lady, your drawers could do with a bit of drying."

The comment was nothing short of out-rageous, but the rascally twinkle in Leo's eyes was so endearing — and my bottom was so wet — that I couldn't resist the invitation.

"Thanks," I said. "We'll be happy to join you."

"Good on ya," Leo said cheerfully, clapping me on the shoulder. "I'll put plates on the table for you."

"Please, don't trouble yourself," said Kit. "I have everything we need."

"In that case," said Leo, "you take my chair, Lori, and I'll fetch something for me and Kit to sit on — unless you've got a sofa in that big pack of yours, Kit." He winked good-naturedly, turned, and headed for the motor home, calling over his shoulder, "Back in two shakes!"

"What a nice man," I murmured after he'd climbed into the motor home. "I'm glad you're okay with him camping here."

"To be honest, I'd rather he stay at the manor house," Kit said softly, "but he strikes me as a man who likes his independence."

When we reached the shelter of the awning, I slung my pack on the relatively dry ground, moved Leo's chair from the place he'd set for himself to the other side of the table, and stood with my back to the fire, drying my "drawers." Kit paused to peer into the stockpot, then set two new places with camping ware he unearthed from his pack.

He was warming his hands at the fire when Leo emerged from the motor home, carrying two camp stools. He handed one to Kit and planted his own in the spot previously occupied by the camp chair. In a little over two shakes, we were all seated at the table, drinking cups of sweet tea and digging into the rich, savory stew Leo had ladled from the pot onto our plates.

"Kit, eh?" Leo said, as we began to eat. "Kit as in Christopher?"

Kit's mouth was so full that he could do nothing but nod in response.

"I knew a bloke named Christopher once," said Leo. "Never left the town he was born in. His patron saint was wasted on him. St. Christopher's for travelers, not stay-at-homes."

Leo's accent intrigued me. There seemed to be several layers to it, though one was more prominent than the others.

"I hope you don't mind my asking," I said, "but are you Australian?"

"No such luck," said Leo, "but I lived there for some forty-odd years — long enough to pick up the lingo. I'm reverting to my old ways, though." He lifted his mug, crooked his pinkie finger genteelly, and feigned an effete English drawl. "By the end of the month, I'll be wholly unintelligible to my chums in the Antipodes."

"Your old ways?" I said when I'd finished

laughing. "Were you originally from England?"

"I'm a Pommy born and bred," Leo answered. "As a matter of fact, I spent a fair amount of time around here, in my younger days. That's when I discovered the old track into the hollow. Many's the time I pitched a tent here. Gypsies used to camp here, too, on their way to the Deeping Fair. It's a good spot — a spring for fresh water; berries, herbs, and mushrooms, if you know where to find them; and plenty of rabbits for the pot." He put a spoonful of stew into his mouth and cocked an inquiring eyebrow at Kit.

"You're welcome to the rabbits," Kit assured him. "We're overrun with them."

I thought instantly of Reginald and felt a slight twinge of guilt as I looked down at my plate, but the stew was delicious and I was too cold and hungry to pass up a hot meal. Apart from that, Kit was right — the Anscombe estate was bursting at the seams with rabbits. No one would begrudge Leo the few that found their way into his pot.

"Has the area changed much since you were last here?" I asked him.

"The weather hasn't," he said, squinting at the cloud-covered sky. "I'll be heading south for the winter, but I wanted to stop here first. You might say I'm on a sentimental journey, revisiting the haunts of my youth. You're a Yank, aren't you?"

"Yes," I said, "but I've lived here for so long that my sons think cricket is their national pastime."

Leo let out a shout of laughter, then proceeded to entertain us with stories about his life in Australia, where he'd worked shearing sheep, mining opals, picking grapes, crewing racing yachts, and tending bars in small towns and big cities alike. It sounded to me as though he'd spent the past forty-odd years exploring the continent rather than pursuing a career, and I admired him for it. What he lacked in material possessions, he more than made up for in memories.

When Kit and I had eaten our fill, Leo looked at us from under his white eyebrows and said with a wry smile, "I hope the pair of you didn't drag yourselves out on such a filthy day just to check up on me."

"We didn't," Kit said. "As a matter of fact, we were looking for someone — a tall, thin man wearing a long cloak and pointed boots. Have you seen anyone like that since you've been here?"

"Sorry, mate, no," said Leo, shaking his head. "I haven't seen a soul since I arrived

— excepting your good selves, that is."

"If you do, will you let me know?" said Kit. "We don't know who he is, and since young children ride at the stables . . ."

"Say no more," said Leo, tapping the side of his nose. "I'll keep an eye peeled for the mongrel."

Kit hauled water from the spring to rinse the dishes, and Leo produced a towel to dry them. By then a steady rain had begun to fall, and Kit decided that it was time for us to return to Anscombe Manor. I didn't argue with him. I thought we'd accomplished quite a bit in the past four hours. Granted, we hadn't laid eyes on Rendor, but we'd proved that the twins hadn't invented him and we'd identified Aldercot Hall as his likely lair. We'd have to gather more hard evidence before I could state conclusively to Bill — or to the police — that a pervert was at large, but we had enough to be going on with.

I'd also had enough of the great outdoors. I couldn't wait to get home, get out of my grungy clothes, and get into a steamy, gardenia-scented bath. I was all ears, therefore, when Leo suggested a return route that didn't involve climbing.

"If you go through there," he advised, pointing to a gap in the trees encircling the hollow, "you can follow the old track along the north pasture."

"I know where the old track is," said Kit, "and I was planning to take it. I grew up here, too."

"You'll know your way round, then," said Leo.

"Well, I *didn't* grow up here," I put in, "so I'm glad you guys are so familiar with the lie of the land. I wasn't looking forward to scaling Emma's Hill again."

"Emma's Hill?" Leo's eyebrows rose. "Is that what you call it? In my day it was called High Point. But I like Emma's Hill better."

I pulled my day pack onto my shoulders and invited Leo to stop by the cottage for a cup of tea before he left the area.

"You can't miss it," I told him. "It's a mile up the lane from Anscombe Manor, on the left. My husband is in London at the moment, but I'd love to introduce you to my sons."

"You must come to the manor house as well," Kit chimed in. "I'm sure the Harrises would like to meet you."

"The Harrises," said Leo. "Do they own the manor now?"

"They've owned it for more than a decade," Kit informed him. "They're good people. You must come and say hello to them before you leave."

"I'll have to check my social calendar," said Leo, grinning, "but I think I might be able to fit them in."

Kit and I thanked him warmly for his hospitality, then made our way through the gap in the trees and onto the rutted, weedy lane that skirted Anscombe Manor's north pasture. I didn't like leaving Leo alone in the rain, but after listening to him recount his adventures in the Australian bush, I agreed with Kit — Leo was a man who liked his independence.

"Well," I said, sidestepping a rain-pitted puddle, "Leo's not Rendor. He's not skinny or pale, and he was wearing the wrong kind of boots. Plus, he's too jolly to be a creepy, child-molesting pseudovampire. So you must have been right about the boot prints in the first place. Rendor must have been heading for Aldercot Hall." I stopped walking and looked at Kit in alarm. "He may be terrorizing the DuCarals as we speak."

"Or he may be their guest," Kit pointed out. "We won't know until we go there, and we're not going there today. It's too far. We'd end up coming back in the dark. Why don't we pay the DuCarals a visit tomorrow morning?"

"Count me in," I said.

Kit nodded. "In the meantime I'll talk to the staff about safety and security. We're always vigilant, but until we find out more about Rendor, we'll need to be extra vigilant."

"You should tell them about Leo, too," I said. "We don't want any of the young bucks tackling him by mistake."

"I'll see to it that no one bothers Leo." Kit paused for a moment, then added, "Although, if you think about it, we don't really know who Leo is. He talked a lot about the years he spent Down Under, but he didn't say much about his life in England."

"He told us he spent a lot of time around here," I said, "and I believe him. Only a local would know how to find his way to Gypsy Hollow."

"True," said Kit. "And only an old-time local would know that the Gypsies camped here on their way to the Deeping Fair, because there hasn't been a Deeping Fair for at least forty years. I remember my parents talking about it. And High Point . . ." Kit smiled reminiscently. "I'd forgotten that Emma's Hill was called High Point, but it came back to me as soon as Leo mentioned it. I must have heard it from my father when I was younger than

Will and Rob."

"I wonder what kind of sentimental journey Leo's on," I mused aloud. "Did he camp there alone when he was young, or did he have company?" I snapped my fingers as a likely scenario presented itself to me. "I know what happened, Kit. Leo fell in love with a Gypsy girl, but she was already betrothed to a dashing young prince in the tribe, so Leo ran off to Australia, to forget."

"Do Gypsies have tribes?" Kit asked. "Or princes?"

"Don't be pedantic," I scolded. "Just think of how *awful* it would be, to have the love of your life within your reach, then lose her to someone else." I gazed dreamily across the soggy pasture, caught up in my own imaginings. "Think of how tragic it would be to have your soul mate snatched away from you, to be robbed of your one chance at happiness. I'll bet, in his heart of hearts, he's still in love with her. I'll bet she's the only girl he ever loved. I'll bet he wishes she'd run away with him to Australia. I'll bet he dreams of her every —"

"Stop it, Lori," Kit cut in, with unaccustomed harshness. "I know what you're trying to do, and I want you to stop *right now.*"

I emerged from my romantic reverie with a start and stared at him in honest confusion. My comments hadn't been aimed at Kit. I'd been thinking solely of Leo.

"I'm not trying to do anything," I protested.

"Just stop it, will you?" Kit said angrily. "You're never going to convince me to marry Nell, so you may as well stop trying. For once and for all, I'm not going to marry her," he went on fiercely. "I'm not going to marry *anyone.*"

I'd seen Kit angry only once before, when a neighbor — the late and utterly unlamented Prunella Hooper — had spread scurrilous rumors about him. I hadn't meant to provoke a second outburst, but his furious overreaction to my idle comments made me consider a possibility I hadn't previously considered.

"Kit," I said gingerly, "are you gay?"

"Oh, for heaven's sake," he snapped, rolling his eyes in exasperation. "No, Lori, I am *not* gay. I'm simply not interested in marriage. It may be difficult for you to comprehend, but some people are *meant* to be *alone.*"

"Okay," I said meekly, "but . . . do you really think you're one of them?"

"Yes, I do," he said, scowling. "It would

be wrong of me to —" He broke off and set his lips in a thin line. "Give it a rest, Lori. I'm perfectly happy as I am."

It didn't seem like the right moment to call him a big fat liar, so I kept my mouth shut. As we walked on, however, I couldn't help feeling a little indignant. If I'd intended to use a story to probe Kit's feelings, I would have come up with something more subtle than a gooey tale about Leo and a long-lost Gypsy girl.

Apart from that, Kit should have known better than to order me to do anything, because he knew how lousy I was at obeying orders. He could holler at me until he lost his voice, and it wouldn't make one jot of difference to me. I might beat a tactical retreat on the Nell front from time to time, but I'd never give up on the battle for his happiness.

A black cloud seemed to hover over Kit as we trudged along the muddy lane, and he didn't say another word until we'd reached the gravel apron in front of the manor house, when he turned to me abruptly.

"Meet me here at nine o'clock tomorrow morning," he said. "Dress for hiking and pray for rain."

Before I could respond, he spun on his heel and stormed into the stable yard, leaving me to wonder what kind of plan he'd hatched for invading Aldercot Hall. Unless it involved boats, I couldn't imagine why we'd need more rain than we already had.

A more immediate concern, however, was to figure out how I'd get the rest of the way home. Annelise and the boys were gone, Emma's car was nowhere in sight, and I wasn't about to ask Kit for a lift in his present mood, so I soon reached a rather depressing conclusion: I had a mile-long slog ahead of me, through rain that was falling harder than ever.

A woebegone sigh escaped me as I turned my back on the manor house, but I hadn't gone more than ten yards down the drive when I heard someone call my name.

"Ms. Shepherd! Wait!"

I turned to see Friedrich marching up the drive with a determined look on his face.

When he reached me, he announced, "I am Friedrich von Hoffenburg. I work for Mr. and Mrs. Harris." He spoke with a charming formality and the slightest hint of a German accent. "You are in need of a lift, I believe. Please, allow me to drive you to your home."

"In your *Porsche?*" I said, flabbergasted.

Friedrich blanched ever so slightly, and when I envisioned the Porsche's immaculate leather interior, I couldn't blame him. I must have looked like a refugee from a village of mud wrestlers.

"Yes, naturally, in my Porsche," he said manfully, and offered me his arm. "Please, you will allow me?"

It wasn't every day that a tall, broad-shouldered youth with flaxen hair and sky-blue eyes appeared out of the rain to offer me his arm. What else could I do but take it?

NINE

I rewarded my escort's gallantry by asking him to fetch a clean blanket from the stables and drape it across the passenger seat before I slid into his precious vehicle. He obeyed with alacrity — and with visible relief — and we were soon cruising down Anscombe Manor's long and curving drive.

Although Friedrich drove with great restraint, I quickly realized that the Porsche wasn't the right car for me. It was lovely to look at, but it didn't offer much in the way of elbow room and it was so low to the ground that I would have had to be as limber as my sons to get in and out of it daily without straining vital muscles. More important, there was no place to put a week's worth of groceries, a deluxe cat carrier, or a pair of wriggly boys.

"Who told you I needed a lift?" I inquired as we made a stately turn onto the lane leading to the cottage.

"Eleanor Harris," Friedrich replied. "She is a friend of yours, I believe."

"She is," I said, smiling at his use of Nell's proper name. "I understand that you met her at the Sorbonne."

"Yes, we met in Paris," he acknowledged, then went on boldly, "I fell in love with her immediately, of course. She is quite . . ." He sighed, and his eyes took on the faraway look common to young men in the throes of Nell-worship.

"Beautiful?" I hazarded.

"She is of course beautiful," Friedrich agreed, "but there are many beautiful girls in the world. Eleanor is more than beautiful. She has a small bear —"

"Bertie," I said promptly. One couldn't know Nell for long without making the acquaintance of Sir Bertram, her chocolate-brown teddy bear. While I kept my relationship with Reginald under wraps, Nell kept hers with Bertie out in the open, for everyone to see.

"Yes, Bertie." Friedrich nodded. "She speaks of this bear without embarrassment. This is character, I think. She is also quite clever, you know. She completed a three-year degree at the Sorbonne in one year. She is altogether remarkable." He glanced earnestly at me. "I have much to offer Eleanor. Not only my love, but comfort, stability, security. My family is quite well-off. We have homes in many beautiful places. Our stables are famous. If you are her friend, you will tell her this."

As Friedrich spoke, it gradually dawned on me that he was driving slowly not because of the inclement weather but because he needed time to convince me that he was the best candidate to marry Nell. He couldn't have been more obvious if he'd held up a sign saying VOTE FOR ME. If he hadn't been so young and so sincere, I would have burst out laughing.

"I think she probably knows about your background already," I said gently.

"But to hear it from a friend may . . . open her eyes," he reasoned.

"I doubt it," I said. "Nell's not easily swayed by other people's opinions."

Friedrich gave me a puzzled look. "But she speaks so highly of you. . . ."

"She does?" I said, astounded. Nell was so superior to me on every measurable scale that I'd never imagined her speaking of me at all, let alone highly. "I'm glad to hear it, but it doesn't mean that I have any influence over her. I'm afraid you'll have to court Nell on your own, Friedrich."

"I see." He lapsed into a disappointed

silence but rallied when we arrived at the cottage. "Your sons are fine equestrians, Ms. Shepherd. If they were my sons, I would be very proud."

"Thank you," I said, climbing out of the car. "And thank you very much for bringing me home."

"It was my pleasure," he said with a courteous nod.

I closed the Porsche's door and gave Friedrich a friendly wave as he drove off. I couldn't think ill of him for trying to win me over. Nell's refusal to go along with his marvelous plans for her future had evidently made him desperate enough to try anything — following her to England, shoveling muck, flattering me. I felt sorry for him, but I also thought Nell would be good for him. She would add the word "humility" to his vocabulary.

As I sloshed up the flagstone path to the cottage's front door, I wondered if I'd be subjected to the same treatment by Mario from Milan, Rafael from Barcelona, and the French boys Annelise had mentioned. If I played my cards right, I thought, giggling, I'd get to ride in every flashy sports car on the market.

I had seldom been so happy to walk into a warm, dry house. Since the twins were still in school and Annelise was browsing the shops in Upper Deeping, Stanley was the only family member to greet me when I came in. He sniffed my boots with the profound concentration of a naturalist examining a new specimen from a foreign land, then followed me through the cottage as I made my rounds.

I threw my hiking clothes into the washer and myself into a blessedly hot bath, then dressed in clean jeans, a sweater, and sneakers and ran downstairs to make dinner. I chose something quick and easy — ham, scalloped potatoes, and broccoli — because I wanted to spend some time in the study while I still had the cottage to myself. I had an awful lot to tell Aunt Dimity.

Twenty minutes later, dinner was ready for launch, my hiking clothes were in the dryer, and I was seated in the study with the blue journal in my hands, a fire in the hearth, and Stanley curled and purring in my lap. Reginald looked beneficently at us from his shelf, as if to say, "I don't mind sharing you with the cat. He needs your warmth more than I do." I gave him a grateful nod, stroked Stanley between the ears, and opened the journal.

"Dimity?" I said. "Want to hear about my day?"

The familiar lines of royal-blue ink spun across the page without a moment's hesitation.

I always want to hear about your days, my dear, but I must confess that I'm particularly eager to hear about this one. I can tell by the tremor in your voice that it was eventful. Did Kit agree to help you with your vampire hunt?

"Yes," I said, "but only after I agreed to take riding lessons."

You agreed to take riding lessons? At last! How clever of Kit to persuade you.

"It wasn't clever," I protested. "It was heartlessly cruel and devious, and he only did it to torment me."

Don't be silly, Lori. Kit is as kind as summer. He would never do anything to torment you.

"He did today," I said. "I gave him the perfect excuse to get away from the stables, and instead of thanking me for it, he used it to blackmail me into doing something I've been avoiding for years. Pure, unadulterated torment."

Why would Kit wish to get away from the stables?

"Because he can't stand the new stable hands," I explained with a slightly malicious smile. "A small, multinational army of rich young bachelors followed Nell home from Paris and volunteered to work at Anscombe

133

Manor. They're falling all over themselves trying to prove that they're worthy of Nell. Emma's taking advantage of them shamelessly, but they're driving Kit nuts."

I imagine they would.

"I could hardly keep up with his mood swings today," I said. "First he blackmailed me into riding, then he got really touchy when I discovered some footprints he missed on Sunday. When I mentioned Nell's name, he went all wistful and sad-eyed, and on the way home he blew up at me."

Defensiveness, irritability, melancholy, unreasonable fits of bad temper . . . The ghost of a bosom-heaving sigh seemed to waft through the room. *He sounds like a man very much in love. Nell's scheme seems to be having the desired effect.*

I frowned uncomprehendingly, then gasped as the penny dropped.

"Dimity," I said, with a note of disapproval in my voice. "You're not suggesting that Nell *invited* those guys to Anscombe Manor, are you?"

I'm suggesting no such thing. Nell is an honorable young woman. I'm certain that her admirers came to Anscombe Manor without any encouragement from her. I'm equally certain, however, that she hasn't gone out of her way to send them packing.

"She's keeping them around to torture Kit?" I said, dismayed.

Kit is torturing himself, Lori. Never forget that. I suspect that Nell is simply using the situation as an opportunity to demonstrate — before his eyes — her unswerving devotion to him. If the scheme fails, I have no doubt that she'll dismiss her young suitors in a trice and think of another way to rid Kit of his foolish conviction that he is too old for her.

"You know what, Dimity?" I said. "I think we may be wrong about the age thing. Kit's always used his age as an excuse to push Nell away, but I have a feeling that something else is going on."

Such as?

"I'm not sure," I said slowly. "When he blew up at me this afternoon, he told me that he has no intention of *ever* getting married. He told me that he's *meant* to be alone. He said that it would be *wrong* of him to marry, not just Nell but *anyone*."

He's meant to be alone and it would be wrong of him to marry. What interesting statements. I wonder what he means by them? Is he, by any chance, homosexual?

"I asked him if he was, and he denied it," I said.

Perhaps he has a physical problem, then, a problem that, in his mind, renders him unfit to

135

play the role of a husband. You must find out if this is indeed what's troubling him.

"How?" I asked uneasily.

Men are, of course, more reticent about such problems than women are, but if you found the courage to ask Kit about his sexual orientation, I'm certain that you'll find a way to discuss with him other subjects of an intimate nature.

I gaped at the blue journal in disbelief. "You want *me* to ask *Kit* about his . . . his manliness?"

You needn't be quite so direct, my dear. You might simply suggest, as a way of opening the conversation, that Nell wouldn't care if he were blind, deaf, and paralyzed from the neck down. She's bound to his spirit, not to his body. You must reassure him on that score.

"I'll do what I can," I said weakly, shooting a horrified look at Reginald. My pink bunny seemed to understand the excruciating awkwardness of the task Aunt Dimity had set for me. Kit was one of my dearest friends, but I wasn't sure he'd remain one if I started quizzing him on subjects of a much-too-intimate nature.

I know you'll do your best, Lori. Now, tell me about the vampire hunt. You mentioned footprints. Did they lead you to Rendor?

"Not yet," I said, overjoyed to move on to

another topic. "But the footprints and a scrap of silk he left behind prove that he's not a figment of the twins' imaginations. Kit thinks he was heading for a place called Aldercot Hall, but before we could follow him there, we smelled smoke. When we went to check it out, we found a man camping in Gypsy Hollow, and we ended up having a very enjoyable lunch with him. I don't know what his last name is, but his first name is Leo, and he's a real charmer. Did you ever hear of him, Dimity? He's spent most of his adult life in Australia, but he grew up in England, and he told us that he spent a fair amount of time around here when he was young."

I've known a number of Leos. It's a pity you didn't ascertain his surname. Did your lunch with Leo put an end to your vampire hunt?

"No, but the rain did," I said. "It started coming down in buckets, so Kit and I decided to storm Aldercot Hall tomorrow." I stroked Stanley absentmindedly, then asked, "Why don't I know about Aldercot Hall, Dimity? It's only a few miles away, but I'd never heard of it until today."

Aldercot Hall is a private residence. It has never been opened to the public, and its owners, the DuCarals, have never involved them-

selves in the affairs of neighboring communities.

"Is that how they've escaped the gossip grapevine?" I asked. "I mean, I'm a card-carrying member of the Finch busybody society, but I haven't heard so much as a whisper about the DuCarals."

You haven't listened to the right people, Lori. Most of the villagers with whom you exchange gossip are relative newcomers to Finch. They are no doubt unaware of certain . . . stories . . . associated with the DuCaral family. If you wish to hear those stories, you'll have to listen to someone who has deep roots in the region, someone whose memories go back a long, long way.

"Like the Pyms?" I asked, referring to a pair of ancient and identical twin sisters who lived between Anscombe Manor and Finch.

No. Ruth and Louise Pym won't be able to help you. As churchgoers they would find it distasteful to discuss the . . . legends . . . that are associated with the DuCarals.

"What does churchgoing have to do with it?" I asked. "What kind of legends are you talking about, Dimity?"

The kind that would make a creature such as Rendor seek sanctuary in Aldercot Hall.

I stared hard at Aunt Dimity's reply, then

glanced foolishly around the study, as though I were afraid of being overheard, before whispering excitedly, "Are you saying that the DuCarals are *vampires?*"

I would never say such a thing, Lori, but there have always been strange rumors connected to the family. Have you ever met a woman named Lizzie Black?

"No," I said. "Who is she?"

She's someone I think you should meet. She has a small freehold on the other side of Horace Malvern's property. It's called Hilltop Farm, and it's been in Lizzie's family for seven generations.

"The Fowlers live on the other side of Mr. Malvern's farm," I reminded her.

Hilltop Farm is tucked between the two properties, at the end of a rather uninviting lane. I'm sure you've passed it many times without giving it a second glance.

I shook my head despondently. "There are way too many gaps in my local knowledge, Dimity. I didn't know about the pet cemetery on Emma's Hill until I stumbled into it today. I'd never heard of Aldercot Hall and the DuCarals until Kit mentioned them. Now you're springing Hilltop Farm and Lizzie Black on me, and I've never heard of them either. I feel like a stranger in my own backyard."

*You're far from a stranger, Lori, but it will
take you many years to become familiar with
every nook and cranny of the countryside surrounding the cottage. As for the DuCaral family and Lizzie Black — they are equally reclu-
sive. I would have been surprised if you'd
claimed an acquaintance with them.*

"Is Lizzie Black related to the DuCarals?"
I asked.

*No, but I believe she knows things about
them that would be of interest to you. Lizzie is
a most unusual woman. She was raised by
her grandmother after her parents died in an
influenza outbreak. The outbreak drove
Granny Black into virtual seclusion. Over the
years, she and her granddaughter became
almost entirely self-sufficient. They grew their
own food and made their own clothes and
learned to do without whatever they couldn't
grow or make.*

"What about other people?" I asked.

*They had little use for other people. Lizzie
was still a young girl when I first met her, but
she was already extraordinarily antisocial. She
stopped attending school at the earliest opportunity, and she made no friends while she
was there. She rarely showed her face in the
village, and when she did, she seldom spoke
to anyone. She had no interest in the modern
world, but she had an in-depth knowledge of*

local lore and legends. Her grandmother told her stories, you see, stories that had been passed down from one generation of Blacks to the next.

"Stories about the DuCarals?" I said.

I heard only vague hints from her about the DuCaral family's curious history, and I had no reason to pursue the matter further. You, however, have the best of reasons: your sons' well-being. I would strongly advise you to visit Lizzie before you visit Aldercot Hall.

"Dimity," I said, "if Lizzie Black is so antisocial, how did you come to know so much about her?"

I met her shortly after Bobby died.

The silence in the study seemed to deepen, and I found myself holding my breath. Bobby MacLaren had been Dimity's fiancé, her heart's delight, the one great love of her life. He'd died in the Second World War, his plane ripped to pieces by enemy fire and his body lost in the English Channel. After his death Dimity had almost lost the will to live. I hadn't seen his name in the blue journal for many years.

I don't remember how I got there, but one stormy night I found myself at Hilltop Farm — delirious, barefoot, and dressed in nothing but my nightgown. Granny Black took me in and nursed me until I was strong enough to return

*to the cottage. Young Lizzie kept watch over
me at night. I can still remember the cool
touch of her hand on my brow and the sooth-
ing sound of her voice, comforting me. I suppose she felt the same pity for me that she'd
feel for an injured animal.*

The handwriting stopped, and a log fell in
the fire, sending up a shower of sparks.
Stanley raised his sleek black head to see
what had caused the commotion, then
tucked his nose under his tail and went back
to sleep. I remained silent, waiting for Aunt
Dimity to go on. A moment later the handwriting resumed.

*After Granny Black died, I was one of the
fortunate few Lizzie allowed into her life —
very occasionally, mind you, because her
tolerance for company was severely limited.
But I went to Hilltop Farm every now and
again, to make sure that Lizzie had everything
she needed. She always did.*

"I'm sure she was glad to see you," I said.
"You grew up here, and you've always had
a way with people. But what makes you
think she'll speak with me, Dimity? I'm not
even English."

*You may not be able to persuade her to
speak with you, Lori, but I think you would be
wise to make the attempt. If anyone can
prepare you for what awaits you at Aldercot*

Hall, it's Lizzie Black.

Since I was beginning to get butterflies in my stomach every time I thought of what awaited me at Aldercot Hall, I decided to follow Aunt Dimity's advice. It would mean missing dinner, but a missed meal would be a small price to pay if I could glean useful information about the DuCarals — and possibly Rendor — from Lizzie Black.

"I'll have to go now," I said, glancing at the clock on the mantelshelf. "I won't have time to visit Lizzie in the morning, and if I wait until after dinner, I'll be intruding on her evening. I'll leave a note for Annelise and take her car."

Don't be put off by Lizzie's manner, Lori. She can be somewhat . . . abrupt.

"Right," I said.

And occasionally aggressive.

"Okay," I said.

As well as abusive.

"Stop fussing," I scolded. "I'll give it a shot, but if she doesn't want to talk to me, I'll leave."

My thoughts will be with you, my dear.

"Thanks," I said, and closed the journal before Aunt Dimity could make me jumpier than I already was.

There was no denying that I was nervous about meeting Lizzie Black. Living alone year after year on an isolated farm could do strange things to a person. Lizzie might be a crazed survivalist by now, or a cackling, one-eyed hag — or an older, creepier version of Miss Archer. The awful possibilities were endless, but as I left the study, I reminded myself that whatever Lizzie Black had become, somewhere deep inside her was the girl who'd shown such kindness to Aunt Dimity.

TEN

I had a sneaking suspicion that Annelise would ask awkward questions if I told her I was going to see Lizzie Black, so I left a note telling her only that I wasn't sure when I'd be back and that she shouldn't hold dinner for me. If there was an emergency, I reasoned, she could always reach me by cell phone.

I left the note on the kitchen table for her to find, fished her spare set of car keys out of The Drawer, grabbed a dry rain jacket from the coatrack in the front hall, and, as an afterthought, pulled on a pair of Wellington boots. My wellies would fare better than my sneakers in a farmyard.

It was nearly four o'clock when I left the cottage, and the sun was sinking low on the horizon, but the rain had stopped, patches of blue sky were showing through the cloud cover, and there was still enough daylight left for me to locate the lane Aunt Dimity had described as "rather uninviting." As it turned out, I *had* driven past it many times, because it had never occurred to me that anyone could drive *up* it. I'd assumed it was a cow path.

By the time I reached the farmyard at the end of Lizzie's lane, I was convinced that I would have to replace the entire suspension system in Annelise's car. Although the small, boxy Ford had survived the deep ruts and bone-jarring potholes that made the lane uninviting, it hadn't done so happily. When I switched off the engine, the beleaguered chassis let out a groan that seemed to say, "I was designed for fuel economy, you fool, not off-road adventuring!"

The sight that met my eyes at the end of the lane, however, soon made me forget about the beginning and the middle. Hilltop Farm was nothing short of enchanting. The outbuildings were old and crooked and clustered companionably atop a modest hump of a hill, behind a small farmhouse decorated with living trees that had been trained and twisted to form arches over the front door and the small windows.

The buildings were made of the same honey-colored limestone as the low walls that encircled the vegetable garden — now banked with straw for the coming winter —

and the sheep-dotted pastures beyond it. The late-afternoon sunlight gave a rosy glow to the golden stone, made the rain-washed fields sparkle, and gilded the rust-colored lichen on the farmhouse's slate roof.

As I climbed out of the car, I felt as if I were leaving the twenty-first century behind and entering an earlier, simpler age. I could hear the homely clucks of unseen chickens, the grunt of a pig, the distant baaing of sheep, and the rush of water dancing downhill in a nearby stream. Smoke curled from the farmhouse's chimney, and its windows were lit from within by a soft radiance that suggested candles rather than lightbulbs. There were no telephone lines, power lines, generators, or satellite dishes to spoil the illusion of stepping back in time. I'd rarely seen a place more at peace with itself.

The peace, alas, was short-lived. The moment I closed the car door, the farmhouse's front door opened and a woman stepped out. She was short and stocky, with pale blue eyes, a round face as weathered as Leo's, and a long braid of white hair wound over the top of her head, like a close-fitting halo. She wore a bulky brown wool sweater over durable canvas trousers, and she had old leather moccasins on her feet, as though she'd finished her farm chores and settled indoors for the evening.

She looked as if she might be somewhere in her mid-sixties, and though she wasn't aiming a shotgun at me, her body language wasn't entirely welcoming. Her shoulders were squared, her hands clenched into fists, and her glare was so potent that I could feel its heat clear across the farmyard.

"Who are you?" she shouted from the doorstep. "And what do you want?"

"I'm Lori Shepherd," I called back, and since I knew that my name would mean nothing to her, I added, "I'm the American who lives in Dimity Westwood's cottage."

"Bought it up, did you?" she sneered. "Going to *improve* it? Going to make it *better?*"

Her questions took me by surprise. My arrival at the cottage had been *the* hot topic of conversation in Finch for at least two years, and I still attracted a goodly amount of attention from the villagers. I was so used to people knowing all sorts of things about me that it came as something of a shock to find someone who knew absolutely nothing. If I'd needed proof that Lizzie Black lived in isolation, I'd just found it.

"As a matter of fact, I inherited the cottage," I answered. "Dimity left it to me in her will. And I haven't done anything to it.

As far as I'm concerned, it's perfect."

Lizzie cocked her head to one side and regarded me suspiciously. "Why would Dimity Westwood leave her cottage to you, Lori Shepherd?"

"My mother was her best friend," I replied simply.

Lizzie's whole demeanor changed. Her blue eyes widened, her balled fists relaxed, and her harsh voice softened as she said, "Your mother would be Beth, would she?"

I blinked, startled to hear my mother's name spoken in a place she'd never seen, by someone she'd never met.

"Yes, my mother was Beth Shepherd," I said. "She died shortly before Dimity Westwood passed away."

Lizzie pursed her lips, then nodded once. "You'd best come in, then, Lori Shepherd."

She withdrew into the farmhouse, leaving the door open behind her. I took a bracing gulp of cold, damp air and followed her into a large, rectangular room with white-plastered walls, a raftered ceiling, and a well-worn flagstone floor. A blanket of warmth enfolded me as soon as I stepped into the cottage, redolent with the tantalizing aromas of fresh-baked bread, roasted meat, and fragrant herbs. The delicious scents made my stomach grumble longingly, but I was too absorbed in my surroundings to regret missing my dinner.

The room was lit not by candles but by three old-fashioned kerosene lamps with bulbous reservoirs, etched bases, and fluted chimneys. Faded rag rugs covered the uneven limestone flags, and hams, bunches of herbs, strings of dried red berries, and skeins of yarn hung from the blackened rafters.

The huge hearth that pierced the north wall had been fitted with a type of black-leaded range I'd seen only once before, in a museum of country life. It had an oven on one side, a boiler on the other, and an open fire burning in a grate in between. A tea-kettle hung on a pivoting pothook above the fire, and woven pot holders dangled from iron hooks set into the mantelshelf.

A wooden rocking chair sat close to the hearth, opposite a three-legged stool and a full-size spinning wheel, and a towering pine dresser beside the hearth was crammed with books and piled with mismatched but beautiful old china.

The south wall held a deep stone sink with a hand pump at one end and a wooden draining board at the other. The rest of the walls were hung with shelves that held too many objects to catalogue at a glance. The remains of a meal littered the oak table that occupied the center of the room — a brown teapot and a blue-and-white striped mug, a crust of bread, an apple core, a plate bearing telltale swirls of gravy.

"I'm so sorry," I said as I closed the door behind me. "I've interrupted your dinner."

"No matter," said Lizzie. "I'd finished." She cleared the table and took the plate to the sink. "Warm yourself by the fire. I'll freshen the pot."

I took off my jacket and sat on the stool with it in my lap while Lizzie prepared tea in the traditional manner, rinsing the teapot with hot water from the kettle, adding three teaspoons of tea leaves from a caddy on the dresser, filling the pot with boiling water, stirring the mixture, then setting it aside to infuse for several minutes. When the tea was ready, she added milk and sugar to my cup without asking whether I wanted them or not and handed it to me. I accepted it gratefully, hoping to appease my growling stomach.

Lizzie didn't refill her own cup. Instead, she sat in the rocking chair, took a pair of knitting needles from a wicker basket filled with balls of yarn, and began to knit so rapidly that I forgot about my tea and watched her, mesmerized.

"Wow," I said, after she'd whizzed through the first five rows. "You're fast."

"I have to be," she said. "I earn my living with my knitting, among other things."

"Doesn't it hurt your eyes to work at night?" I asked, glancing at the kerosene lamps.

"I don't need to look," she said. "My hands know what to do."

"They certainly do," I said respectfully, and because she'd shown no sign of resenting my first question, I asked another. "Where do you sell your knitting?"

"In an exclusive little shop in Upper Deeping," she replied. "The owner comes by once a month to fetch what I've finished." A hint of amusement lit Lizzie's eyes as she added, "She walks in. Doesn't like to risk her motorcar."

"Smart woman," I muttered.

The needles kept clicking while Lizzie's pale eyes traveled from the spinning wheel to the skeins of yarn hanging overhead. "I raise the sheep and shear them, spin the wool, and make the dyes from berries, onion skins, lichens. People feel closer to nature when they wear one of my jumpers, and these days people pay dearly to feel close to nature."

"It sounds like hard work," I commented.

"Hard work keeps me healthy," she returned. "I'm seventy-five years old, and I've never had a day's illness in my life."

"You're seventy-five?" I said, impressed. "I thought you were younger."

"That's because I live alone," she said, nodding wisely. "Mark my words, Lori Shepherd, the less you have to do with people, the healthier you'll be, in mind as well as body. People are good for nothing but germs and arguments."

"What about Dimity?" I asked.

"She was different," Lizzie allowed. "She didn't yammer on at me about finding a husband and having babies. As if I ever needed either." She tossed her head disdainfully. "People think children will look after them in their old age. In truth, most children would as soon poison their old parents as look after them. As for husbands — I sleep much better without a man hogging the bed or raising the roof with his snoring or telling me to put out the light before I've finished reading."

It suddenly struck me that Lizzie was as different from the Pym sisters as it was possible to be. Where they were vague and gentle, Lizzie was as sharp as an axe and just as lethal.

"Your animals depend on you, though," I

said. "What would happen to them if you fell ill?"

"A young couple, Rhys and Kim, live over the hill," she said complacently. "I gave them a place to park their caravan ten years ago, and in return they help me with the heavy work. They drop in from time to time, to make sure I'm still ticking, but otherwise we leave each other be. When I pop my clogs, they'll get the animals, the land, everything."

She put down her knitting, picked up a poker, and stirred the fire vigorously. I sipped my tea and basked in the fire's warmth.

"Did Dimity tell you about my mother?" I asked after a moment's silence.

"She mentioned her best friend, Beth, from time to time," said Lizzie, returning to her knitting. "I'd forgotten that Beth had a daughter." She tilted her head toward me. "You'd be the one with the rabbit."

I grinned. "Yep. I'm the one with the rabbit. His name is Reginald, and he lives with me, my husband, and my sons in Dimity's cottage."

"Husband and sons, eh?" Lizzie shrugged. "To each her own."

"I'll drink to that," I said, and took a sip of the sweet, milky tea.

"Why did you come to see me, Lori Shepherd?" Lizzie eyed me shrewdly. "You're not doing a piece on me for the *Upper Deeping Despatch,* are you?"

"I'm not a journalist," I assured her. "I came here on my own account, to ask you about Aldercot Hall."

The knitting needles stopped moving. "Why would you come to me with questions about Aldercot?"

I phrased my answer carefully. "Dimity Westwood left her personal journal to me along with the cottage. In the journal she wrote that you knew about certain legends associated with Aldercot." I skated delicately around the fact that the journal entry had been written posthumously and continued, "I'm interested in local history, but I haven't been able to find out anything about the DuCaral family or their home. So I decided to come to you. Was Dimity right? Can you tell me about Aldercot?"

"Oh, I can tell you about Aldercot," Lizzie said darkly. "Whether you'll believe me or not is another question."

"Try me," I suggested.

"Your sons," she said, after a moment's silence. "How old would they be?"

"They'll be six in March," I told her. "They're twins."

"Babies," she murmured. After another pause she laid her knitting in her lap and nodded decisively. "All right, Lori Shepherd, I'll tell you what I know. You can do with it what you will, but if you're half as clever as I think you are, you'll keep those sons of yours away from Aldercot Hall."

A shiver of anticipation passed through me, and I hunched forward on the stool so as not to miss a word that Lizzie said. She rested her arms on the chair's, began to rock in a slow but steady rhythm, and turned her gaze to the fire. The flickering flames cast a reddish glow over her wrinkled face and lit her pale eyes with golden sparks.

"In 1899," she began, "a great storm drove a ship ashore near the town of Whitby in North Yorkshire. The crew was dead and the ship's sole passenger missing, so no one could explain the queer cargo the ship carried. Fifty crates filled with dirt seemed an odd thing to ship to England, but the crates were loaded onto a wagon and sent to London, in accordance with papers found in the captain's cabin. The crates were the property of the ship's missing passenger." Her fire-flecked eyes swiveled toward me. "His name was Count Dracula."

"I've heard of him," I said solemnly. It seemed impolite to point out that her story, so far, had been stolen directly from Bram Stoker's famous novel, a copy of which might very well be sitting on one of the pine dresser's crowded shelves.

"Everyone's heard of Count Dracula," Lizzie acknowledged, looking again into the fire. "And some have heard of the crates he shipped to London. But only a few — a scant few — know that the wagons carrying those crates interrupted their southward journey with a stop at Aldercot Hall."

"Ah," I breathed. The Aldercot Hall connection was a new twist on the old tale, a subplot not derived from Stoker's novel.

"The Aldercot family had died out years before, and the hall was derelict," Lizzie went on. "But a short time after the wagons made their unexpected stop, a new family — the DuCarals — took possession of the hall, claiming a distant kinship with the Aldercots. They kept themselves to themselves and were never seen in the nearby villages. The DuCarals ordered everything they needed from London" — Lizzie gave me a meaningful sidelong glance — "including servants."

"Why did they bring servants up from London?" I asked. "There must have been plenty of people around here who needed jobs."

"Too many questions would be asked if a local girl went missing," Lizzie replied.

"Went missing?" I repeated, frowning.

"The girls that entered Aldercot Hall were never seen again," Lizzie intoned.

"Didn't their families —" I began, but Lizzie cut me off.

"They had no families," she declared. "They were orphans, all of them. When they disappeared, no one noticed or cared."

"What happened to them?" I asked, though I thought I knew the answer.

"The DuCarals needed blood to live," Lizzie said bluntly. "They used those girls to keep themselves alive, and when they'd drained them dry, they ordered new ones. There are more graves in the DuCaral family graveyard than there ever were Du-Carals to bury. And most of them are unmarked."

The wind moaned in the chimney, and the twisted tree branches scratched at the windowpanes, like clawed fingers searching for a way in. I clutched my teacup in both hands and tried to ignore the gooseflesh that was creeping up my arms.

"It couldn't go on, of course," Lizzie continued. "Times change, and the DuCarals changed with them. When disposable humans became more difficult to come by, they turned to animals. A herd of fallow deer roams their property, to make the place more picturesque — or so they would have you think."

"They drink the deer's blood?" I said, grimacing.

"The DuCarals came from a foreign land, but they're English now," said Lizzie. "They don't like to draw attention to themselves. Missing deer draw far less attention than missing housemaids." She stopped rocking and turned her pale blue eyes toward me. "You'll know them by their sharp white teeth, their rancid breath, the strength in their cold hands. They live in shadows, and unless they're killed the right way, they never die."

"The . . . the right way?" I faltered.

Lizzie leaned forward and lowered her voice. "Ask them, if you dare, about the murder that took place there forty years ago. Ask them why it was never reported to the police. Ask them how a man could be dead one day and alive the next."

"A d-dead man came b-back to life?" I stammered, my eyes widening.

"No," Lizzie said softly. "He never died. The bullet missed his heart, you see. You have to hit the heart to kill a *vampire*."

She picked up the poker, heated it in the

fire, and used the soot on its tip to write the name "DuCaral" in spiky capital letters on the hearthstone. Then she wrote the name a second time, but this time she rearranged the letters to spell . . .

"Dracula," I whispered, thunderstruck.

"The count never came to Aldercot," Lizzie said in what she must have thought was a reassuring tone. "But his cousins did. And they never left."

While I stared, dumbfounded, at the anagram Lizzie had scrawled upon the hearthstone, she sat back in the rocking chair and resumed knitting. The hissing fire and the clicking needles made me acutely aware of sounds that were missing from Lizzie's house — the hum of a refrigerator, the rumble of a furnace, the ticking of a clock, the background noises I associated with normalcy. But I was so caught up in the abnormal by then that I found myself straining to hear a wolf's howl rising from the valley or a bat's claws scrabbling at the door. When Lizzie spoke, I jumped in fright and splashed tea across the spiky letters, making the soot run in rivulets, like black blood spilled upon the hearth.

"Keep your sons away from Aldercot," she warned. "You can see yourself out."

"Uh, yes," I said, tearing my horrified gaze

from the hearthstone and getting unsteadily to my feet. "Thank you for a . . . a fascinating evening. And for the tea." I wiped my tea-streaked hand on my jeans, took my cup to the sink, put on my jacket, and headed for the door.

"Wait," said Lizzie. She placed her knitting atop the balls of yarn in the wicker basket, stood, and pulled a string of shriveled red berries down from a hook on one of the rafters. She tied the string into a loop and hung it around my neck. "Rowanberries. The undead can't abide rowans. I plant them around my fields to protect my flocks."

I looked at the room's tiny windows. "The trees arched around your windows, your door . . . ?"

"Rowans," Lizzie confirmed. Without warning she seized my shoulders and drew me to her, until her cheek was nearly touching mine. "If you go there, go by day," she whispered hoarsely. "That's when they're weakest." She released me, turned toward her rocking chair, and said over her shoulder, "Good night, Lori Shepherd."

"Good night," I said.

I opened the door, hesitated, then stepped outside. I would never admit it to Bill or to Kit or to the incurably sensible Emma

Harris, but without the rowanberries I might not have had the courage to face the darkness.

Eleven

Few drives have tried my patience more severely than the one I took that night down Lizzie's lane. Each dead leaf streaking past my windshield made me squeak like a frightened mouse, and the headlights picked out grotesque shapes in the hedgerows — leering faces, staring eyes, twisted hands with grasping fingers.

I wanted to fly home at the speed of light, but I was forced instead to inch along at the speed of sludge, dodging potholes and bumping gingerly in and out of the yawning craters I couldn't dodge. The only thing that kept me from panicking completely — and destroying what was left of Annelise's car — was the wholly irrational but nonetheless comforting thought that the trees lining the lane might be rowans.

I floored the accelerator the moment I hit the paved road, and I didn't lift my foot until I reached the safety of my driveway and saw the beautiful pools of bright, electric light spilling from the cottage's many windows. Since I didn't want Annelise, Will, or Rob to know how spooked I was, I took a moment to collect myself, then pasted a winning smile on my face and strode jauntily up the flagstone path to the front door.

My hand was on the latch when I realized with a jolt that I was still wearing the rowanberry necklace. I removed it hastily, to avoid unwanted questions, stuffed it into my jacket pocket, hitched my smile back into place, and walked into the cottage.

"Mummy!"

The twins' shouts and the familiar sound of their slippered feet pounding down the staircase turned my fake smile into a real one. I swept each of them into a hug and felt my tightly wound nerves unwind as I breathed in the tranquilizing scent of freshly bathed little boys.

Rob and Will helped me out of my jacket and my wellies, then came with me to the kitchen, where Annelise was dishing up a plate of rewarmed ham and scalloped potatoes for me. The boys chattered like magpies while I ate, telling me about the clay ponies they'd made at school, the flock of sheep that had blocked the road on their way home, and the new toy they'd brought home for Stanley, which turned out to be a ball of raw wool they'd retrieved from a hedgerow while waiting for the sheep to pass. Annelise assured me that she'd washed and dried the wool before presenting it to Stanley, who'd chased it all over the cottage before depositing it on Bill's armchair.

I was still eating — and the twins were still chattering — when Bill called, so I handed the telephone to them. They kept their father occupied until I'd finished, then passed the telephone back to me and repaired to the living room to play with their knights and dinosaurs. Annelise went with them, to make sure that none of the pterodactyls "accidentally" flew into the fire.

"How's life in cat land?" I asked Bill after they'd gone.

"Littered with complications," he replied dryly. "Did I mention the educational scholarships Mrs. Shuttleworth endowed?"

"Is Miss Muffin going to college?" I asked, laughing.

"Thankfully, no," said Bill. "The Shuttleworth scholarships will be awarded to humans, but only if they promise to dedicate their lives to curing cats. Not dogs. Not hamsters. Not parrots. Just cats."

"A laudable aim," I said. "Stanley approves."

"Wait until I tell him about the cat spa," Bill said. "What's up with you?"

I reminded myself of my own laudable aim — to protect my husband from unnecessary distractions — and said, "Nothing much. I'm pretty beat from all the walking Kit and I did today, so I'll probably turn in early."

"Me, too." Bill sighed wistfully. "It's barely seven o'clock, and we're already talking about going to bed. We must be getting old."

"I don't mind," I said, "as long as we get old together."

"That's the plan," said Bill, sounding more cheerful.

"There is one thing you should know, though." I turned away from the kitchen door and lowered my voice. "We have to buy Annelise a new car."

There was a long pause before Bill asked resignedly, "What happened to Annelise's car, Lori? You didn't drive it into a ditch by any chance, did you?"

"No, I did *not* drive it into a ditch," I responded indignantly. I'd driven *my* car into a ditch once, and even though I'd been the innocent victim of an ice-covered road and a sharp bend, my husband had always chosen to believe that my bad driving had caused the accident. "I don't make a habit of driving cars into ditches, Bill."

"What happened to Annelise's car, Lori?" he asked again.

"Potholes," I replied. "I hit some really nasty potholes while I was driving it this afternoon. It could have happened to anyone."

"They *must* have been nasty if we have to replace the car," Bill observed. "Where were you driving?"

"Near Mr. Malvern's farm," I said, as truthfully as I could. "I went down a lane I'd never explored before, and suddenly I was surrounded by potholes. The car made some really strange noises when I finally got it out of there. It'll probably cost less to replace than to repair." I heaved a remorseful sigh. "I'm sorry, Bill. If I'd known how bad the lane would be, I wouldn't have driven up it."

"It's all right," he said. "Annelise's car has reached its sell-by date anyway. I was planning to replace it, as a wedding present. I'm sure she won't mind getting it a few months early."

"You are the nicest man on earth," I said fondly.

"I am, aren't I?" Bill marveled. He paused, as if he were contemplating the awe-inspiring magnitude of his niceness, then chuckled softly and asked, "What's on your agenda for tomorrow?"

"Kit and I are going to see a historic house," I said, hoping that Bill wouldn't ask which one. "It'll give him another excuse to get away from the stables and me another whack at convincing him to marry Nell."

"Good luck," said Bill.

"Luck," I observed loftily, "will have nothing to do with it. Matchmaking is a finely honed *skill.*"

We chatted for a few more minutes, and by the time we rang off, the last vestiges of atavistic terror had left me. The dishwasher was humming, my sons were making dinosaur noises in the living room, and my husband was casting aspersions on my driving. Everything was back to normal. What had seemed eerily believable in the flickering firelight at Hilltop Farm seemed utterly ludicrous in my well-lit and well-lived-in cottage.

"If I'm going to worry about something," I murmured, "I'll worry about something real — like finding a car that doesn't sound as if I've dropped a box of wrenches under the hood."

Bill's offer to buy Annelise a new car was nothing short of princely, but it didn't solve my immediate transportation problem. Annelise needed the Range Rover to ferry the twins hither and yon, and however tempting it was to use Nell's rich young suitors as my personal chauffeurs, I didn't want to be dependent on their goodwill. I needed a set of wheels of my own.

I picked up the telephone and called Mr. Barlow. The local handyman enjoyed tinkering with cars and usually had a few fixeruppers parked behind his cottage. As soon as I explained my situation to him, he offered to loan me a Morris Mini he'd just finished repairing. I knew that Bill would rib me endlessly when he found out what I was driving, because the car I'd put into a ditch had also been a Morris Mini, but it seemed a small price to pay for mobility.

"That'd be great, Mr. Barlow," I said. "Do you think you could drop it off at Anscombe Manor tomorrow? I can get a lift there from Annelise in the morning — she'll be taking the twins to the stables for their Saturday trail ride — but I'll need the Mini later on, when I'm ready to come home."

"No problem," said Mr. Barlow. "Where have you been keeping yourself, Lori?" he went on conversationally. "Haven't seen you in the village for ages."

"I was at the Guy Fawkes Day committee meeting yesterday," I said, taken aback.

"Were you?" he said. "You must have been keeping your head down — a wise thing to do when Peggy Taxman's in charge. Did you stay for tea and buns afterwards?"

"No," I said. "I had to get home."

"Well, don't be in such a hurry to leave next time," Mr. Barlow scolded. "I miss our little chats. I'll drop the Mini off at Anscombe Manor by noon tomorrow."

I thanked him, said good night, and hung up. I was bemused by his comment regarding our little chats. I didn't think it had been "ages" since he and I had enjoyed a tête-à-tête, but perhaps it had seemed like ages to him. He was, after all, an old man living on his own. I made a mental note to visit him soon, then turned to the next item on the evening's agenda.

I called Annelise into the kitchen, to give her the bad news as well as the good news about her car. She accepted both calmly — Annelise was preternaturally unflappable — but when I described the exact location of the potholes, she folded her arms and surveyed me disapprovingly.

"Why were you going to Lizzie Black's?" she asked.

"Who's Lizzie Black?" I responded artlessly.

"She's a crackbrained old crone who

believes in all sorts of outlandish nonsense," Annelise replied, "and she lives at the end of the lane you *say* you were exploring. Did someone in the village tell you about her?" She raised an eyebrow. "Did someone in Finch tell you to ask Lizzie Black about vampires?"

"Why would I ask anyone about vampires?" I said with a tolerant smile.

"Because you've been looking for reasons to fret about Rob and Will ever since they started school," she replied. "If it's not chlorine gas, it's measles. After what they told us the other night, I'm willing to bet my wedding dress that you've worked yourself into a lather about Rendor, the Destroyer of Souls."

"I haven't worked myself into a —" I began, but Annelise silenced me with an impatient cluck.

"Let me tell you about Lizzie Black, Lori," she said. "My youngest brother, Tony, bumped into her while she was collecting berries in the woods, and do you know what she told him?"

"No," I said.

"She sat Tony down on a tree stump and told him all about the Butterfly Man," said Annelise. "Sounds sweet, doesn't it? Harmless?"

"Butterflies don't exactly fill me with terror," I admitted.

"Just wait." Annelise's voice took on a sugary, singsong quality, as if she were telling a fairy tale to a young child. "The Butterfly Man catches little children in his net and takes them to his dark house in the forest. When he gets them inside, he pins them to a board and drops *camphor* on their heads until they're *dead*." Annelise flung her hands into the air. "Tony was eight years old, Lori! He believed every word that mad old biddy said! It took us the longest time to figure out why he was afraid to leave the house, but when we did, Mum went up to Hilltop Farm to have a word with Lizzie. And do you know what Lizzie told Mum?"

"No," I said.

"Lizzie told my mother that *she'd* better watch out for the Butterfly Man or he'd pin *her* to one of his boards!" Annelise shook her head. "Lizzie's barking, Lori, daft as a brush, and she enjoys frightening gullible people. You shouldn't get mixed up with her."

"Thanks for the warning," I said. "As a matter of fact, I have one for you, too. The twins may have embroidered their story the other night, but I have reason to believe that they saw someone in the woods on Sunday.

Kit and I reexamined the ground today and found footprints up there."

Annelise's eyebrows rose.

"Kit's putting the stable hands on high alert," I went on, "and I'd like you to keep a close watch on the boys while you're at Anscombe Manor tomorrow. Not that you don't always keep an eye on them, but —"

"I won't let Will and Rob out of my sight," Annelise stated firmly. She would have said more, but a shuddering yawn interrupted her.

"Why don't you turn in?" I suggested. "I'll take the boys upstairs and get them settled."

"All right," she said, suppressing another yawn. "I don't know why I'm so tired. It must be the weather."

"It's dreary enough to make anyone tired," I agreed.

Annelise went up to her room and I went to the living room to round up the twins. As I shepherded them upstairs, I kept thinking about Lizzie Black and the Butterfly Man. I couldn't imagine why Aunt Dimity had encouraged me to pay attention to someone who was so clearly out of touch with reality. Perhaps, I thought, Lizzie had misplaced a few marbles since Aunt Dimity had known her.

By half past eight, Annelise and the boys

were in bed and asleep, and I was seated in the high-backed leather armchair before the fire in the study, with the blue journal open in my lap and Reginald nestled in the crook of my arm. Stanley had elected to spend the night with Will and Rob.

"Aunt Dimity?" I said. "I went to Hilltop Farm. I met Lizzie Black."

Aunt Dimity's fine copperplate curled instantly across the page. *Would she speak with you?*

"Yes," I said, "after I told her that I was your best friend's daughter."

Your mother would be pleased to know that she'd smoothed the way for you. Did Lizzie tell you about the DuCarals?

"She told me that they were *Dracula's cousins,* Dimity." I giggled. "If she read Bram Stoker's novel, she must have mistaken it for history rather than fiction. According to her, the DuCarals drank the blood of orphaned housemaids until the supply dried up — so to speak. Now they live on deer's blood. I guess good help really *is* hard to find these days." I stifled a gurgle of laughter and tried to sound more sympathetic. "I'm sorry, Dimity. I know that Lizzie was your friend, but she's become rather eccentric in her old age. Annelise called her a crackbrained old crone," I added gently.

Elderly women who live on their own are often ridiculed, Lori. Did you think her crack-brained?

"No," I admitted candidly. "When she talked about the way she lives, she sounded perfectly sane, if a bit fed up with the human race. And when she talked about the other stuff, about the bloodsucking DuCarals and the unmarked graves at Aldercot Hall, I sort of . . . got caught up in it. She's a convincing storyteller, Dimity, and her farmhouse is . . . atmospheric. It was easy to fall under her spell. But once I got home, I snapped out of it and realized that she was spouting nonsense."

Bram Stoker was a convincing storyteller, too, because he did extensive research before writing his novel. He based his fictional Count Dracula on the historical figure of Vlad the Impaler, a Romanian ruler who lived in the fifteenth century.

"Yes, but his Dracula was still fictional," I pointed out. "Fictional characters don't have cousins living in the Cotswolds."

I know they don't, Lori. I'm merely suggesting that Lizzie's story, like Mr. Stoker's, may contain a kernel of truth. Why are the DuCarals associated with bizarre tales of unnatural monsters and unmarked graves? Why do they keep their neighbors at bay? Why are they so reluctant to welcome visitors? Are they perhaps hiding something — or someone — at Aldercot Hall?

A shiver slithered down my spine like a slowly melting ice cube. I stiffened in my chair and tightened my grip on the blue journal as I asked, "What do you mean?"

I don't wish to upset you.

"Too late," I said. "If you're thinking what I think you're thinking, I'm already upset. So tell me what you're thinking."

Very well. I'm thinking of the man who shot you. His family knew that he was a murderous madman, but instead of turning him in to the proper authorities, they shielded him, protected him, locked him away in a private institution from which he ultimately escaped. What if a similar scenario is being played out at Aldercot Hall?

I lifted my eyes from the curving lines of royal-blue ink and stared into the fire uneasily. Aunt Dimity's thoughts corresponded almost too closely with my own. I'd already suggested to Kit that the footprints and the scrap of crimson silk we'd found on Emma's Hill might have been left there by a man with a vampire fixation. What if the man wasn't a guest at Aldercot Hall but a member of the DuCaral family? What if the family knew that he was insane but kept him

176

under lock and key in the hall instead of in an institution?

"You could be right," I said, looking down at the journal. "The DuCarals might be shielding a killer. Lizzie told me that someone was murdered at Aldercot Hall, not in the dim and distant past but forty years ago. She said the murder was never reported to the police."

I doubt that the DuCarals would report a murder that had been committed by one of their own. The crime would draw the family into the public eye and destroy their privacy forever.

"So instead of calling the police and having Rendor carted away to an asylum, they put him under house arrest, buried the victim's body in an unmarked grave, and isolated themselves completely from the rest of the world, to keep others from discovering what they were hiding behind closed doors — what they're *still* hiding behind closed doors. Bloody hell, Dimity . . ." Tears of frustration pricked my eyes, but I blinked them away impatiently. "We're not dealing with another Abaddon, are we? Does every wealthy family in England have a homicidal maniac locked in the attic?"

I sincerely doubt it, Lori. But the DuCarals might. I suggest that you find out. If history is repeating itself, the madman has found a way out of the attic.

"Maybe Lizzie caught a glimpse of him in the woods, in his vampire regalia," I said wonderingly. "Maybe *he's* the kernel of truth in Lizzie's story."

It's possible.

I wrinkled my nose, perplexed. "But the footprints led me and Kit *to* Aldercot Hall. Why would Rendor go back there if he knew his family would lock him up again?"

Rendor may be slipping in and out of Aldercot Hall without his family's knowledge.

"That does it," I declared, smacking my hand on the arm of the chair and nearly dropping Reginald on his snout. "I'm not having another lunatic stalk my sons. I'm calling the police right now."

You're getting ahead of yourself, Lori. The police don't respond to speculation, and speculation is all you have to offer them at the moment. We don't know for certain that a murder ever took place at Aldercot Hall, or that the DuCarals are harboring a criminal, or that a disturbed member of the family is currently stalking Will and Rob. Unless you can substantiate your claims with hard evidence, the police won't listen to a word you have to say. Given your recent history, one can hardly blame them.

Although I'd said much the same thing to Kit when he'd suggested calling in the police, I was too angry to view the situation rationally.

"What should I do, then?" I demanded. "Tear Aldercot Hall apart with my bare hands?"

The destruction of private property would certainly attract the attention of the police, but not in a way you would find helpful. If you wish to conduct a successful investigation of the goings-on at Aldercot Hall, you must first calm down.

It was sound advice. The DuCarals would undoubtedly set the dogs on me if I showed up on their doorstep breathing fire, so I relaxed my grip on the blue journal and rubbed my cheek against Reginald's ears until the red mist before my eyes dissipated.

"All right," I said finally. "I'm calm."

You must remain so when you and Kit visit Aldercot Hall. While there, look for evidence that supports Lizzie's story. See how many kernels of truth you can glean. There may be more than you expect.

"But I should focus on the murder, shouldn't I?" I asked.

You should gather as much information about the DuCarals as you can. If a member of the family died accidentally, or of natural causes, and the family chose not to report it, there's no reason for you to be unduly alarmed for your sons' safety. If, on the other hand, a passing stranger was killed in a savage attack and the family chose to cover it up . . .

"Then I'll have something to take to the police," I said grimly.

Speak with the servants if you can, Lori. There's no better source of information than a chatty servant.

"I know how to handle chatty servants," I said.

Do you? Apart from an occasional committee meeting, you haven't spent much time in Finch lately, honing your news-gathering skills. I'm afraid you may be losing your edge.

"I'm not losing my edge," I said, stung by Aunt Dimity's lack of faith in me. "I've just been more interested in what the boys are doing at school than in what Peggy Taxman is doing with the greengrocer's shop in Finch. Don't worry, Dimity. I'll get the skinny on the DuCarals."

Please remember, Lori, that the DuCarals are not fond of visitors. You must approach them with great delicacy. If you find it difficult to keep your temper in check, you must allow Kit to do the talking. His charm is irresistible.

"Right," I said. "And while Kit keeps them

occupied, I'll run upstairs and break into the attic."

I do hope you're being facetious, Lori.

"I am," I said, with a wry smile. "I'll be on my best behavior tomorrow, Dimity. I'll keep my eyes and ears open and my mouth shut."

There's a first time for everything, I suppose. I'll be very interested to hear what you discover.

"I'll keep you informed," I promised.

I know you will. Run along to bed, now. You've had a busy day, and I suspect that tomorrow will be even busier.

"Good night, Dimity," I said.

Good night, my dear.

I waited until Aunt Dimity's handwriting had vanished from the page, then closed the journal, but instead of returning it to its shelf, I gazed down at its blue cover reflectively.

When I'd entered the study, I'd been ready to laugh at Lizzie Black and her bizarre fantasies. Now I was almost ready to believe that everything she'd said was true. I'd gone from chiding myself for taking Lizzie too seriously to scolding myself for not taking her seriously enough. It was a strange turn of events. Aunt Dimity usually pulled me back from the edge of hysteria,

181

but tonight she'd waved a red flag in my face.

"Thank heavens for Dimity," I said to Reginald. "I gave too much weight to Annelise's opinion of Lizzie Black. If I hadn't spoken with Dimity, I would have written Lizzie off as a crackpot and ignored the possibility that she might know more about the DuCarals than Annelise does. But I know better now. Lizzie's version of history might be garbled, but it's based on one true thing: Something bad happened at Aldercot Hall forty years ago, and the person responsible for it is still there. If I don't find him and stop him, bad things will start happening again. So he'd better watch out, because I'm on my way."

Reginald's eyes gleamed with approval. I gave him a hug, stood, and returned the blue journal to its shelf. As I returned Reginald to his, I felt the full weight of the day close in on me. It was all I could do to shut off the lights and drag myself upstairs.

"I'm coming to get you, Rendor," I murmured sleepily as I crawled into bed. Then I added, at Kit's request, a short and fairly sincere prayer for rain.

TWELVE

My prayer was answered with such ferocity that the boys' trail ride was canceled the next morning.

"It's been raining like blazes all night," Emma told me over the phone, "and it doesn't look as though it's going to stop anytime soon. The trails have turned into waterfalls, the outdoor rings are flooded, and the arena's roof is leaking. I've canceled tomorrow's sessions as well as today's. Thunder and Storm will stay in the stables, along with the rest of the horses, until the monsoon passes."

"I'll let the boys know," I said. "By the way, Emma, has Kit spoken to you about tightening security around the stables?"

"He has," Emma replied. "And we're on top of it. I'm sorry that I didn't take the twins seriously the other day. It sounds as if we might have a voyeur on the premises. If he shows his face around here again, I'm notifying the police." She paused to speak with someone on her end of the line, then said to me, "I've got to run, Lori. The buckets in the arena need emptying. Tell the boys that if they want to spend their Saturday doing stable chores, they're welcome to join us."

"I'll tell them," I said, and rang off.

The twins took the news of their washed-out trail ride philosophically, explaining to me that it was never a good idea to go riding in a heavy downpour because slick footing could be hazardous for both rider and pony. Preoccupied as I was by an entirely different kind of hazard, I listened with only half an ear.

Neither Annelise nor I was surprised when the twins leapt at the chance to spend the day at Anscombe Manor doing stable chores — my sons shared an inexplicable enthusiasm for shoveling muck — but Annelise was frankly astonished when I appeared in the front hall dressed in my hiking gear.

"You're not going rambling *today,* are you?" she asked incredulously.

"Why shouldn't I?" I said. "A little rain never hurt anyone." And since Kit had asked me to pray for it, I added silently, he wouldn't cancel our trip to Aldercot Hall because of it.

"A *little* rain?" Annelise said, and her tone of voice indicated in no uncertain terms that anyone who would voluntarily spend time outdoors on such a filthy day had to be as mad as Lizzie Black.

If Annelise had spotted the rowanberry necklace I was wearing beneath my rain jacket or glimpsed the array of nonstandard supplies filling my day pack, she probably would have made an emergency call to Bill — after locking me in my bedroom — so I kept my jacket zipped and my pack securely closed while we bundled the boys into the Range Rover.

It was raining so hard that the drops exploded when they hit the road surface, creating a mist that made it hard to see where the lane ended and the hedgerows began. If I'd been driving, I would have turned back, but Annelise handled the challenging conditions with her usual aplomb, and we reached Anscombe Manor without incident.

We parted company in the stable yard, Annelise and the boys heading for the ponies' stalls while I made for the courtyard. Kit was waiting for me in the shelter of the doorway that led to his spartan second-floor flat. His shoulders were hunched against the gusting downpour, and he'd pulled the hood of his rain jacket so far forward on his head that from a distance I could see only the tip of his perfectly shaped nose.

"If I ever doubt the power of prayer," I called as I strode across the courtyard, "remind me of today."

"I will," he said, and came out of the doorway to meet me. "Listen, Lori, I'm sorry that I was so ratty yesterday. I shouldn't have raised my voice to you."

"Don't worry about it," I told him, with a careless wave of my hand. "I find it somehow reassuring to know that you *can* be ratty."

He glanced fleetingly at the manor house, then looked down at his boots. "I realize that you view me as some sort of saint, Lori, but I'm not a saint. I'm a deeply flawed human being."

For one slim whisker of a second, I was tempted to pursue the line of questioning Aunt Dimity had suggested and ask Kit if his flaws included an inability to perform adequately — or at all — in certain intimate situations, but I chickened out. He seemed to be in a fairly good mood, and I didn't want to risk spoiling it so early in the day.

"If *you're* deeply flawed, my friend, then there's hope for the rest of us," I said bracingly. "Can we get going? If I stand still much longer, I'll get moldy."

Kit managed a small smile and led the way out of the courtyard. Much to my relief, he didn't return to the absurdly steep game trail we'd climbed to reach the gnarled apple tree, but went instead to the splendidly level track that ran alongside the north pasture. The track was a swampy mess, to be sure, but at least it hadn't turned into a waterfall.

"Do you know a woman named Lizzie Black?" I asked as we squelched along.

"Lizzie of Hilltop Farm?" said Kit. "Yes, of course, I know her. She's extraordinarily wise in woodlore. Knows when and where to find the best berries, mushrooms, nuts. She's mad as a spoon, of course — believes in banshees and werewolves and such — but she's very reliable when it comes to berries and nuts. Why?"

Since Kit's opinion of Lizzie Black seemed to match Annelise's, I decided not to tell him about my visit to Hilltop Farm. Annelise had already told me how crazy Lizzie was. I didn't need to hear it all over again from Kit. Aunt Dimity had convinced me to keep an open mind about Lizzie's claims, and I intended to do just that.

"Idle curiosity," I replied lightly. "I heard someone mention her name and I just wondered if you knew her. Are we going to Gypsy Hollow?"

"We'll pass through it on our way to Aldercot Hall," Kit replied.

"Good," I said. "I want to make sure that Leo's okay. It can't be much fun for him to be cooped up in his little motor home on a day like this."

"I was planning to look in on him," Kit assured me, "but I suspect that he's coped with worse things than a rainy day."

I gave him a curious glance. "Why were you so eager for it to rain today?"

"It's part of my cunning plan to gain access to Aldercot Hall," he informed me with a wily, sidelong glance. "The DuCarals have a reputation for being standoffish when it comes to visitors, so I doubt that we'd get very far with them if we drove over there. I think we'll have a better chance of getting our boots inside the hall if we present ourselves as a pair of hapless ramblers who've lost their way."

"Okay," I said. "But I still don't see why we need an extra helping of rain."

"We're going to appeal to their sense of humanity," Kit explained. "If we're drenched and freezing when we arrive on their doorstep, they'll be more likely to take pity on us and let us in. Once we're inside, we'll try to find out more about Rendor. Is he a member of the family? A friend?"

"A voyeuristic pervert?" I interjected.

"Let's not leap to any conclusions," Kit advised. "He may simply be a shy man who enjoys watching children at play."

"And I may be the rightful heir to the throne of England," I said sardonically.

Kit pursed his lips and began, "Now, Lori —"

"All right, all right," I interrupted. "I'll reserve judgment until I meet him face-to-face. And I like your plan. I get lost naturally, so I won't have any trouble acting like a hapless rambler."

"I'm glad you approve," he said.

The rain was still hammering down when we reached Gypsy Hollow. The lowest spots in the hollow had turned into quagmires, and the rest of the ground was so thoroughly saturated that I half expected to see mushrooms sprouting up before our eyes. Leo had evidently brought his belongings into the motor home, because there was no sign of the awning or of the furniture that had been clustered beneath it when we'd eaten lunch with him.

There was no sign of Leo either, and when we walked up to the motor home, we found a note taped to the door.

Sorry to miss you, whoever you are. I've gone out and I don't know when I'll be back. If you're desperate, take what you need. If not, please respect my home.

"He must have gone to Finch," I said. "You don't think he walked, do you?"

"He has a bicycle," Kit reminded me. "I imagine he cycled to the village in order to save petrol. I wish I'd known. I'd have given him a lift."

"He'll be fine once he reaches the village," I said confidently. "Sally Pyne will give him a hot breakfast in the tearoom, and the Peacocks will let him spend the rest of the day in the pub. And Mr. Barlow will give him a lift when he decides to come back to the motor home."

"You have great faith in the villagers," Kit commented.

"I have great faith in the vicar," I retorted. "He'll skin them alive if they treat Leo the way they treated you when you were down and out."

Kit flinched as if I'd slapped him, and turned away.

"I'm sorry," I said quickly. "I didn't mean to —"

"It's all right," he murmured.

"Those days are long gone," I pointed out,

wondering what had come over him. We'd always discussed his troubled past quite openly. I'd never known him to be sensitive about it.

"Of course they are," he said with a brittle sort of cheerfulness. "Let's move on, shall we?"

"Right," I said, trying not to show how flustered I was. "So how do we get to Aldercot? Through the cleft between the hills?"

"The cleft will be a running stream by now," said Kit.

He looked at me, then at the slope I'd slithered down the day before. My heart sank as I followed his gaze.

"You're not suggesting that we climb the hill, are you?" I asked. "There must be an easier way."

"There are lots of easier ways, but imagine how awful we'll look after we take this one," said Kit, starting forward. "It'll add authenticity to our story."

I emitted an entirely authentic groan, tightened the straps on my day pack, and clambered up the hill as best I could. By the time I had crawled on all fours onto the familiar shelf near the top of the hill, I was gasping, red-faced, and as muddy as a wallowing warthog. Kit reached down to pull me to my feet, then stood back to survey me critically.

"I knew you could play the part, Lori," he said. "But now you *look* like a hapless rambler."

I gave him the evil eye, then raised my grimy hands and smeared mud across his beautiful face, like war paint. "There," I said. "Now you look the part, too."

Kit wiped a streak of damp clay from his lips and grinned. "Touché," he said. "You'll be happy to know that it's all downhill from here, on a well-drained and gently sloping trail."

He led the way around the shoulder of the hill to the ledge on which he'd discovered Rendor's most suggestive boot print, then paused to gaze down at the valley below. Shredded wisps of river mist curled sinuously through the dense grove of trees that concealed Aldercot Hall.

"Look," I said, pointing to a patch of open ground to the right of the grove. "The family cemetery."

"So it is," said Kit.

A border of stately yew trees delineated the graveyard, in which smaller headstones surrounded a boxy white tomb.

"There aren't many graves," I noted nervously.

"There may be some we can't see from

up here," said Kit. "And the mausoleum may contain the remains of more than one family member."

If I were Lizzie Black, I thought, I'd argue that there aren't many graves because the vampires who live at Aldercot Hall are virtually immortal. Since I'm Lori Shepherd, however, I'll go with Kit's explanation and hope to high heaven he's right.

I glanced toward the overcast sky, then followed Kit onto a trail Will and Rob could have handled without difficulty. It took us less than fifteen minutes to reach the valley floor and less than ten to find a graveled drive that led through the grove of trees to Aldercot Hall. As Kit and I trudged down the drive, I peered into the woods surreptitiously, searching for a herd of anemic deer, but the only animal I saw was a damp pheasant.

I'd come to associate Aldercot Hall so closely with the undead that I expected it to be a grim, gray, gargoyle-infested Gothic monstrosity — the kind of place Miss Archer could call home. I felt a pinch of disappointment, therefore, when I saw the restrained lines and classical proportions of the stately, cream-colored Georgian mansion that stood at the end of the drive. I could detect nothing sinister in its appearance, except perhaps for the river mist that swirled around it like a ghostly veil and a certain air of neglect that made it appear unloved, almost abandoned.

Although the plane trees surrounding the house were magnificent specimens, the flower beds in the unkempt lawn had been left to languish, and a dank tangle of shrubbery seemed to be all that remained of a formal garden. Dead weeds straggled from the marble urns flanking the columned porch, balusters were missing from the roof's parapet, and birds' nests bristled on every window ledge. All the windows, save those on the topmost floor, were shrouded with black-lined drapes. The ones on the top floor had been boarded up.

"As if," I said under my breath, "those who live here can't bear the light of day."

"Pardon?" said Kit, inclining his head toward me.

"The DuCarals must not like sunlight," I said, jutting my chin toward the windows.

"Sunlight fades furniture," said Kit. "Those are blackout drapes, Lori. They protect carpets and upholstery from the bleaching effects of ultraviolet rays. They're quite common in historic houses."

Kit's commentary was so crushingly level-headed that I suppressed the urge to ask him if he thought the humps in the patchy lawn looked like the unmarked graves of orphaned housemaids.

But I couldn't help asking what he thought of the boarded windows.

"They conserve heat," he said succinctly.

"Of course," I said, and although I had my own ideas about why the attic story had been enclosed, I decided not to share them with Kit just yet.

"We'll try the front entrance first," Kit proposed. "And, Lori, it might be best if you let me —"

"Do the talking," I broke in resignedly. "Go ahead. I'll be as quiet as a mouse."

We climbed the steps to the columned porch, where I stood back, trying to look like a waif from a Dickens novel, while Kit rang the brass-mounted doorbell. I was starting to wonder if the doorbell was out of order when we heard the sound of locks and latches shifting from within. A moment later, the door was opened by a bald, pink-faced elderly man in a neatly pressed black suit. Although he was a few inches shorter than Kit, he still managed to look down his nose at both of us.

"May I help you?" he said in an icy drawl.

"I hope so, sir," said Kit. "My friend and I are in trouble, and we *need* your help."

For the next few minutes, I did nothing but savor the sound of Kit's exquisitely modulated voice as he crafted a tale so rich in pathos that it made *me* want to cry. By the time he finished, I felt so sorry for us that I wanted to whip out my cell phone and call in a rescue helicopter.

"You *are* in a pickle," said the bald man, thawing just enough to employ a slang word. He regarded us through narrowed eyes, as if weighing the pros and cons of granting us shelter from the storm, then nodded. "Very well. You may wait here until the storm abates, but I'll not have you tracking filth on my clean floors. Go around to the kitchen entrance. Mrs. Harcourt will give you a cup of tea while you wait."

"Thank you, sir. Is Mrs. Harcourt the cook?" Kit inquired politely.

"She is, and I am Mr. Bellamy, the butler." The old man leaned in close to Kit and said in an audible murmur, "Your friend there, is she mute?"

Kit had a sudden coughing fit that rendered him incapable of speech, so I had no choice but to answer.

"Too cold to talk," I croaked feebly.

"You'd best get indoors, then," opined Mr. Bellamy. "The kitchen entrance is around the side. Mrs. Harcourt will attend to you."

As soon as the door closed, Kit leaned against one of the pillars, saying in short bursts between guffaws, "You. Mute. So funny. Thought I'd burst . . . a blood vessel . . . trying not . . . to laugh."

"I'm beginning to wish you had," I grumbled.

"Sorry." Kit caught his breath and wiped his eyes, then bowed me off the porch like a proper gentleman.

I smiled grudgingly but took his arm as we walked down the steps, because I wasn't really annoyed with him. I was such a chronic chatterbox that anyone who knew me would have found Mr. Bellamy's question highly amusing. Apart from that, Kit's cunning plan had succeeded in a way that would delight Aunt Dimity. She'd urged me to *speak with the servants,* and here we were, on our way to the kitchen.

I doubted that we'd get much out of icy Mr. Bellamy, but cooks were notorious talkers, and the kitchen was the heart of every home. Mrs. Harcourt would know if a shy man who liked children was sitting down to dinner in the dining room at Aldercot Hall or if a vampiric psychopath was chowing down on raw deer meat behind the boarded windows in the attic. If she'd been at the hall long enough, she might even be able to fill us in on the forty-year-old murder.

I knew in my bones that if anyone could be enticed into revealing the DuCarals' lurid family secrets, it would be Mrs. Harcourt. I was equally convinced that if anyone could entice her, it would be me. I was determined to prove to Aunt Dimity that I hadn't lost my edge when it came to extracting information from chatty servants.

"I'll do the talking in the kitchen," I told Kit. "*You* may be irresistibly charming, but *I'm* a world-class gossip."

THIRTEEN

The kitchen entrance was down a short flight of stone steps toward the rear of Aldercot Hall. The kitchen windows were the only ones I'd seen so far that weren't covered by drapes or plywood, but since the kitchen was practically underground, I suspected that the extra light was both needed and welcomed by those who worked there.

Kit had barely withdrawn his finger from the doorbell when the door was flung open by a middle-aged woman of such imposing stature that we both fell back a step. She wasn't fat, exactly, but she was several inches taller than Kit and at least twice his width, and her bosom was simply massive. If ever a woman were a bloodsucking fiend's dream-date, it was this one, but as I scanned her neck for bite marks, it occurred to me that she could probably hold her own in a fight with a vampire, however supernatural his strength.

It wasn't the woman's size alone that startled us. She was also as brightly colored as a parrot. Her vermilion hair was quite short and stylishly spiky, and her vivid green eyes were set off by her florid face. She wore a floaty lemon-yellow cotton top with short sleeves and a deep V neckline over the kind of loose-fitting lavender trousers usually worn to yoga classes. A pair of dazzling turquoise socks showed through the straps of the orange huaraches that graced her astonishingly large feet.

She was, in fact, dressed as though it were high summer instead of mid-October, and when the blast of heat from the kitchen hit us, I understood why.

"Well, if ever there was a pair of drowned rats," she said, planting her hands on her hips and looking us up and down.

"We're —" Kit began, but he didn't get any further.

"I know, I know," boomed the woman. "Mr. Bellamy rang to warn me. Whatever were you thinking, going out on a day like this? Come in, come in, before I'm as wet as you are."

She didn't wait for us to step over the threshold but grabbed each of us by a shoulder and hauled us effortlessly into a small foyer with a door in every wall. Once we were all inside, she gestured to an enameled pan sitting on the flagstone floor.

"Bung your boots in there and give me your socks and your jackets," she said. "I'll put them near the Aga to dry. I'd ask for your trousers, too, but we don't run that kind of house." Her eyes crinkled to slits, and her whole body shook as she laughed at her own risqué joke.

"We have dry socks," Kit offered timidly.

"Dry socks won't do much good on wet feet," she declared. "You can leave your packs in the scullery to drip, and you can wash your hands and faces in there, too." She looked askance at us, then barked, "Well? What are you waiting for?"

"Where's the scullery?" I asked in a small voice, looking desperately from door to door.

"Oh, for pity's sake," she said, and grabbed each of us by a wrist.

After that it was a bit like taking a ride in a spin dryer. Mrs. Harcourt pushed and pulled us from place to place until I didn't know if I was coming or going. She actually cleaned Kit's face for him with the corner of a dampened towel, and she inspected my hands closely after I'd scrubbed them. She signaled the end of the cycle by dragging us into the spacious, overheated kitchen and planting us, barefoot and somewhat dazed, on a pair of wooden chairs near a dark-red four-oven Aga cooker that was emitting the wonderful scents of baking pastry.

While we recovered our equilibrium, she went on bustling. First she stuffed our boots with newspaper and placed them near the cooker, then she hung our socks and jackets on a wooden rack suspended above the cooker, and then she removed a tray of little cakes from the cooker and placed it beside several others that were cooling on a counter. After testing a few of the cakes with a fingertip, she turned to tower over us.

"There, now, that's better, isn't it?" she said cheerfully.

"Yes, thank you, Mrs. Harcourt," we chorused, like a pair of ten-year-olds.

"Don't 'Mrs. Harcourt' me," she scolded, lifting a steaming teakettle from the Aga and filling the brown teapot that sat on the oversized kitchen table. "It's only Mr. Bellamy calls me that, because he's got it fixed in his head that all cooks should be called 'Mrs.,' whether they're married or not. I'm not married and never will be, because there isn't a man alive I'd have for a husband, though I might make an exception in your case, ducky." She returned the kettle to the

Aga and gave Kit a roguish wink. "What a pretty face you have, and pretty manners, too. My name's Henrietta. What's yours?"

I couldn't swear to it, of course, but I'm almost certain that Kit's entire body blushed.

"Kit," he said weakly. "Kit Smith."

"And you?" she said, turning to me.

"Lori Shepherd," I said.

She beamed at us. "Welcome to Aldercot Hall, Kit and Lori. Put your trotters by the Aga while I set out a few nibbles."

Henrietta Harcourt's idea of a few nibbles was as expansive as her personality. The table was soon littered with a savory assortment of meat pies, sausages, cheeses, breads, chutneys, mustards, and pickles. It wasn't the sort of fare I'd normally serve with tea, but apparently the tea was meant only to warm us, because as soon as we'd downed our first cup, she beckoned us to the table and brought out the beer.

I'm not a beer-drinker by nature, but I'm also not suicidal. I accepted the foaming glass Henrietta offered and refrained from making faces while I sipped it. When she took a seat across from us and filled her plate with substantial portions of everything she'd laid out on the table, Kit and I dutifully followed suit.

203

"You sound like an American, Lori," she said, adding a wedge of creamy Stilton to her plate.

"That's because I *am* an American," I said, helping myself to a hunk of cheddar. "I was born and raised in Chicago."

Henrietta responded to my pronouncement as so many English people before her had responded when I mentioned the name of my hometown, by raising her hands as if she were holding a machine gun and making guttural rat-a-tat noises in the back of her throat.

"Al Capone," she said brightly, when she'd finished rat-a-tatting.

"That's right," I said. "I never knew Al personally, but his legend lives on. Are you from around here?"

"Heavens no," she said. "I'm a Londoner."

My ears pricked up as I recalled Lizzie Black's ominous words: *The DuCarals ordered everything they needed from London . . . including servants.*

"How did you find a job way out here?" I asked.

"Answered an ad in the *Times,*" said Henrietta. "Miss Charlotte had trouble keeping staff after her mum passed on — except for Mr. Bellamy, of course, and he won't leave Aldercot until they carry him out feetfirst."

She popped a chunk of sausage into her mouth, but the act of chewing did not in any way impede her ability to speak. "The rest of the old-timers took their pensions and ran, and the new cooks and housemaids disappeared just as fast as Miss Charlotte could hire them."

I thought uneasily of the humps in the unkempt lawn.

"I wasn't the only experienced cook to answer Miss Charlotte's ad," Henrietta went on, "but I was the only one who liked the look of the place and wanted to stay on."

"I suppose the others thought that life here might be too . . . quiet," I ventured.

"Quiet's what *I* wanted." Henrietta leaned forward aggressively, still gripping her knife and fork. "I grew up with four brothers and six sisters in a cramped council flat on a dirty, noisy street in a neighborhood the tour buses don't include in their itineraries. When I was a kid, all I wanted was to live in the country, have a room of my own, and enjoy some peace and quiet. Aldercot suited me to a tee. I couldn't wait to move in."

She sat back and reached for her glass. While she took a long draft of beer, Kit mouthed the words "You're *good*" at me, but I didn't deserve the praise. Henrietta was too easy. Getting her to talk was about as difficult as getting Will and Rob to ride their ponies.

"It must be a lot of work, though," I said, "catering to such a large household."

Henrietta lowered her glass and gave a shout of laughter. "The house may be large, but the household isn't. It's just Miss Charlotte upstairs, and me and Mr. Bellamy and Jacqueline downstairs. Jacqueline took the job for the scenery," Henrietta explained, smearing mustard on a forkful of meat pie. "She wants to be a nature photographer." Her green eyes swerved abruptly toward Kit. "You're not saying much, ducky. I can tell you have a brain behind your pretty face, so what's the problem? Cat got your tongue? Or are you the strong and silent type?"

Kit's face flamed red again. "I'm . . . um, er . . ."

"He's shy," I said.

"I like 'em shy." Henrietta waggled her eyebrows, then reached across the table and chucked Kit under the chin.

I was so impressed by the length of her arm that I almost missed the chuck under the chin, but Kit, as the chuck's recipient, was unable to ignore it. He mustered a pained grimace that, in a dim light, could have passed for a smile, then lowered his chin to his chest and began furiously dissecting a gherkin.

"Does Jacqueline help you in the kitchen?" I asked quickly, to distract Henrietta from Kit's undeniably pretty face.

"I don't need help in the kitchen," she said. "Mostly Jacqueline runs up and down stairs so Mr. Bellamy and I don't have to."

"Wow," I said. "Just the four of you in this big house . . . Are you allowed to have guests?"

"No," said Henrietta, "but I have all the company I need. A cleaning crew comes up from London every couple of months to dust the place down, and another crew comes up to mow the lawn."

"You have a lawn service?" I asked, unable to conceal my surprise.

"They don't maintain it," said Henrietta. "They don't roll it or fertilize it or grub up the weeds. They just keep it from overrunning the house, is all. It's an easy day out in the country for them. They're nice blokes. They bring me the news from London, and I give them slap-up meals. They like my cooking," she added, with the quiet pride of a woman who enjoys feeding people. "Miss Charlotte, now, she eats like a bird. Hardly touches a morsel I send up. Some cooks would take offense, but I see it as a challenge. I'm always on the lookout for dishes that might tempt her."

I was about to recommend a plateful of blood pudding or a dainty feast of venison tartare when a painfully thin young woman drifted into the kitchen. She was dressed in ripped jeans, a wooly turtleneck, and sneakers, and she'd pulled her straight blond hair back into a ponytail.

"Have your ears been burning, Jacqueline?" Henrietta asked amiably. "I was just telling my new friends about you."

The girl turned her pale face toward us and shrugged incuriously. Without saying a word, she proceeded to take a can of diet soda from the refrigerator and drift out of the kitchen.

"A very inward sort of person, is our Jacqueline," Henrietta observed, sawing a slice of bread from a dense brown loaf. "Artists often are, you know."

"She doesn't look too healthy," I said cautiously.

"Iron deficiency," said Henrietta.

Blood deficiency, I thought, and lost what little appetite I had left.

"I do my best to feed her properly." Henrietta sighed as she mashed a wedge of Stilton on the slice of bread. "But you know what girls are these days. They'd rather be starving sparrows than fat pheasants."

Her words brought to mind the damp pheasant I'd seen in the woods when I'd been looking for the herd of fallow deer that, according to Lizzie, served as the Du-Carals' private blood bank.

"I was told that a herd of deer roams the property," I said, "but I didn't notice one when Kit and I were in the woods."

"There haven't been deer at Aldercot since old Mrs. DuCaral passed away," said Henrietta. "Mr. Bellamy told me that Miss Charlotte sold the herd to a deer park up in County Durham after her mother died, to save herself the trouble and expense of looking after it."

I wondered distractedly if the herd's sale had coincided with the arrival of a series of disturbingly thin maids-of-all-work like Jacqueline. It stood to reason that once the deer were gone, the lunatic in the attic would require another source of fresh blood. If the servant girls were in his thrall, they'd go to him willingly, and they wouldn't tell Henrietta what was happening to them. They'd just fade away before her worried eyes until one day they'd simply "disappear," and others would be brought from London to take their place.

I must have been lost in disquieting

thought for some time, because Kit finally worked up the courage to speak to Henrietta.

"Did you know Mrs. DuCaral?" he inquired.

"No," she replied, twinkling at him. "And between you and me, Kit, it's just as well. God rest her soul and all that, but from what Mr. Bellamy's let slip, it sounds as if she was too proud for her own good. Only the finest London shops would do for her. She wouldn't have anything in the house that was made or grown round here, except milk, and that was left at the gates, so Mr. Bellamy had to send the girl down there to fetch it every morning. Mrs. DuCaral never got to know her neighbors, never took an interest in county affairs. From what I've gathered, she just stayed at home, looking down on the rest of the world."

"Does her daughter take after her?" I asked, slipping back into my role as chief interrogator.

"In some ways," Henrietta allowed. "Miss Charlotte keeps herself to herself, and she still orders lots of things from London — force of habit, I suppose — but the milk's delivered to the kitchen door as it should be, along with local butter, cheese, veg, and fruit. I told her when she interviewed me that I couldn't do my job without fresh ingredients, and she took it to heart. Mr. Bellamy's devoted to her, of course, and Jacqueline seems content enough, and I've never had a cross word from her, so I can't find a reason to complain. To tell you the truth, I've only laid eyes on her a handful of times since she interviewed me for the job. I don't go upstairs, and she's not the sort of woman who comes down to the kitchen for a cuppa with the cook."

"It sounds as if she leads a lonely life," I commented. "Does she ever entertain?"

"Never," said Henrietta, taking a bite of the cheese-slathered bread. "I wish she would. I'm a dab hand at banquets."

I gave Kit a meaningful glance, and he returned it with a thoughtful one. It had evidently occurred to him, as it had to me, that, if Henrietta wasn't allowed to have guests and Miss Charlotte never entertained, then Rendor couldn't be a visitor to Aldercot Hall. Ergo, he had to be a family member.

"Does Miss Charlotte have brothers or sisters?" Kit asked.

"An older brother," Henrietta replied, "but I don't know anything about him. Mr. Bellamy mentioned him once — not by name, you understand, just as 'the young master' — but he clammed up after that. Considering the state of the house, I'd say that Miss Charlotte's brother disgraced himself financially — cards or the gee-gees or some such — and got himself booted out of the family. You know how it is with the gentry. There's always a naughty boy in the bunch. All I know is, he's never set foot in Aldercot Hall since I've been here."

While Henrietta washed down the bread and cheese with a swig of beer, a voice inside my head cried out, *The brother's in the attic!* Luckily, no one but me heard it.

"For all practical purposes," Henrietta continued, patting at her mouth with a napkin, "Miss Charlotte is the only surviving member of the DuCaral family. Her mother died two years ago — a year before I came on board — and from what I've heard, the old lady's death was a blessed release for Miss Charlotte."

"How so?" I asked.

"Old Mrs. DuCaral had a stroke after her husband died," Henrietta informed me, "and she never really recovered from it. Miss Charlotte waited on her hand and foot until she passed."

"Did Mr. DuCaral die a long time ago?" I asked. "Like, say, forty years ago?"

"More like three," said Henrietta. "The

date's out there, in the mausoleum. But he'd been an invalid for nearly forty years before that."

Lizzie Black seemed to whisper in my ear: "Ask them, if you dare, about the murder that took place there forty years ago. Ask them why it was never reported to the police. Ask them how a man could be dead one day and alive the next."

I stared down at my plate, certain that I'd found the answers Lizzie had dared me to find, the kernels of truth in her garbled story. Mr. DuCaral hadn't been murdered forty years ago, as Lizzie had intimated, but he had been viciously attacked, perhaps by his own mysteriously missing son. Though the attack hadn't killed Mr. DuCaral outright, it had turned him into an invalid and caused the lingering illness that had led to his death.

Mrs. DuCaral hadn't wanted her son to go to prison — what mother would? — so she'd sequestered him in the attic — drugged him, perhaps, to control his violent behavior. When she died, Charlotte had taken over the tasks of controlling and concealing her brother. Charlotte was the last DuCaral left to guard the family's secrets.

"Poor Charlotte," I murmured, caught up

in my own musings.

Henrietta seemed to think I was talking to her. "Poor Miss Charlotte, indeed. Her brother a ne'er-do-well and her parents invalids . . . What a burden her family has been to her."

Kit and I were nodding sympathetically when the kitchen door opened and Mr. Bellamy entered the room with his arms wrapped around a large bundle of cloth.

"Hello, Mr. Bellamy," boomed Henrietta. "What've you got there? Curtains for me to wash?"

Mr. Bellamy acknowledged her query with a nod but didn't answer. Instead, he crossed to stand wordlessly behind me and Kit. Kit and I exchanged questioning glances, then turned our chairs around to face him.

"I beg pardon for intruding," he said, with a formal half bow, "but I have explained your plight to Miss Charlotte, and she wishes to be of further assistance to you. Since your garments are besmirched, she hopes that you will allow Mrs. Harcourt —"

Henrietta snorted.

"— to clean them properly for you before you leave," Mr. Bellamy continued, ignoring Henrietta and holding the bundle out to us. "Miss Charlotte offers these garments to you to wear while your own are being cleaned. She has also expressed an interest in conversing with you and would be most grateful if you would join her in the music room."

Henrietta let loose an astonished squawk, but her astonishment was nothing compared to mine and Kit's when we realized that the bundle Mr. Bellamy had presented to us was, in fact, a pair of bathrobes and two pairs of bedroom slippers.

Kit looked as though he'd rather die a slow and painful death than take his clothes off within a hundred miles of Henrietta, but I would have worn a bathing suit and flippers if it meant we could have an audience with Miss Charlotte. When Kit opened his mouth to express what I was sure would be a resolute refusal, I deftly beat him to the punch.

"How thoughtful of Miss Charlotte," I said, jumping to my feet. "Where do we change?"

FOURTEEN

I changed in the servants' bathroom, Kit in the butler's pantry, and we met afterward halfway down the adjoining corridor, where Mr. Bellamy stood waiting for us. He took our "besmirched" hiking clothes from us with a faint moue of distaste and conveyed them at arm's length to the kitchen.

"You are *brilliant*," I said to Kit in an ecstatic whisper when the kitchen door had closed behind the butler. "Hiking over here in the rain, climbing that horrible hill — strokes of genius! We couldn't have looked more authentically awful if we'd tried! And Shakespeare himself would have cried his heart out if he'd heard your tragic soliloquy at the front door! Your plan is working *perfectly!* Look at us! We're on our way to see Miss Charlotte in the music room!"

Kit was clearly unmoved by my panegyric. He stood with his arms wrapped tightly around himself, looking utterly mortified.

"Yes, look at us," he said through gritted teeth. "We're wearing *dressing gowns.*"

I nodded happily. I had a hunch that Mr. Bellamy had come up with the idea of asking us to change into clean garments — he hadn't wanted us to muddy his precious floors with our boots, so it stood to reason that he wouldn't want us to soil the music-room furniture with our filthy trousers — but I didn't much care whose idea it had been. I loved my robe so much that I wanted to sneak it out of Aldercot Hall in my day pack when we left.

Mr. Bellamy — I presumed — had selected for me a fluid, floor-length, kimono-like gown made of silk woven with a pattern of snow-white cranes in flight on a silvery background. It wasn't the sort of thing I could wear while frying bacon for Bill or scrubbing mud off the twins, but it satisfied my girlie side in a way that blue jeans and sweaters never could. I felt as though I shimmered when I walked. Kit's plum-colored paisley silk dressing gown was classy, but not nearly as beautiful as my kimono.

"How could you do this to me, Lori?" he demanded in a high-pitched, outraged whisper.

"I don't know what you're complaining

about." I flapped a hand toward his robe. "It's not as if you're naked under there." I hesitated, then asked uncertainly, "You're not, are you?"

"Of course I'm not," Kit said irritably.

"Neither am I," I said. "So why are you making such a fuss? At least your slippers are practical sheepskin models. Look at the slippers Mr. Bellamy picked out for *me*." I lifted the kimono's hem and held up a foot to display a confection of beaded midnight-blue velvet trimmed in fluffy blue feathers. "They have pointy little *heels,* for pity's sake. What woman in her right mind wears bedroom slippers with pointy *heels?*"

"If Henrietta comes after me," Kit murmured, casting a hunted look over his shoulder, "I'm going to use your pointy heels to fend her off."

I scarcely heard what he was saying, because the sight of my slipper had inspired a magnificent new scheme to spring, fully formed, into my mind. I peered up at Kit and explained excitedly, "If I sprain an ankle because of these stupid slippers, Miss Charlotte will *have* to let us stay overnight. We'll have *all night* to search the house from cellar to —"

"Don't even think about it," Kit broke in, looking daggers at me. "Rendor may not be a vampire, but Henrietta Harcourt is, and I'm not spending the night with her scratching at my bedroom door."

"I'll protect you," I whispered, giggling.

"I don't think she's afraid of garlic," Kit said glumly. "I've tasted her sausages."

We fell silent as Mr. Bellamy emerged from the kitchen and beckoned us to follow him down the service corridor. It wasn't until he closed the kitchen door that I noticed how cold the corridor was. As I tottered toward the butler, I tucked my hands into the wide sleeves of my kimono and wished I'd donned my spare wool socks instead of the feathery slippers.

I'd seldom taken part in a more curious procession. Bald Mr. Bellamy, in his immaculate black suit, led the way, as erect and solemn as an undertaker. Kit came next, with his arms folded across his chest and his broad shoulders hunched forward, looking as though he'd rather be cleaning Mount Everest with a toothbrush than walking through a strange house clad in someone else's dressing gown. I took up the rear, enjoying the touch of smooth silk against my skin and peering avidly at my surroundings.

My first impression was, appropriately, one of gloom. The service corridor was lit by just two light fixtures, and they were fitted with low-wattage bulbs and spaced widely apart. Every door we passed was shut, and the only sounds that disturbed the heavy silence were the shuffling of Kit's sheepskin slippers, the faint squeaking of Mr. Bellamy's leather shoes, and the tapping of my ridiculous heels on the plank flooring.

When Mr. Bellamy led us up a wooden staircase and through a baize-covered door, I expected to be temporarily blinded by the light in the upper room, but it was no brighter there than it had been in the service corridor. The dim glow of a single wall sconce guided us across a parquet floor to the foot of a gold-streaked white marble staircase that was the centerpiece of what appeared to be an entrance hall.

I'd visited quite a few stately homes since I'd moved to England, and I'd seen my share of entrance halls. The grand foyers tended to be elaborately dressed to give visitors a good first impression. Most held family portraits, gilt-framed mirrors, console tables, spindly chairs, potted ferns, and perhaps an oak settle or two. Many featured a fireplace around which guests could gather after divesting themselves of their coats.

Aldercot's entrance hall bore little resemblance to any entrance hall I'd ever seen. Granted, it had a fireplace, but there was no fire burning in it, nor was there so much as a smudge of ash to suggest that a fire had *ever* burned in it. The buff-colored walls were devoid of both paintings and mirrors, and the furnishings consisted of exactly three shabby items clustered forlornly near the front door: a chipped blue-willow-patterned umbrella stand, a frayed coir mat, and a freestanding metal coatrack that would not have looked out of place in a dentist's office.

The murky light emphasized the room's cavernous emptiness. Blackout drapes hid the tall windows on either side of the front door as well as the round window above it. The lightbulbs had been removed from the hall's fabulous crystal chandelier and from all but one of the gold-leafed wall sconces. As my gaze traveled down the blank walls to the uninterrupted expanse of parquet floor, I felt as if I were looking at the bones of a room that had been stripped of its decorative flesh.

The starkness reinforced the air of abandonment I'd sensed when I'd first seen Aldercot Hall. The neglected garden, the missing lightbulbs, the chill in the air, and the reduced staff suggested to me that Miss

Charlotte might not be as wealthy as she'd once been.

I thought of Mr. DuCaral's long illness and Mrs. DuCaral's debilitating stroke and wondered if Miss Charlotte had fallen on hard times after her parents' deaths. Perhaps, I thought, she'd been forced to sell her possessions and reduce her living expenses drastically in order to maintain ownership of Aldercot Hall, the repository of the dark secrets she'd sworn to keep.

"If you'll come this way, please, Ms. Shepherd?" said Mr. Bellamy, his voice echoing hollowly in the gloom.

I realized with a start that I'd wandered away from the foot of the stairs and come to a standstill beneath the unlit chandelier.

"Sorry, Mr. Bellamy," I muttered, and hastened to follow him and Kit up the marble staircase and along a second-floor corridor.

The buff-colored wallpaper continued on the second floor, as did the spare lighting, the silence, and the depressing absence of furniture. When Mr. Bellamy finally ushered us into the music room, it was like reaching an oasis after a long sojourn in a desert.

The music room, unlike the entrance hall, was simply but elegantly furnished. The Aubusson carpet looked as though it had been dyed to match the soft greens and pale golds in the silk wall-coverings and the stiff brocade drapes. A half dozen gilt-framed landscapes hung on the walls, and a few choice antiques — two George III armchairs, a mahogany drum table, a Chippendale sofa — had been arranged around the handsome Adam fireplace. A modest coal-fire burned in the grate, and a row of porcelain figurines graced the mantelshelf — a shepherd, a shepherdess, a winsome milkmaid. A pair of floor lamps with fringed shades flanked the sofa, and, much to my surprise, both were lit.

There were other notable antiques scattered around the music room, but the crowning glory was a gleaming black grand piano. It projected into the room from a U-shaped alcove with windows that would have framed magnificent views of the grove if they hadn't been covered from ceiling to floor by the heavy brocade drapes.

A middle-aged woman sat at the piano's keyboard, playing music so sweetly plaintive that it brought a lump to my throat and made my heart tremble with undefined longing. She went on playing after Mr. Bellamy led us into the room, as though she were so absorbed in the melancholy tune that she hadn't noticed our entrance.

Mr. Bellamy raised a fist to his mouth and cleared his throat, to catch the woman's attention. She played one last poignant chord before looking up from the keys.

"Your guests have arrived, Miss Charlotte," the old man informed her.

"Thank you, Bellamy," said the woman. "You may go."

The butler bowed to her and exited the room, closing the door silently as he left.

I hadn't realized how clearly I'd envisioned Charlotte DuCaral until she rose from the piano bench and crossed the room to greet us. In my mind's eye, she was an attenuated, white-faced ghoul with raven hair and bloodred lips, dressed in a tight-fitting black gown with a plunging neckline and a hemline that trailed behind her spiky heels. Her fingernails, like her canine teeth, were long and pointed, and her eyes were outlined in black and shadowed with dark makeup.

I'd unconsciously assumed that she would have rancid breath, cadaver-cold hands, an unnaturally strong grip, and the sort of twitchiness that came with heightened senses, but I'd also assumed that her oddities would be offset by her immense charm, because, as Aunt Dimity had pointed out, a vampire could be *immensely charming . . . when it's attempting to seduce a potential victim.* I had, of course, labeled myself and Kit as potential victims the moment we'd entered Aldercot Hall.

My preconceived notions crumbled into dust as soon as Mr. Bellamy spoke his employer's name, and when the real Charlotte DuCaral left her place at the piano and walked toward us, I felt myself shriveling with embarrassment at my own foolishness.

Miss Charlotte was tall and slender, but by no means attenuated, and she'd pinned her long hair up in a tidy bun. She had the fair skin of a woman whose white hair had once been blond, but she wasn't unnaturally pale, and although her face was careworn, she'd made no effort to conceal it or her blue-gray eyes behind a mask of makeup.

Instead of a clingy black gown, she wore a matronly navy-blue cardigan over a pale blue blouse tucked into a gray tweed skirt, and there was nothing spiky about her plain black pumps. Her only adornments were a pair of simple pearl earrings and a double strand of pearls around her neck.

When she smiled at us, she revealed a row of perfectly normal teeth, and when she held her hand out to shake mine, I saw that her nails were trimmed to a length that wouldn't impede her piano playing.

Her handshake was firm, but not over-whelmingly so, and her hand was warmer than mine. I didn't even try to smell her breath.

"How do you do?" she said. "As you may have gathered, I am Charlotte DuCaral, the mistress of Aldercot Hall, but there's no need to observe the formalities. You must call me Charlotte, and with your permission, I shall call you Lori and . . . Kit, is it?"

"Yes," said Kit. "It's short for Christopher. And yes, you may call me Kit."

"Everyone calls me Lori," I chimed in. "You play the piano beautifully, Charlotte. What piece were you playing when we came in?"

"It doesn't have a name," said Charlotte. "I like to improvise." She shrugged as if to ward off further compliments, then put a finger to her lips and peered anxiously at our unusual attire. "Oh, dear. How dread-fully awkward you must feel. Won't you sit down? Awkwardness is always reduced by half when one is sitting down."

She motioned us toward the armchairs, and when we were seated, she sat midway between us, on the Chippendale sofa. The fire's warmth almost made me forget the chilly corridor.

"Bellamy insisted on the dressing gowns," Charlotte explained apologetically. "They belonged to my late parents, who were rather more extravagant than I am." She sighed. "Dear Bellamy. He's terribly protective of my things."

"He has every right to be," I said. "We were filthy."

"Yes, he told me that the storm caught you out," she said. "I do hope you'll be able to find your way when you leave."

"We will," I assured her.

"Bellamy tells me that you're an American, Lori," said Charlotte. "How long have you been in England?"

"Nearly eight years," I replied. "I live in a cottage not far from here, with my husband and my sons. And a nanny and a cat," I added, in the interest of full disclosure.

I thought my answer would pique Charlotte's curiosity, but she simply nodded politely, then turned her attention to Kit.

"And you, Kit?" she said. "Where do you live?"

"I have a flat in Anscombe Manor," he said. "It's not far from Lori's cottage."

"Anscombe Manor," she said, and something seemed to freeze behind her eyes. "How long have you lived there?"

"Several years, recently," said Kit. "But I

spent the earliest years of my childhood there as well. My family once owned the manor. I should be familiar with the trails by now, but the storm —" He broke off, interrupted by Charlotte's short gasp of surprise.

"You're Christopher," she said, putting a hand to her breast. "Christopher Anscombe-Smith. You're Sir Miles's son."

Kit looked as startled as Charlotte, and I thought I knew why. Only a handful of his closest friends knew his full name, and none of us ever used it. And no one, including Kit, ever talked about his father.

"Did you know my father?" he asked Charlotte.

"Not well," she said, shaking her head. "But I knew your mother. She was closer to my age than your father was. She married quite young."

Kit shifted his gaze from Charlotte's face to the fire. "My mother was twenty-one when she married. She was nearly twenty years younger than my father."

"She died young, too." Charlotte sighed. "What happened to Sir Miles? I lost touch with him after he remarried."

I watched Kit from the corner of my eye, wondering if he would tell Charlotte Du-Caral the truth. Would he tell her that his father had hanged himself after a long battle with severe mental illness? Or would he tell her simply that Sir Miles Anscombe-Smith had died?

"He died nine years ago," said Kit.

I looked down at my hands. I couldn't blame Kit for withholding the details of his father's death from Charlotte. If my father had committed suicide, I would have been equally reluctant to discuss it with someone I'd just met.

"I'm so sorry," said Charlotte, and she sounded as if she meant it. "Ah, here's Bellamy with the tea. I know it's too early for tea, but I thought you might enjoy it after your adventures."

A soft knock had sounded at the door, and Mr. Bellamy reentered the music room, pushing a three-tiered tea trolley. A splendid old silver tea service and three bone china cups and saucers sat on the top tier, but the lower two held serving dishes filled with the cakes and cookies I'd seen cooling on the counter in the kitchen. Mr. Bellamy rolled the trolley to within Charlotte's reach, bowed, and departed.

"Shall I pour?" Charlotte asked, placing the silver tea strainer on one of the cups.

Her question made me uncomfortably aware of how much I'd already had to drink in the kitchen.

"Excuse me," I said. "May I use the rest-room?"

"Of course," said Charlotte. "It's at the opposite end of the corridor from the staircase, on the right."

"Please don't wait for me," I told her, getting to my feet. "I may be a while."

"Take your time, dear," she said.

I could feel Kit's suspicious gaze follow me out of the room, but I chose to ignore it. After closing the door behind me and making sure that I had the corridor to myself, I took off my slippers and held them in one hand while I hiked up my kimono with the other. Then I ran full-tilt for the lavatory. I planned to use it as speedily as nature would allow, because I also planned to make a small excursion before I returned to the music room.

If Kit was unhappy about being left alone with our inquisitive hostess, he had only himself to blame. Since he refused to stay overnight at Aldercot Hall and since I refused to stay overnight there without him, I had no choice but to make the most of today's visit. If I didn't dash up to the attic right then, I reasoned, I might never have another chance.

"I won't break down the door, Dimity," I

muttered. "But I can't leave Aldercot Hall without trying the handle."

FIFTEEN

Charlotte DuCaral might not be the monster I'd imagined her to be, but I hadn't yet given up on her mysteriously missing brother. I had to find out if she was hiding the young master behind the attic's boarded windows, and in order to do that, I had to go to the attic.

Although my day pack — with its specialized contents — was inaccessible in the kitchen, I wasn't wholly unprepared to deal with a potentially violent pseudovampire on my own. Before I left the lavatory, I pulled Lizzie Black's rowanberry necklace from beneath my kimono and let it fall in plain sight upon my breast. Wearing the necklace might not be as effective as threatening the young master with a stake, but I figured that if push came to shove, it would buy me enough time to escape the attic with all my veins intact.

"It doesn't matter whether *I* believe in it

or not," I said, my voice echoing from the lavatory's tiled walls, "as long as *he* does."

My feet were absolutely freezing by the time I left the lavatory, but they warmed up when I sprinted back down the corridor. I slowed my pace as I approached the music room, tiptoed stealthily past the door, then took off again at full speed, hoping to reach the attic before Mr. Bellamy returned to retrieve the tea trolley. I didn't think Charlotte would notice my absence. She seemed far more interested in Kit than she was in me.

I paused at the end of the corridor to listen for the telltale squeaking of Mr. Bellamy's leather shoes, but I heard only the distant drumming of rain on the porch's roof. Reassured, I darted onto the staircase, wincing as my feet came into contact with the frigid marble.

Again I paused, this time to peer upward. Since I didn't have a flashlight, I was relieved to see a weak golden glow above me in the otherwise impenetrable gloom. I remembered the wall sconce that had guided our steps in the entrance hall and guessed that Mr. Bellamy left a handful of sconces on at all times, like night-lights, to illuminate the stairs. After all, I told myself, Miss Charlotte would want to visit the attic, as would poor deluded Jacqueline, though for very different reasons.

My impulse was to take the stairs two at a time, but the lighting was so poor that I forced myself to climb at a measured pace. I didn't want to risk falling, not only because I might hurt myself but because I might drop the slippers. If anything would end my private tour of Aldercot Hall prematurely, it would be the sound of those ridiculous pointy heels clattering down the stairs.

The marble staircase ended at the third-floor landing, where, as I had predicted, a wall sconce like the one in the entrance hall glimmered faintly in the darkness. I was at a loss as to where to turn next until I caught sight of another sconce shedding a soft pool of light halfway down the corridor on my left.

I sprinted to the pool of light and cautiously opened the doors nearest it. The first three opened onto empty, echoing chambers that might once have been used as bedrooms.

"Why hang blackout drapes in empty rooms?" I muttered as I closed the third door. Then I shivered as the answer came to me.

Since the bedrooms, like the entrance hall, contained no carpeting or upholstery, the drapes hadn't been hung to protect precious fabrics from the sun's harmful rays. Blackout drapes had been hung throughout Aldercot Hall in order to protect someone who couldn't bear the touch of sunlight on his skin *because he lived his life as though he were a vampire.* It was the only rational explanation.

The fourth door opened onto a flight of wooden stairs leading upward. In a house like Aldercot, wooden steps signaled behind-the-scenes rooms meant for servants rather than guests.

"The attic," I breathed, and the chill that gripped my heart had nothing to do with the unheated corridor. Will's drawing had flashed into my mind unbidden, and I knew that if I closed my eyes, I would see the crimson tips of Rendor's vicious fangs as clearly as if the drawing were in my hand. But I didn't dare close my eyes.

The feeling of dread that trickled through me was so unnerving that I might have had second thoughts about tackling the young master on my own if I hadn't suddenly recalled Kit's plan to fend off Henrietta with my slippers. I promptly placed one slipper on the floor of the corridor and gripped the other like a hammer, with the heel pointed away from me. I was pretty sure that no one had ever confronted Count Dracula armed with nothing more than a string of dried berries and a fluffy slipper, but they were the only weapons I had to hand, and I was fully prepared to use them.

Emboldened, I lifted my kimono clear of my feet and started up the wooden stairs. No light fixture had been mounted in the staircase, but my eyes had become so accustomed to the darkness by then that the faint glow from the corridor was all I needed to see the vague outline of the door at the top of the steps.

I held my breath as I crept closer to the door, afraid that the slightest sound would give me away. If a stair had creaked, I would have shrieked loudly enough to shatter windows in Finch, but fortunately the staircase was solidly built.

The sense of dread that had chilled my heart at the bottom of the stairs became stronger with every upward step I took. I felt as if I were caught in a countdown to a terrible explosion from which there was no turning back. When I finally reached the door, it took every ounce of courage I possessed to release my kimono and place a cold and shaking hand upon the doorknob. I raised the feathered slipper, ready to strike, grasped the doorknob firmly, and discovered that it wouldn't turn.

I tried turning it in the other direction, with the same result. I placed the slipper on the top stair and wrapped both hands tightly around the doorknob, but no matter how I tugged and twisted, it refused to budge. After a few seconds of futile struggle, I groped furiously for my slipper, found it, and was on the verge of beating the door-knob into submission when I heard a sound that made the hairs on the back of my neck stand on end.

A floorboard had creaked on the other side of the door. *Someone was in the attic.*

I stood paralyzed with terror, expecting the young master to fling the door open at any moment and drag me into his den of iniquity, but nothing happened. The door didn't open, the young master didn't appear, and I wasn't dragged anywhere.

Slowly, with infinite care, I pressed my ear to the door, but although I listened with all my might, I heard nothing. I was beginning to think that I'd imagined the floorboard's creak when the blood-chilling truth struck home: The young master had his ear pressed to the door, too. His face was mere inches from mine. If I put my nose to the keyhole, I would probably smell his rancid breath.

My courage evaporated. I grabbed the

hem of my kimono and fled. I ran down the wooden stairs, snatched my other slipper from the floor, and kept running until I reached the door to the music room, where I tucked the rowanberry necklace inside my kimono and shoved my feet into my slippers. It took a little longer to pull my heart out of my throat, but I eventually managed to calm down enough to present a relatively tranquil face to Kit and Charlotte.

My tranquillity was short-lived, however, because the sight that met my eyes when I entered the music room sent my heart back into my throat. Kit appeared to be wiping a smear of blood from his lips, and Charlotte seemed to have drops of blood on her fingertips.

"What are you *eating?*" I blurted, aghast.

"Hello, Lori," said Charlotte, turning her head to look at me. "It's a treat from my nursery days." She held up a dish of cookies that looked like little flying saucers leaking blood. "Jammy biscuits."

"They're filled with Mrs. Harcourt's homemade raspberry jam," said Kit. "Delicious."

"If a bit messy," said Charlotte, smiling down at her fingers.

"Jam," I repeated breathlessly. "Raspberry jam."

"Won't you try one?" Charlotte asked.

I waited until my pulse slowed from a gallop to a walk, then crossed the room and sank weakly into my chair.

"No, thank you," I said. "I'm not hungry. I don't think Mrs. Harcourt's sausages agreed with me."

"They can be a bit of a trial," Charlotte said sympathetically. "I may be old-fashioned, but I find that Mrs. Harcourt is rather heavy-handed with the garlic."

A passion for garlic might explain Henrietta's ruddy complexion as well as the absence of bite marks on her neck, I told myself.

"May I offer you a cup of tea?" said Charlotte, setting the jammy biscuits aside. "It's still hot."

"Yes, please," I said fervently, hoping that a hot drink would chase off the chill I'd brought with me from my close encounter with the creature in the attic.

Once I'd sipped enough tea to still my chattering teeth, I began to take an interest in the other items on the trolley. Apart from the bleeding biscuits, which I had no intention of ever trying as long as I lived, there were petits fours, brandy snaps, chocolate eclairs, ladyfingers, and Eccles cakes, but I concentrated on the crustless sandwiches, sampling the watercress, the smoked salmon, and the deviled egg in turn.

"You seem to be feeling better," Kit observed dryly.

"Tea is a powerful restorative," I said. "What did you two talk about while I was gone?"

"Kit was telling me of the many difficulties you encountered during your most unfortunate walk," said Charlotte. "You must have been relieved when he kept you from tumbling into the river."

"I was," I said, realizing at once that Kit had been having a little fun at my expense while I'd been away, to repay me for leaving him with Charlotte.

"And you must have been so very grateful when he caught the branch that was about to fall on you," said Charlotte.

"I was relieved *and* grateful," I agreed, nodding earnestly.

"And if he hadn't pushed you to the ground when the lightning struck," said Charlotte, "heaven knows what might have happened."

"It wouldn't have been pretty," I said.

"I hope you don't mind," said Charlotte, "but I'm forced to agree with Kit. It was ill-advised of you to propose an outing in such inclement weather."

"Yes, it was incredibly stupid of me, wasn't it?" I said. "I don't know what I was thinking."

"When Bellamy informed me of your unexpected arrival," Charlotte went on, "I thought you might be the campers responsible for the column of smoke I saw rising above the hills yesterday."

I popped a last bite of smoked salmon into my mouth and waited for Kit to tell Charlotte how he'd put out the forest fire I'd started after he'd saved me from the river, the falling branch, and the lightning bolt, but she'd evidently hit upon a subject they hadn't yet discussed, because he responded truthfully for a change.

"No," he said, "that wasn't us. There's a man camping in Gypsy Hollow, in a small caravan. Lori and I had lunch with him yesterday."

"He's absolutely charming," I said. "He's spent most of his adult life in Australia, but he lived around here when he was younger. His name is Leo, and he was so kind to Kit and me, and so funny." I looked at Kit and grinned. "Remember his story about the sheep shearing contest and the . . ." My voice trailed off when the expression on Kit's face changed from one of amusement to one of deep concern.

"Charlotte?" Kit asked. "Are you all right?"

I looked at Charlotte. She looked as though she'd seen a ghost. Her mouth had fallen open, and she'd gone white to the lips. Although she blinked slowly, her breathing was too fast, and she swayed on the couch, as though she were going to faint. She looked so dazed that Kit and I both started forward with our arms outstretched to catch her before she hit the floor. When she managed to stay upright, we sat back, exchanging looks of utter bewilderment.

"Charlotte?" Kit said again. "Would you like me to fetch Mr. Bellamy?"

"I'm . . . I'm perfectly well," she said, though there was a distinct tremor in her voice. "Lori? Did you say that the man's name is . . . Leo?"

"Yes," I replied.

"How old is he?" she asked.

Kit and I looked at each other and shrugged.

"Sixty?" I guessed. "Give or take a few years."

Charlotte pressed a trembling hand to her lips, rose from the couch, and walked stiffly to the fireplace. She stood in silence for a moment, staring down at the porcelain shepherd on the mantelshelf. Then she lifted the delicate figurine from the shelf and held it level with her eyes.

"The man's eyes," she said, with her back to us. "Are they blue?"

"Yes," I replied, mystified.

"Bright blue?" she asked.

"Yes," I said again. "They twinkle."

"I can't believe it," she whispered. The nape of her neck flushed red, and she began to speak in jerky spurts, as though she were choked by a fury so intense that she could barely get the words out. "The *nerve* . . . show his face . . . after he . . . My father would have . . . *Unforgivable* . . . All these *years* . . . How dare he? How *dare* he?"

Although I couldn't see her face, I could hear her spittle sizzling on the grate and almost feel the waves of rage radiating from her. With a sudden, savage movement, she hurled the shepherd into the fire, where it shattered into a million tiny fragments. Kit and I goggled at her. In the space of a few minutes, Charlotte had undergone a transformation so complete that she was scarcely recognizable. We didn't know what she might do next.

"I'm going for Mr. Bellamy," Kit said under his breath.

"I'm coming with you," I whispered back.

We were halfway out of our chairs when the hall door opened and Mr. Bellamy returned, with our clean pullovers, shirts, socks, and trousers folded neatly in his arms. His gaze flitted from Charlotte, who was now muttering to herself nonstop, to the scattered slivers of shepherd that littered the hearth and finally came to rest on me and Kit.

"Please, come with me," he said to us, without betraying a flicker of emotion.

I thought it was an excellent suggestion, but Kit hesitated.

"Will your mistress be all right?" he asked.

"Miss Charlotte is none of your concern, sir," said Mr. Bellamy. "If you will come this way, please?"

Mr. Bellamy followed us into the corridor, handed each of us our clothes, and ushered us into separate unfurnished rooms down the hall from the music room.

"You will dress here," he instructed us. "You will then meet me in the entrance hall, where I will be waiting with your boots, your packs, and your coats. Please do not dawdle."

If Kit and I had been in a quick-change contest, we would have tied for first place. In less than ten minutes, we were in the entrance hall, fully dressed and swapping our lovely robes for our rain jackets.

"Mr. Bellamy," Kit said as he shrugged the straps of his day pack into place, "please believe me when I tell you that whatever we did to upset Miss Charlotte, we did inadvertently."

"I believe that the storm has slackened, sir." Mr. Bellamy opened the front door. "Good day."

Kit and I pulled our hoods over our heads and stepped out onto the porch. The wind had let up, but the rain was still falling steadily. The river mist clung like cobwebs to the branches of the towering plane trees, and by the time we'd gone a few yards down the graveled drive, Aldercot Hall had become a mist-shrouded ghost. Kit paused for a last look at the stately mansion, then ducked his head self-consciously and turned his back on it.

"Don't look now," he said, "but we're being watched."

I looked, of course, and saw Charlotte gazing down at us from the music room.

"Damn," I muttered. "I wanted to visit the family cemetery, but I'm not going to do it with her watching us from on high."

"Why do you want to visit the cemetery?" Kit asked as we walked on.

"To check some names and dates," I

replied. "We don't know nearly enough about the DuCaral family."

"I don't know anything at all." Kit shook his head. "What *happened* back there?"

I studied him for a moment, to make sure he wasn't joking, then said, "It's obvious, isn't it?"

"Not to me," he said.

"Didn't you listen to Henrietta?" I asked.

"I was too busy watching her hands," Kit replied.

"In that case, I'll summarize the main points for you," I offered. "Father dies after a long illness. Mother dies of a stroke. Charlotte lives in a huge empty house. Big brother is persona non grata."

Kit waited for me to go on. When I didn't, he said, "So?"

"All right, then, I'll spell it out for you," I said, with the long-suffering sigh of an experienced gossipmonger teaching the basics to a neophyte. "Charlotte's rotten older brother ran up gambling debts that drove both of his parents to their graves and forced Charlotte to sell almost everything she owned. When the family ran out of money, big brother legged it to Australia to escape the heavies that were after him. Now he's come back to see if he can squeeze any more cash out of his sister."

"Australia?" said Kit, frowning. "But Henrietta didn't say anything about Austra—" He came to a sudden halt and clapped a hand to his forehead. *"Leo."*

"Knew you'd get there in the end," I said serenely.

"*Leo* is Charlotte DuCaral's rotten older brother," Kit marveled as we resumed walking. "It would explain why he knows so much about our corner of the world. If he grew up at Aldercot, he'd know that Emma's Hill used to be called High Point, and that Gypsies once camped in Gypsy Hollow. And his name did seem to trigger Charlotte's . . . episode."

I nodded. "She was going along just fine until I mentioned Leo's name. Then she went ballistic."

"It all fits." Kit paused. "Except that Leo doesn't seem like a rotten person. Do you remember the note he left taped to the motor home? 'If you're desperate, take what you need.' It's not the sort of message a rotten person would leave, is it?"

"Maybe he's changed," I said. "He's been away an awfully long time. A lot can happen to a person." I kicked gravel aimlessly, sighed, and dug my hands into my pockets as we entered the grove of trees.

"I think we should speak with him before

we write him off," said Kit, "but I have to admit that your version of events is plausible." He nudged me with his elbow. "Why don't you look more pleased with yourself?"

"Because none of it has anything to do with *Rendor,*" I said irritably. "Remember him? The creepy psycho pervert voyeur my sons spotted lurking in the woods? If Leo is Charlotte's brother, then Charlotte's brother can't be Rendor. So I've figured out everything *except* what I came here to figure out. Who left the boot prints on Emma's Hill? Who left the scrap of crimson silk in the pet cemetery? Above all, who's living in the attic?"

"Is that where you were while Charlotte and I were eating jammy biscuits?" Kit asked. "In the attic?"

"Not quite," I said. "The attic door was locked, so I couldn't get inside. But someone was in there, Kit. I heard a floorboard creak, and I . . . I *sensed* someone listening at the door." I smacked a fist into my open palm. "We have to find out more about the DuCarals."

"Why?" Kit asked.

"It's the only way we're going to nail Rendor," I explained. "He's obviously not a houseguest, because Charlotte doesn't entertain guests and the staff isn't allowed to have them."

"Therefore," said Kit, "Rendor must be a DuCaral. But if he isn't Leo, then who . . . ?" He left the sentence hanging and glanced at me expectantly.

"Charlotte must have another brother," I said thoughtfully, "a brother Henrietta doesn't know about. He must be the one who's locked in the attic."

"How could Henrietta not know about him if he's living in the attic?" Kit asked.

"Because Charlotte doesn't want her to know," I said. "He's the crazy brother, the one who thinks he's a vampire, so Charlotte wouldn't want the world to know about him."

"So you still think a vampire's involved?" said Kit.

"A *pseudo*vampire," I corrected him. "And yes, I do. Think about it, Kit. Did you see a mirror in Aldercot Hall, or a family photograph? Vampires don't have reflections, and they can't be photographed, because they have no soul, so if someone thought he was a vampire —"

"He'd avoid decorating his house with mirrors and photographs," Kit cut in, nodding. "I see."

"And what about the blackout drapes?" I said. "They're all over the place, but the only furniture we saw was in the music room. So tell me: What are they protecting?"

"Mr. Pseudovampire," Kit answered obediently, "because vampires can't stand sunlight."

"That's right," I said. "Mr. Bellamy must be in on the secret, and I'll bet Jacqueline is, too, but Henrietta's such a blabbermouth that they wouldn't dare tell her."

"She did say that she never went upstairs," Kit recalled.

"Exactly," I said. "She's out of the loop."

"We're now assuming that Charlotte has two brothers," said Kit. "Leo the reprobate, and . . . well, let's continue to call the other one Rendor until we learn his real name."

"We may as well," I said. "For all we know, he patterned himself after the Destroyer of Souls in the comic book. Do you think the parents were mentally ill, too? Maybe they had the same vampire fixation as the crazy son. After seeing Charlotte's schizophrenic turn, it wouldn't surprise me to discover that insanity runs in the family."

"It often does," Kit murmured. Then he laughed. "Fixation, schizophrenic . . . You're tossing off jargon like a pro, Lori."

"I'm not an expert," I conceded, "but I do know that normal people don't spy on little kids and live inside locked attics." I stopped short and stared down at my trouser legs. "Do your trousers feel *starched?*"

"They are a bit stiff," Kit acknowledged.

"They're spotless, too," I said. "It's unnatural."

"I have the perfect solution," said Kit. "Let's talk with Leo right now. He'll know whether he has a brother or not."

I looked up at him, stricken. "But that means we'll have to —"

"Climb down the hill into Gypsy Hollow," Kit finished for me, grinning mischievously. "It'll take the starch out of your trousers."

"It may also take away my will to live," I grumbled, but I agreed to Kit's plan nonetheless.

My desire to interrogate Leo far outweighed my desire to avoid yet another undignified slide into Gypsy Hollow.

Sixteen

I somehow managed to land in Gypsy Hollow in a dignified, upright position, but I was so pleased with my accomplishment that I failed to watch my next step, slipped on a slimy rock, and sat with a splash in a murky puddle.

"Yeah, I know," I said wryly as Kit hauled me to my feet. "Pride goeth before a pratfall."

"I wasn't even thinking such a thing," he protested, though a smile was playing on his lips. "But I *was* thinking that we should rename this place 'Lori's Bottom.'"

I laughed along with him, even though it was a bit depressing to realize that I wouldn't be able to dry my wet drawers at Leo's campfire, because there was no campfire, nor was there any sign that Leo had returned.

"The note's still there," I said, pointing to the message Leo had taped to the motor home's door.

"Let's have a look inside," said Kit, striding forward. "He may be ill or injured and need our help."

The door was unlocked, so a desperate person could have taken what he needed from the motor home, but after surveying its cramped quarters I decided that a person would have to be *truly* desperate to need anything that Leo owned. His possessions were so shabby that they would have been rejected by a thrift shop.

Kit nodded at a neat pile of logs that filled the space between the bed and the small table. "He carries his own firewood."

"Now we know how he got a fire going in such damp weather," I said.

"He must still be in the village," said Kit.

"I hope so." I looked from the dented teakettle to the frayed blanket that covered the tiny bed. "It's easy to see why he needs an infusion of cash. He doesn't exactly live in the lap of luxury."

"He seems happy, though," Kit said.

"I know," I said. "He's cheerful, charming, generous. . . . How could such a nice man make Charlotte so angry?"

"Families are funny things," said Kit. "He might show one face to us and an entirely different face to his sister."

"Multiple personality syndrome," I said wisely as we climbed out of the motor home.

"I wish you'd give the jargon a rest, Lori," Kit said, with a tired sigh. "Not every character trait is a mental illness, and as you said before, you're not an expert on the subject."

I blinked at him, then ducked my head and colored to my roots, suddenly aware of how tactless it had been of me to harp on mental illness in the presence of a person whose father had suffered so cruelly from depression that he'd eventually hanged himself. I felt terrible, but I didn't know how to apologize without mentioning Sir Miles, which would only make matters worse.

"Sorry," I mumbled, too embarrassed to meet Kit's eyes.

"Forget about it," he said shortly. "Do you want to wait for Leo, look for him in Finch, or head home?"

"Home," I said unhesitatingly. With my trousers soaked through again, I didn't want to stay outdoors any longer than I had to.

"Let's go," said Kit.

We made our way through the gap in the trees to the muddy track that led to Anscombe Manor. An awkward silence hung between us until, at last, Kit spoke.

"I'll look in on Leo in the morning," he said. "In the meantime I'll run an online search and see if the Web can tell us anything about the DuCarals."

"Thanks," I said. "I'm as useless with computers as I am with horses."

"You won't be useless with horses for much longer," said Kit. "I hope you haven't forgotten your promise to take riding lessons."

"I haven't," I said, grimacing. "But I was hoping you had."

"There's nothing to worry about, Lori," said Kit. "I'm a superb instructor."

"Humble, too," I muttered.

Kit smiled, and the tension between us dissolved.

"If there's nothing on the Web," he said, returning to the main topic of our conversation, "and if I fail to connect with Leo, I have another idea. How would you like to spend a day in Upper Deeping?"

"What's in Upper Deeping?" I asked.

"The *Upper Deeping Despatch,*" he replied. "It's been the local newspaper for nearly a hundred years. We might find some mention of the DuCarals in the *Despatch*'s archives."

"It's worth a try," I said, brightening. "In fact, I'd like to search the archives regardless of what happens with Leo and the Web. We could find some valuable information there — like birth announcements for *two* DuCaral brothers."

"It'll have to wait until Monday," Kit warned. "The office is closed on Sunday."

"Monday's fine by me," I said. "I couldn't go tomorrow anyway. Annelise is spending the day with her fiancé, and I promised to take Will and Rob to the Cotswold Farm Park after church."

"All right, then," said Kit. "I'll pick you up at the cottage at nine on Monday morning, and we'll see what we can find in Upper Deeping."

Kit offered to drive me home when we reached Anscombe Manor, but I was able to turn him down because, as I explained to him, Mr. Barlow had kept his promise. An old, beat-up, rust-red Morris Mini sat among the sleek sports cars parked in front of the manor house, looking like a potato in a bouquet of tulips.

"Now, *there's* a car I can drive in dirty trousers," I said.

"I don't think Mr. Barlow will mind," Kit agreed.

"I don't think Mr. Barlow will *notice*," I said contentedly.

I dumped my day pack in the Mini, then

went with Kit to the stables to check in with Annelise. I found her chatting with Fabrice, one of Nell's many French admirers, while the twins watched the local farrier shoe Rocinante, Nell's chestnut mare. Kit had evidently worked out a signal with Will and Rob, because before I quite knew what was happening, the twins' hands were in mine and I was being led, gently but inexorably, to Toby's stall.

The old gray pony stood with his head over the stall door. He snuffled when he saw the boys.

"Toby's saying hello, Mummy," Rob explained.

"You can let him smell your hand," said Will. "He won't bite."

"Go ahead," Rob coaxed. "You can do it."

"But not too fast," Will cautioned.

"You don't want to spook him," said Rob.

I raised my hand with infinite care until it was close to Toby's nostrils, and the old pony rubbed it gently with his velvety nose.

"He likes you," said Will.

"He rubs people he likes," Rob added earnestly.

And for some reason I will never understand, I believed them.

Kit came up behind me, put his hands on my shoulders, and said quietly, "Here endeth the first lesson."

I felt an unexpected twinge of regret when the boys led me away from Toby, and before I left the stables, I turned back to give him a little wave. He snuffled again, as if to say, "See you later!" and a tiny part of me began to believe that learning to ride him might not be an irredeemably bad idea.

Since it was just past noon and the farrier had several more horses to shoe, the boys were not ready to leave the stables. I told Annelise that I'd see them at home and headed for the Mini.

Mr. Barlow had left the keys in the ignition, but before I got into the car, I placed a hand on its rusty roof and vowed solemnly that I would never drive it down Lizzie's lane. It must have sensed my good intentions, because it started right away and puttered along without a squeak or a groan as I cruised down Anscombe Manor's curving drive.

I stopped when I reached the end of the drive, and looked in both directions. A left-hand turn would take me to the cottage, but if I turned right, I'd soon be in Finch. I tapped the steering wheel thoughtfully.

I'd had plenty to eat at Aldercot Hall, so I wasn't hungry, and the Mini's heater was already drying my trousers, so I wasn't in a hurry to change clothes. Annelise and the boys wouldn't be home for several hours, so I didn't need to put dinner on the table for a while. I could, in fact, think of no compelling reason to go straight back to the cottage. So I turned right.

I watched carefully for Leo as I negotiated the lane's winding curves, paying particular attention to the hedges and ditches, in case he'd had an accident and was lying by the side of the road, injured. I even stopped the car once, to peer into the ditch Bill liked to call mine, but I made it all the way to Finch's humpbacked bridge without seeing a soul, which wasn't unusual. Even on a gorgeous spring day, there was rarely any traffic on my lane.

As I drove over the bridge, all of Finch lay before me, looking rather damp and deserted. Rain gushed out of downspouts and rushed down the cobbled street, and a small pond had taken shape just below the war memorial on the village green. No one was window-shopping or bench sitting or doing anything outdoors, except for Jasper Taxman, who was scurrying from the Emporium to the greengrocer's shop next door, with a bucket of mauve paint in one hand and several paintbrushes in the other.

The Emporium, which served as Finch's

general store as well as its post office, was owned by the all-powerful Peggy Taxman. Peggy had recently purchased the greengrocer's shop from old Mr. and Mrs. Farnham, who had retired and moved to Derbyshire to be near their three grown daughters. To judge by Jasper's harassed expression, it looked as though Peggy had assigned to her husband the task of redecorating the latest addition to her empire.

Jasper paused beneath the shop's green awning when he saw me, and I drove over to crank my window down and say hello.

"Keeping busy?" I said, looking pointedly at the paintbrushes.

"You don't know the half of it," he replied with a heavy sigh. "But better busy than bored, I always say. How is life treating you? I haven't seen your face in Finch for quite a while."

"I was at the Guy Fawkes Day committee meeting on Thursday," I told him, experiencing a flutter of déjà vu. Hadn't I said the same thing to Mr. Barlow just last night?

"Were you?" said Jasper. "I must have missed you. How are the boys getting along at Morningside?"

"They're doing great," I replied. "They couldn't be happier. Listen, Mr. Taxman, I was wondering — have you seen a stranger in town today? An older man, with white hair and blue eyes. He would have been riding a bicycle."

Jasper shook his head. "I don't think so, Lori, but I've been so busy running back and forth that I may have missed him."

"Better busy than bored, eh?" I teased.

"That's right." Jasper held up the can of mauve paint. "And I'd best *get* busy or Mrs. Taxman will have something to say about it."

"Thanks, Mr. Taxman," I said.

"You're welcome, Lori. And don't stay away so long. People will begin to think you don't like it here." He gave me a friendly nod and went into the greengrocer's shop.

I rolled up my window, parked the Mini near the tearoom, and sat in it for a moment, gazing perplexedly at the raindrops drizzling down the windshield. Why hadn't Mr. Barlow or Mr. Taxman noticed me at the committee meeting on Thursday? I wondered. I'd often wished to be invisible during meetings, especially when Peggy Taxman had a bone to pick with me, but I was fairly sure I'd never actually disappeared. And why were both men under the impression that I'd been avoiding Finch?

"It hasn't been that long since I've been to the village," I said to the rearview mirror.

"Mr. Barlow and Mr. Taxman must be losing track of time. It's easy to do in the fall, when the days all look alike."

I nodded confidently at my reflection and went into the tearoom, where I was greeted like a long-lost relative by Sally Pyne, George Wetherhead, Lilian Bunting, Miranda Morrow, and several other neighbors. Sally, who owned the tearoom, bustled off to make a pot of tea I hadn't ordered, and the others proceeded to bombard me with questions.

"What's Bill up to these days?"

"Are the twins enjoying school?"

"What do you think of the paint Peggy picked out for the greengrocer's?"

"Have Will and Rob made lots of new friends?"

"Why are you driving Mr. Barlow's old Mini?"

"What's all this about a pervert on Emma's Hill?"

"Do the boys like their teacher?"

"Here you go, dear," said Sally Pyne, drawing a chair out from a table she'd set for me. "Have a seat and tell us how you've been."

I looked at the circle of smiling, inquisitive faces and bowed to the inevitable. I took a seat, let Sally fill my teacup, and began firing off answers.

"Bill's in London, arranging trust funds for cats. Peggy's never had much color sense, but if you tell her I said so, I'll deny it. I'm borrowing Mr. Barlow's Mini because Annelise's car has developed a few hiccups. Everyone at Anscombe Manor is on the lookout for the pervert. Will and Rob love their teacher, their new friends, and everything about Morningside. I've been perfectly well, thank you."

My answers led to a gabfest that lasted for over an hour and proved to be very informative. I learned that Miranda Morrow's cat had given birth to four snow-white kittens; that Mr. Wetherhead had purchased a new locomotive for his elaborate train set; and that Sally Pyne's cellar had been knee-deep in water for the past two days. I didn't know where to look when Lilian Bunting, the vicar's wife, informed me that someone had been pilfering holy water from the baptismal font in St. George's, but I made a mental note to drop a large donation on the collection plate the next time I was in church.

Neither Lilian nor anyone else present in the tearoom knew anything about the Du-Carals. They had a vague notion that Aldercot Hall was somewhere in the general vicinity of Finch, but its exact location eluded them, and they weren't nearly as interested in what went on there as they were in finding good homes for Miranda's kittens. As I listened to them chatter, I realized that Kit's wry description of my neighbors as "a bit parochial" had been accurate, if grossly understated.

I also reminded myself that none of them had lived in Finch for more than twenty years. As relative newcomers, they couldn't be expected to be as well versed in local history as someone like Lizzie Black, whose family had lived in the area for many generations.

I was disappointed to discover that although everyone had seen Leo drive his motor home through the village on his way to Gypsy Hollow, no one had seen him since. The villagers had assumed that he was a late-season camper and felt sorry for him for having such bad luck with the weather, but he hadn't aroused their curiosity.

After promising to return very soon, I managed to extricate myself from the tearoom and cross the village green to the pub, but I struck out there as well. Christine and Dick Peacock, the pub's proprietors, had never heard of the DuCarals *or* Aldercot Hall, and they hadn't seen Leo since he'd driven through Finch.

They had, however, seen Miranda's kittens, Mr. Wetherhead's locomotive, and Sally Pyne's flooded cellar, and they were intensely curious to know how the twins were doing at Morningside, if Bill would be back in time for the darts tournament, and what I thought of the paint Peggy Taxman had chosen for the greengrocer's shop.

After I'd filled them in, they asked where I'd been keeping myself.

"I was at the Guy Fawkes Day committee meeting on Thursday," I informed them stoically.

"We know," said Dick, "but you didn't open your mouth once, and you didn't stay for tea and buns afterwards."

I was pathetically grateful to Dick for confirming that I had been at the meeting, but I was reluctant to explain why I'd bailed on the tea and buns. I would have ignited a firestorm of speculation that would have burned for several decades if I'd told them that I'd had to run home to talk to Will and Rob about the vampire they'd seen on Emma's Hill, so I said instead that I'd simply wanted to spend the evening with my husband before he left for London.

"You'd think the two of you were still on your honeymoon," Chris cooed, with a romantic sigh.

"Speaking of honeymoons," said Dick, leaning on the bar. "Have you seen the new crew at Anscombe Manor? Kit had better get a move on, or one of the new boys will carry Nell off."

"I'm working on it," I said.

"Work harder," Chris urged. "We want our Nell to marry Kit. We don't want to lose her to some foreigner who has more money than sense."

"I'll do my best," I promised, and after assuring them yet again that Will and Rob were doing wonderfully well at school, I left the pub.

I didn't have the stomach to enter the Emporium and ask Peggy Taxman about Leo, and I didn't really think it was necessary. Sally Pyne, Miranda Morrow, George Wetherhead, Lilian Bunting, and the Peacocks were more useful than a host of spy satellites when it came to observing the goings-on in Finch. If they hadn't seen Leo ride his bicycle into Finch, then he hadn't ridden his bicycle into Finch. Period.

Where *had* he ridden it? I asked myself as I climbed into the Mini. Where had Leo spent the day?

I drummed my fingers on the steering wheel and pondered what to do next. My trip to the village had been a waste of time.

The only good thing to come out of it was the strangely satisfying realization that I, a foreigner and the newest newcomer to Finch, knew more than any of my neighbors about the DuCarals of Aldercot Hall. The only person who knew more about the DuCarals than I did was Lizzie Black, and she'd lived in the area longer than anyone except —

"Ruth and Louise," I said, and thumped a fist on the steering wheel. "Of course!"

I backed the Mini away from the tearoom and turned it toward the humpbacked bridge. I couldn't believe that I'd left two such obvious stones unturned. Ruth and Louise Pym had lived in or near Finch for just over a hundred years. They couldn't have lived so close to Aldercot Hall for so long without picking up a few tidbits about the DuCaral family.

I wouldn't be able to ask them about vampires — Aunt Dimity had warned me against mentioning such an unsavory subject to the churchgoing sisters — but I was bound and determined to find out what they knew about Leo.

And churchgoers were *always* eager to discuss black sheep.

SEVENTEEN

Ruth and Louise Pym lived a half mile outside of Finch, in a thatched house made of mellow orange-red brick. Their house was an architectural oddity in a region where most buildings were made of locally quarried limestone and roofed with slate, but I loved it nonetheless. The shaggy thatch and the weathered bricks made the house seem warm and inviting even on the dreariest of days.

I parked the Mini on the grassy verge in front of the house and let myself through the wrought-iron gate between the short hedges that separated the front garden from the lane. The Pyms' front garden was a thing of beauty in the spring and summer, but the recent rains had left it looking decidedly bedraggled.

The soggy, windblown plants reminded me of my own disheveled state, so I paused on the doorstep to brush the dried mud from my trousers before turning the handle on the old-fashioned bell.

The sisters opened the door together, but it was beyond my poor powers of observation to figure out which one was Ruth and which one was Louise. As the mother of identical twins, I'd grown accustomed to the idea of two people looking alike, but Ruth and Louise Pym looked so *exactly* alike that it was impossible for a mere mortal to tell them apart.

They were, as always, dressed identically, in matching dove-gray gowns with long sleeves, lace collars, and pearl-shaped buttons that ran in two rows from their tiny waists to the matching gray-and-cream cameos pinned at their throats. Their interchangeable black shoes were profoundly sensible, and their white hair was wound into identical buns on the backs of their identical heads. It wasn't until they greeted me that I could identify them as individuals. Louise's voice was softer than Ruth's, and Ruth invariably spoke first.

"Lori!" she exclaimed. "What a . . ."

". . . delightful surprise," continued Louise. "It's been an age and an age since we . . ."

". . . last saw you," Ruth went on. "Do come in!"

Listening to the Pyms was not unlike watching a tennis match. Both activities required concentration and supple neck muscles.

The sisters would have taken me straight into their front parlor, but I insisted on leaving my hiking boots with my jacket in the foyer and stopping in their powder room to freshen up. Since I couldn't bear the thought of besmirching their lovely needlepoint chairs with my unfortunate trousers, I brought a towel with me when I joined them in the parlor and spread it on my chair before sitting down.

While I'd been washing up, the sisters had set the walnut tea table with an assortment of cakes, muffins, and sandwiches that Henrietta Harcourt would have looked upon with approval. As I took my seat near the fire, the teakettle's whistle called Louise to the kitchen. She returned a short time later, carrying a tray with cups, saucers, and the hand-painted tea set the sisters always used when they had company.

"Don't stir, Lori," said Ruth. "I'll toast a muffin for you and . . ."

". . . I'll fill your cup," said Louise.

Although I found it deeply embarrassing to be waited on by a pair of centenarian spinsters, I made no effort to stop them.

The sisters might look as frail as frost, but they were, in fact, as tough as old tree roots. They kept their house spotless; gardened in all weather; canned, preserved, bottled, pickled, and dried the fruits of their labors; and participated in village life with a vigor that put women half their age to shame. They were perfectly capable of toasting muffins and pouring tea without any help from me.

After a few minutes of industrious fluttering, they came to rest in chairs facing mine across the tea table, which was now amply supplied with hot, buttered muffins, and asked about Bill, the twins, Stanley, Annelise, and me. While I answered their questions, their bright bird's eyes flitted interestedly over my less-than-formal attire.

"I'm sorry I'm such a mess," I apologized, dabbing melted butter from my lips with a lace-edged linen napkin. "Kit Smith and I hiked over to Aldercot Hall this morning, and the trails were pretty muddy."

"Aldercot Hall?" said Ruth. "A splendid house. So sad that it fell into the hands of such dreadful people."

"The DuCarals, you know," said Louise. "Maurice and Madeline. Not one of our old families. They made their money . . ."

". . . in washing-machine parts," said

Ruth, "and once they'd struck it rich, they left their old life behind and bought . . ."

". . . Aldercot Hall, to impress their old friends," said Louise. "They hired people to decorate the house and to tend the gardens, and they hired their help through a London agency. They bought a herd . . ."

". . . of fallow deer," said Ruth, "because they'd seen one at another stately home and thought it was de rigueur. They hired a gamekeeper . . ."

". . . to manage the deer, the grouse, and the pheasants," said Louise, "and a stable-man . . ."

". . . to look after a pair of hunters they never learned to ride," said Ruth.

"So silly of them," said Louise. "Maurice DuCaral didn't know the first thing about shooting . . ."

". . . or riding . . ."

". . . or fishing," said Louise, "but he bought the right outfits and the most expensive guns and rods and went about . . ."

". . . pretending to be lord of the manor." Ruth tilted her head to one side and peered vaguely at the ceiling. "He had no idea what it *means* to be lord of the manor. Maurice and Madeline thought local matters . . ."

". . . were beneath their notice," said Louise. "They never took an interest in their neighbors, and they never allowed their children to mix with . . ."

". . . anyone who had less money than they did. They thought their money made them superior, you see." Ruth clucked her tongue. "Poor things. They were wholly unsuited to country life."

Louise nodded sadly. "They simply didn't have a clue."

"It must have been hard on the children," I said.

"Ah, yes," said Ruth. "Poor Charlotte. She had one chance to escape her parents' clutches, but the young man . . ."

". . . failed her," said Louise. "She shouldn't have put her faith in Leo. He never was very reliable."

"Leo?" I said, startled. "Leo in the motor home?"

The sisters bobbed their heads in identical nods.

"He drove past our house yesterday morning," said Ruth. "But of course . . ."

". . . we ignored him," said Louise. "We haven't quite forgiven him . . ."

". . . for his ill-treatment of poor Charlotte," said Ruth.

"Let me get this straight," I said. "The Leo you saw in the motor home used to be Charlotte DuCaral's *boyfriend?*"

"He was more than a boyfriend, I'm afraid," said Ruth. "Leo and Charlotte were going to elope. They planned to run off in the dead of night. It was the only way . . ."

". . . Charlotte could break free from her parents," said Louise. "But Leo never came. He left her waiting — so humiliating for the poor girl — and disappeared without a word of warning . . ."

". . . and Charlotte never saw him again," said Ruth. "Then the accident happened and she had to stay at home because her mother was . . ."

". . . a thoroughly incompetent nurse," said Louise, "and her father was such a demanding invalid that the nurses they hired wouldn't stay . . ."

". . . for more than a week," said Ruth. "But Charlotte wouldn't have left Aldercot . . ."

". . . even if she'd hadn't had to care for her father," said Louise. "Leo broke her heart, you see. She never recovered from the blow."

I ran my hand through my hair dazedly. Leo was undoubtedly the black sheep who'd earned Charlotte's ire, but he wasn't in the right flock.

"To tell you the truth," I said, "I thought

Leo was Charlotte's *brother.*"

"Her brother?" said Ruth, blinking in surprise. "Oh, my, no, Leo wasn't her brother. Her brother was a trial to her, of course, but in an entirely different way."

"The shame, the guilt, the effort it took to conceal the truth . . ." Louise sighed regretfully. "One can't blame him for his desires, but . . ."

". . . it would have been better for all concerned if he had controlled them," Ruth concluded. "Have another muffin, dear."

"And another cup of tea." Louise refilled my cup, and both sisters began to chat about Miranda Morrow's kittens.

I went with the flow, because I knew that no matter how hard I tried, I wouldn't be able to steer the conversation back to Maurice, Madeline, Charlotte, Leo, or the nameless brother with the shameful desires. When the sisters closed the door on a subject, it was impossible to get them to open it again, and they'd clearly closed the door on the DuCarals.

I couldn't complain, though. Ruth and Louise might not have answered all my questions about the DuCaral family, but they'd answered at least as many as they'd raised. After indulging in one last buttery muffin, I left their house feeling as though the hour I'd spent with them had not been wasted.

As I climbed into the Mini, it occurred to me that Leo might have returned to his motor home while I'd been visiting the Pyms, but I quickly dismissed the notion of looking for him there. The Mini would never make it down the track to Gypsy Hollow, and I had no intention of walking down it. Leo, I decided, could wait until the morning. I was sick of traipsing through mud. I wanted to go home.

By the time Annelise, Will, and Rob returned to the cottage, I'd showered, changed, checked the freezer for ice cream, and thrown together a homemade pizza. Pizza, ice cream, and a movie were our Saturday-night treats, so after the boys were bathed and we were all fed, we gathered in the living room with bowls of ice cream to watch *The Black Stallion* for what had to be the seven-thousandth time. This time, however, I found myself thinking of old Toby and wondering idly what it would be like to bond with him the way the boy bonded with the stallion. I was almost sorry when the film ended and bedtime arrived.

Annelise worked on her wedding dress for a while after I'd put Will and Rob to bed, but she retired relatively early because she wanted to look her best for her fiancé the next morning.

Bill called right after she'd gone upstairs — he knew better than to interrupt our Saturday-night movie by calling earlier — but he was too tired to talk for very long. Mrs. Shuttleworth's daughters had just discovered that their shares of their mother's estate were smaller than Mr. Muddy-Buddy's, and Bill had spent the day fielding telephone calls from them and their irate lawyers.

I cheered him with the news from Finch. He was so amused by the thought of Jasper Taxman painting the greengrocer's shop mauve that he forgot to ask me about the historic home Kit and I had spent the day visiting, and I didn't feel the need to mention it to him.

"I'm going to sleep in tomorrow," he said finally. "What about you?"

"Church and the Cotswold Farm Park," I said. "No rest for the weary mother."

"Say hello to the polka-dotted pigs for me," he said.

"I'll give them your best," I promised, and rang off.

I turned off the lights in the kitchen and went to the study, where I smiled at Reginald, lit a fire in the hearth, and curled up in the tall leather armchair with the blue journal in my lap. I paused for a moment to marshal my thoughts, then opened the journal and gazed down at the blank page.

"Dimity?" I said. "I hope you're comfortable, because I have an awful lot to tell you."

I smiled as Aunt Dimity's response began to scroll across the page in her familiar, old-fashioned copperplate.

One of the great advantages of being disembodied is that one is always comfortable. Fire away!

I leaned back in the chair, stretched my legs out on the ottoman, and gave Aunt Dimity a detailed account of everything I'd done that day, both with Kit and without him. I described our fascinating — and thoroughly disquieting — visit to Aldercot Hall, our fruitless journeys to Gypsy Hollow, my solo tour of Finch, and the remarkable conversation I'd had with the Pym sisters.

After a lengthy digression, during which I had to answer Aunt Dimity's questions about Miranda Morrow's kittens ("Four — white"), Sally Pyne's flood ("Knee-deep"), Peggy Taxman's paint color ("Mauve"), and George Wetherhead's locomotive ("No idea, I haven't seen it yet"), I presented her with a scenario based on what I'd seen at Aldercot Hall and what I'd heard from Lizzie Black, Henrietta Harcourt, and the Pyms. I thought it was a pretty impressive piece of work.

"One day," I began, "perhaps when he was in his teens and showing the first signs of instability, Charlotte's brother rearranged the letters of his last name and convinced himself that he, a DuCaral, was the direct descendent of the prince of darkness, Count Dracula."

Ah. Yes, of course. It's exactly the sort of thing an unstable young man might do. I expect we'll call the brother "Rendor," since we still don't know his Christian name.

"Yes, we will," I said, and went on. "Rendor became gradually more violent and more delusional until, some forty years ago, he decided to claim dominion over Aldercot Hall by murdering his own father. The Pyms think Maurice DuCaral was crippled by an accident, but he wasn't. He was attacked by his own son."

My goodness.

"The attack left Maurice incapacitated," I continued, "and the DuCarals were finally forced to admit that their son was a dangerous lunatic. They couldn't bring themselves to turn him in to the police, though, or to plunk him in an institution, because they

279

didn't want their old friends to find out about him."

Because they couldn't bear the humiliation of admitting to their old friends that their seemingly superior family was tainted with mental illness?

"Exactly," I said. "So they called the attack an accident, shot Rendor full of tranquilizers, and locked him in the attic." I snapped my fingers as a fresh new idea occurred to me. "They may have put the tranquilizers in glasses of deer's blood. Since Rendor thought he was a vampire, he'd drink it down lickety-split."

What a perfectly appalling image, Lori. How did they explain Rendor's disappearance?

"They didn't have to," I said, "because from that point on they made do with a severely reduced staff and kept everyone else at bay. No guests, no visitors, and no mixing with the locals — they even made the milkman leave his deliveries at the gates."

Ingenious. Go on.

"Maurice, Madeline, and Charlotte Du-Caral made a solemn vow to take the family secret with them to the grave," I said, "and two of them succeeded. Maurice died of his wounds three years ago, and Madeline died a year later."

Leaving Charlotte to cope with Rendor on her own.

"She's not completely on her own," I pointed out. "I think Mr. Bellamy must be in on the secret by now. And I'm fairly sure that Jacqueline is just the latest in a string of household helpers who've let Rendor have his way with them."

Some girls might think it thrilling to have their necks bitten. I can't see the attraction myself.

"Nor can I," I said impatiently. "But my point is, Charlotte's too unstable to control her brother. When her mother died, she let Rendor get the upper hand. She cleared the house of anything that might upset him — mirrors, photographs, sunlight."

Why did she get rid of nearly all of the furniture?

"She's too unstable to earn a living," I said, "so she sold the furniture to bolster her inheritance."

I see. Sorry to interrupt. Please, go on.

"Charlotte sold the deer," I said, "and hired girls like Jacqueline, hoping to satisfy Rendor's lust for human blood, but it wasn't enough. Now she's allowing him to leave the attic and roam the countryside, looking for fresh prey."

If Charlotte is allowing her mad brother to leave the attic, why did you find the attic door locked?

I stared pensively into the fire, then replied, "He locks himself in out of habit."

Well, you've certainly been hard at work, Lori. Your explanation of the affairs at Aldercot Hall is stunningly comprehensive. I wish, for your sake, that it was also conclusive, but, alas, it isn't. You haven't proved that Rendor exists. Until you do, you'll find it difficult to prove to the police that Will and Rob saw him in the woods.

"Kit and I are going to Upper Deeping on Monday," I informed her. "We're going to search the archives of the *Upper Deeping Despatch.* Our original plan was to look for anything concerning the DuCarals, but you've just given me a better idea."

I'm always glad to help. What idea have I given you?

"I think we should focus our efforts on finding references to Rendor," I said. "That is, references to a DuCaral son. If we can find a birth announcement, or a piece about his school days, or any article that mentions him in any way, maybe we can file a missing-person report and get the police to start an investigation. They won't let a locked door stop them, and once they're inside the attic, they'll know I'm right."

I wish I could take credit for the idea, Lori, but it's all yours and it's quite brilliant. I'm sure the Despatch *will provide you with the information you need. There is one other loose end that intrigues me, however. It's not directly related to Rendor, but it troubles me nonetheless.*

"What's that?" I asked.

Your description of Leo as a kind, thoughtful, generous, charming man doesn't square with the Pyms' description of him as a cad, a bounder, a heartless scoundrel who would toy with a woman's affections, then abandon her.

"Kit said the same thing, when we still thought Leo might be Charlotte's rotten brother," I acknowledged. "I guess Leo's changed."

Human nature isn't as malleable as all that, Lori. If Leo was a cruel and selfish young man, he'd more than likely be a cruel and selfish old man.

"But he isn't cruel or selfish," I said. "He shared his stew with us. He made us laugh. He left his door unlocked today, in case someone needed to take shelter in his motor home."

It does make one wonder what actually happened all those many long years ago. Is the Pyms' version of events accurate? Is Char-

lotte's? I suggest that you hear Leo's side of the story before you pass judgment on his younger self.

"We'll try," I said, "but he isn't the easiest man to find."

I'm sure he'll turn up sooner or later. When he does, listen to him. By the way, did you make any progress with Kit while you were out and about today?

"None," I admitted. "I managed to hurt his feelings, though."

Shame on you, Lori.

"I didn't do it on purpose," I protested. "He never used to mind it when I talked about the bad old days, when he was living on the streets, but when I brought it up today, he flinched."

What inspired you to mention it today?

"Kit was worried that Leo might be cold-shouldered in Finch," I explained. "And I told him that the villagers wouldn't dare treat Leo the way they'd treated him when he was down and out, because the vicar wouldn't let them."

And he flinched?

"As if I'd smacked him in the face," I said guiltily. "But I haven't told you the worst part yet. After we left Aldercot, I started yammering like an idiot about mental illness. I didn't stop to think about what had

284

happened to Kit's father until Kit finally told me to shut up. And then I wanted to kick myself, or let Kit kick me, for being so incredibly insensitive. I felt awful, Dimity, just awful."

I can imagine. Did you say anything else that upset him?

"No," I said. "I put my foot in my mouth twice, but otherwise I was positive and upbeat with him. When he started going on about being a deeply flawed human being, I told him that if he was deeply flawed, then there was hope for the rest of us." I shook my head. "Tell me, Dimity: Why do saints always think they're flawed?"

Because they're saints.

"But what flaws could Kit possibly have?" I demanded. "A disgraceful streak of kindness? An overabundance of patience? A bigger heart than the law allows?"

Perhaps Kit doesn't see himself as you see him, Lori. Or perhaps he sees something in himself that you don't see. Or something that isn't there.

"Sorry, Dimity," I said, squinting at the page. "You've lost me."

Never mind. It's not important. Have you anything else to report?

"Not tonight," I said. "But I hope that I'll have more to tell you on Monday."

As do I. Good night, Lori, and good luck at the Despatch. *I hope the archives will lead you to the truth.*

"Thanks," I said. "Good night, Dimity."

When the graceful lines of royal-blue ink had faded from the page, I closed the journal, held my feet out to the fire, and contemplated the trip to Upper Deeping with a purely girlie sense of satisfaction.

"Finding the truth is a good and noble thing, Reg," I said, looking up at my pink bunny. "But so is a day without mud."

Eighteen

Since Rob and Will approved of Annelise's fiancé, they didn't mind in the least when he spirited her off before church the following morning, although the questions they asked while we were in church made me wonder what kind of comic books Clive Pickle had been bringing to school lately.

Peggy Taxman's head snapped in our direction when Will inquired, loudly, if Annelise and Oliver would have babies, and the vicar faltered in the middle of his sermon when Rob announced, after some thought, that Annelise would have *lots* of babies, because she had such a nice, soft tummy. I could do nothing but bow my head, not only to hide my blushes but to give heartfelt thanks to God that Annelise wasn't there.

The boys and I trooped over to the vicarage after church, to apologize to the vicar for interrupting his sermon and to meet the white kitten he and Mrs. Bunting had adopted the night before. While Will and Rob played with Angel, Mr. Bunting took me to his study to admire the armchair his wife had given to him for his birthday.

"Your birthday!" I exclaimed, mortified. "It was last month, wasn't it? I'm so sorry. I forgot all about it."

"I didn't bring you in here to make you feel guilty for forgetting my birthday," said Mr. Bunting.

"I know, but I feel guilty anyway," I said. "How could I have missed your birthday?"

"You haven't been to see us since the boys started school," he said gently.

"You're kidding," I said, gazing up at him in surprise.

"I'm not." He smiled. "You've also been rushing off after Sunday services as if the church were on fire. We've hardly had a chance to say hello." He ran a hand across the back of his new armchair. "I do understand, Lori. It's not an easy transition for any mother to make, and you've had more reasons than most to worry about your little ones. My wife tells me, however, that the boys are doing wonderfully well at Morningside. Perhaps the time for worrying is over?" He smiled again. "It's for you to decide, of course. I simply want you to know how pleased the whole village will be when you find time for us again. Now, let's see if the boys have taught Angel a trick or two — or vice versa!"

I was grateful to Mr. Bunting for turning his attention to the kitten's antics, because I was so choked up I couldn't speak. I hadn't believed my neighbors when they'd told me that I'd been gone for "an age and an age," but the vicar's kindly remonstrance had made me realize, finally, that they'd been telling me the truth.

It had been six weeks since the twins had started school, six weeks since I'd dropped out of village life to obsess about their safety, and in a tightly knit community six weeks was an age. I wondered how many other birthdays I'd forgotten, how many neighborly duties I'd neglected. Every role was vital in a tiny place like Finch, and I'd failed to play mine for six long weeks.

"Thank you," I said to the vicar as the boys and I prepared to leave the vicarage. "Your message came through loud and clear. I'll be at the nativity-play committee meeting on Friday evening, and *everyone* will know I'm there. And," I added as we reached the doorstep, "I will most *definitely* stay for tea and buns afterwards."

I stopped to chat with everyone I saw as I

drove through the village, and instead of taking the twins back to the cottage for breakfast, we filled up on bacon and eggs — and plenty of gossip — at the tearoom. By the time we returned to the cottage to change out of our Sunday clothes, I felt as if I'd made up some of the ground I'd lost since the boys had started school.

We had a wonderful time at the Cotswold Farm Park, feeding the friendly, curious goats and petting the rabbits and sheep. My prayer for rain had evidently run its course, because the weather was fine enough for us to eat our picnic lunch at the park's outdoor tables.

After lunch, we paid our respects to the oxen, the pigs, and the chickens. I said hello to the Gloucester Old Spots for Bill, and they grunted their best wishes back to him. The highlight of the boys' visit was, of course, the stately Shire horses, and we spent the entire homeward journey discussing the many ways in which horses had served mankind.

Annelise floated into the cottage shortly after we'd eaten dinner. She was so love-drunk after her day with Oliver that she did nothing but smile seraphically when I informed her, very cautiously, that her tummy had been mentioned in church.

When Bill called, I spoke to him freely and without restraint, because for the first time since he'd left for London, I'd made it through an entire day without thinking once about Rendor.

"Look at it!" I expostulated as I climbed into Kit's pint-size pickup truck on Monday morning. "Look at the sky! Bright sunshine, no clouds, not a hint of rain!"

"The old folks would tell you that St. Luke's Little Summer has arrived," said Kit, turning the truck toward the Upper Deeping road. "I believe it's called Indian summer in the States."

"I don't care what it's called," I said grumpily. "What use is a beautiful day if we're not outdoors to enjoy it?"

"If you're going to start playing the imponderable-questions game, I have one for you," Kit retorted. "Where's Leo? I went to Gypsy Hollow twice yesterday and again early this morning, and I'm willing to swear that he hasn't been back there since you and I saw him on Friday. So where is he? Where has he been for the past two days?"

"I don't know," I said, "but I'm fairly sure we can rule out both Finch and Aldercot Hall."

I told Kit about my foray into Finch and

my visit with the Pym sisters, then outlined for him the scenario I'd revealed to Aunt Dimity on Saturday evening. When I finished, he gave a low whistle.

"No wonder Charlotte reacted so strongly when she heard Leo's name," he said. "She's a woman scorned."

"She was scorned an awfully long time ago," I pointed out.

"Which means," said Kit, "that she's had an awfully long time to brood over it. She was a ticking time bomb waiting to explode. Leo's name set her off."

"Why did he come back?" I asked pensively. "He said he was on a sentimental journey, but what kind of sentimental journey takes you back to a place where you broke someone's heart?"

"Perhaps he didn't intend to break Charlotte's heart," Kit suggested. "Perhaps he came back to explain."

"I seriously doubt that Charlotte will listen to any explanation Leo has to offer," I said. "But I will. We have to find him, Kit."

"I've asked Emma to keep an eye on Gypsy Hollow," he said. "If Leo turns up while we're in Upper Deeping, she'll ring me on my mobile."

"Charlotte must have felt so lonely after he walked out on her," I said. "All those years, stuck in that house with her invalid father and her snooty mother and her crazy brother . . ." I sighed. "It's not hard to understand why she's still so angry with Leo."

"She did have one friend, apart from Leo," Kit said. "While you were running around Aldercot Hall in your bare feet, Charlotte told me that my mother rode to Aldercot almost every day, after she married my father and moved into Anscombe Manor. She and Charlotte used to walk along the river and talk about everything under the sun, the way women do. She went there less often after she became pregnant with me, and when the car accident happened, Charlotte lost her best — her only — friend."

"And you lost your mother," I said. "How old were you when the accident happened?"

"I was barely a year old," said Kit. "My mother was twenty-four."

"So young," I said, shaking my head. "Do you remember much about her?"

"I remember her smile," Kit answered. "I think she must have been a very happy young woman, because her smile stands out so clearly in my memory. I'm almost glad that she didn't live long enough to see my father . . . deteriorate."

"Some blessings are extremely well disguised," I murmured. I gazed somberly at the passing scenery for a while, then turned to Kit and asked, "Any luck with the online search?"

"Ah," he said, giving me a sidelong glance. "I didn't actually do an online search. Emma spent the weekend reformatting all the computers in the manor."

"The new stable hands must have their own laptops," I said. "Why didn't you borrow one of theirs?"

"I didn't wish to inconvenience them," Kit said stiffly.

I suspected that I would be an Olympic equestrian champion before Kit would ask one of Nell's rich young swains for a favor, but I said only, "Don't worry about it. There's always the *Despatch.* I had a brilliant idea about the *Despatch,* by the way."

"Only one?" Kit said, raising an eyebrow.

"Yes," I said, "but it's a good one. I want to prove beyond a reasonable doubt that Rendor is alive and well and menacing my children, right?"

"Right," said Kit.

"I want solid proof that I can take to the police," I said. "So instead of searching the *Despatch* for articles about the DuCaral family in general, I think we should focus on finding articles about the troublesome brother with the shameful desires. The police will laugh at me if I tell them a vampire's on the loose, but I don't think they'll laugh about a missing person."

"They might even try to find a missing person." Kit reached over to pat me on the head. "Brilliant."

"I told you so," I said smugly, and watched through the windshield as the church spires of Upper Deeping came into view.

The *Upper Deeping Despatch* offices took up the first two floors of a four-story building just off the main town square. Kit had to settle for a parking space six blocks away, but the weather was so mild that I didn't mind the walk. We'd just reached the square when Kit stopped short and announced that he'd had his own brilliant idea.

"I know how we'll talk our way into the archives," he said. "You, my American friend, have come to Upper Deeping to do genealogical research, and you hope the *Despatch*'s archives will help you with your project."

"I always wondered where Aunt Penelope came from," I said, rubbing my chin thoughtfully. Then I reached up and patted Kit on the head. "Brilliant."

I felt a pang of regret when we left the

sunshine and balmy breezes behind and stepped into the newspaper's utilitarian and fluorescently lit front office. A chest-high counter separated a waiting area — two plastic chairs, a low table, and an upright rack filled with dog-eared copies of the *Despatch* — from a large, untidy desk and a swivel chair that was, at the moment, unoccupied.

"Hello?" Kit called.

A muffled bellow sounded from afar. *"Coming!"*

The door behind the untidy desk sprang open, and a pudgy young man in a tweed jacket and twill trousers bustled up to the counter. He had a round, shiny face, thinning brown hair, a ballpoint pen parked behind his right ear, and a pair of horn-rimmed glasses perched halfway down his nose.

"Sorry," he said. "Our receptionist is . . . um . . ." He peered nearsightedly around the reception area, as though the receptionist might be playing hide-and-seek. "Not here, apparently. No idea where she's got to, but never mind, I'm here. Desmond Carmichael, at your service. How may I help you?"

Kit gestured toward me and began, "My friend is —"

"I know who your friend is," Desmond broke in, staring avidly at me. "You're the lady who was shot by the stalker on Erinskil Island, aren't you? I read about you in the *Times.*"

"That's me," I said. "Want to see my scar?"

"Whoops. Sorry," Desmond said, with an apologetic grimace. "It must have been a harrowing experience for you, but to be perfectly honest" — he pushed his horn-rimmed glasses up his nose and leaned his elbows on the counter — "reading about it was a thrill for someone like me, who spends his life writing about church fetes and gymkhanas." His eyes brightened, and he pointed a finger at me. "I've seen you at gymkhanas, too! Your sons ride with the Anscombe Manor team, don't they?"

"The junior team," I admitted modestly.

"The Willis twins," said Desmond, nodding, but his knowing look was rapidly replaced by one of puzzlement. "But *your* name is —"

"Lori Shepherd," I said. "That's right. I didn't change my name when I married, but we decided to reduce confusion all around by giving my husband's last name to the boys."

"Well, I'm delighted to meet you," said

Desmond, straightening. "What brings you to the *Despatch* today?"

"As you'll know from the articles in the *Times*," said Kit, "Lori is an American. She's doing genealogical research, and she thought she might find some pertinent information in your archives."

My hard-won celebrity status had its uses. Desmond bounced into action as if he'd been shot from a cannon, ushering us around the counter and through the door behind the desk, past several offices, and down a stairway at the rear of the building.

"The archives are housed in the cellar, I'm afraid," he said, pulling a ring of keys out of his pocket and inserting one in the door at the bottom of the stairs. "We were afraid the upper floors wouldn't take the weight."

The cellar wasn't too bad, as cellars go. It had a high ceiling and finished walls, a tiled floor and ample lighting, which Desmond turned on with the flick of a switch near the door. A computer sat on the large metal desk that occupied the only floor space that wasn't filled with shelves, and a single plastic chair sat facing the computer.

"How far back would you like to go?" Desmond inquired. "We've got the last ten years on disk, but it's bound volumes before that, six months per volume. We're trying to put it all on disk, of course, but we never seem to have the budget or the manpower to make much progress. We do have indexes to each year's run, though, going right back to the beginning. They're not as detailed as I'd like them to be, but you might find them helpful."

Desmond showed us how to use the computer, explained how the bound volumes were organized, fetched an extra chair from upstairs, and gave us his cell-phone number, in case we needed to call on him for further guidance. After wishing us the best of luck, he closed the door and left us on our own.

"What a helpful young man," I said.

"I'm surprised he didn't ask for your autograph," said Kit.

"I'm surprised he didn't want to see my scar," I said. "Well? Shall we get to work?"

"I don't see the point of consulting the indexes if they're incomplete," said Kit. "The computer files won't help us either. I don't think much news about Rendor has come out of Aldercot Hall in the past ten years."

"Charlotte looks as though she's in her late fifties or early sixties," I said. "Let's go back seventy years and work our way forward."

We turned to face the heavily laden shelves.

"I'm glad we got here early," Kit murmured.

An hour passed, then two, the silence broken only by the ruffle of turning pages and the shuffle of our shoes as we retrieved fresh volumes from the shelves. Although I resisted the temptation to read every single article that caught my eye, I couldn't help noticing that the function of a small-town newspaper hadn't changed much over the years. For more than a century, the *Upper Deeping Despatch* had faithfully kept its readers abreast of local births, deaths, marriages, accidents, inquests, court cases, fashions, competitions, and celebrations.

"Gymkhanas and church fetes," I mumbled, rubbing my eyes.

"Sorry?" said Kit, peering blearily at me across the metal table.

"Time for lunch," I said, more loudly. "We need a break."

We rang Desmond, and he came down to lock the cellar door after us. He recommended his favorite café to us as well, but we bought sandwiches at a nearby bakery and ate them on a bench in the town square, surrounded by sun-starved townspeople who'd also decided to take advantage of the fine weather. Then we plunged back into the dusty fray.

We took another break at two o'clock. When Kit suggested that we walk over to Morningside, to look in on Will and Rob, I steeled myself and suggested that we walk to the park instead.

"I'm sure the boys are just fine," I said, with only a slight tremor in my voice.

Kit put his arm around my shoulders and gave me a sideways hug. "Well done, Lori. Let's go and feed the ducks."

We buckled down to our task after the ducks, flipping through volume after volume without discovering one word about the DuCarals. It didn't dawn on me until nearly four o'clock that the *Upper Deeping Despatch* was exactly the wrong place to look for news about them. At which point I closed the volume I'd been scanning, leaned my weary head in my hands, and groaned.

"We're not going to find anything about Rendor here," I said dejectedly. "Maurice and Madeline were too arrogant to announce their children's births in a local rag. They'd place an ad in the *Times.* The same goes for anything the kids might have done in school, and I'll bet they didn't go to local schools, because local schools wouldn't have been good enough for them. And after Ren-

301

dor went bonkers, they shut up shop completely. They wouldn't let the milkman near the house, so I doubt that they put out a welcome mat for reporters and photographers. We've spent a *whole day* barking up the wrong tree."

I released another groan, expecting to hear an echoing groan from Kit, or at least a disappointed sigh. When I heard nothing, I lifted my head from my hands and looked at him.

He wasn't scanning the page before him. He was staring at it, with an arrested expression on his face.

"Kit?" I said, suddenly alert. "Have you found something?"

"Yes," he said, still staring down at the page. "It's a police report about a nineteen-year-old young man who was brought up on charges for being drunk and disorderly. It happened thirty-eight years ago."

"Some things never change," I said, shaking my head.

"The young man's name was Leo Sutherland," said Kit.

"Leo?" I leaned forward. "Do you think he might be *our* Leo?"

Kit lifted his gaze from the page and said wonderingly, "Sutherland was my mother's maiden name. Before she married my father

— thirty-eight years ago — my mother was known as Amy Sutherland."

"Whoa," I said, falling back in my chair. "Now, there's a coincidence."

"Is it a coincidence?" A slight frown creased Kit's forehead. "Our Leo told us that he spent a lot of time near Anscombe Manor when he was young, and we know from the Pym sisters that he was going to elope with my mother's closest friend." He rapped the page once with his knuckles. "Now I find a Leo with my mother's maiden name, written up in the local newspaper around the time my mother came to live at Anscombe Manor. It's entirely possible that our Leo is . . . was . . . related to my mother."

"And to you," I said. "How much do you know about your mother's family?"

"I don't know anything about them," Kit admitted. "My father remarried less than a year after my mother's death, and he never talked about her. I grew up knowing my stepmother's family, and my father's, but not my mother's."

I glanced toward the shelves. "Have you found any other references to Leo Sutherland?"

"No," said Kit. "Just the one police report. But Ruth and Louise said he was unreliable. Perhaps it was their polite way of saying that he had a drinking problem."

"I'd expect to find more than one police report if he had a drinking problem," I said, "and I didn't see any liquor bottles in Leo's motor home."

"Even so . . ." said Kit, tilting his head to one side.

"Yeah," I said, nodding. "The rest of it does seem to stretch the boundaries of mere coincidence. We *have* to talk with Leo." I picked up the bound volume I'd been scanning. "Call Desmond. Tell him we're leaving. We'll call Emma on the way back and find out if anyone's seen Leo."

I returned the bound volumes to their proper places on the shelves and thanked Desmond sincerely when he showed up to escort us out of the building. Kit telephoned Emma on the way to the pickup truck, but she had no joy to report. Leo hadn't yet returned to Gypsy Hollow.

Since Leo was still on our missing-persons list, Kit dropped me off at the cottage, where I ate warmed-over macaroni and cheese and listened distractedly to the twins' chatter. They were in the midst of describing the rat Clive Pickle had brought to school for show-and-tell when the telephone rang. I jumped up from the kitchen table to answer it.

"Lori?" Kit said, sounding rather breathless. "Smoke's rising from Gypsy Hollow."

"Don't you *dare* go there without me!" I cried, and slammed down the phone.

I pulled on my hiking boots and a warm sweater, grabbed my rain jacket from the coatrack in the hall, called to Annelise that I didn't know when I'd be back, and dashed out to the Mini.

I couldn't explain why my hand shook as I turned the key in the ignition or why I gunned the tiny engine all the way to Anscombe Manor. I was going purely on instinct, and my instincts were telling me that the man in Gypsy Hollow held the keys to more mysteries than the ones swirling like river mist around Aldercot Hall.

NINETEEN

I forced myself to putter at a snail's pace down Anscombe Manor's drive, to avoid the cardinal sin of frightening the horses, but as soon as I pulled in beside Friedrich's Porsche, I leapt from the Mini and ran to the courtyard so fast that I sprayed gravel in my wake. Kit was waiting for me there, standing half hidden in his shadowy doorway, with his hands buried deep in his jacket pockets.

I would have appreciated five seconds to catch my breath, but Kit took off before I'd stopped gasping, and I raced after him, splashing willy-nilly through assorted puddles in my attempt to keep up with his long strides. When we moved beyond the courtyard's floodlight and onto the muddy track, the darkness compelled us to slow down, until Kit pulled a flashlight from his pocket, switched it on, and sped up again.

"Good . . . thinking," I panted, scampering around potholes caught in the flash-light's bobbing beam.

Kit glanced down at me, as if he were noticing me for the first time. "Sorry, Lori. Am I going too fast for you?"

"Nope," I managed, clutching the stitch in my side. "I'm as eager to talk to Leo as you are."

"I don't think you can be." Kit moderated his pace, out of kindness to me, but his voice quavered with suppressed excitement as he explained. "When I invented the story about doing genealogical research at the *Despatch,* I never expected it to come true. What if Leo is my uncle or my cousin? He might be able to tell me things about my mother, things my father never told me, things I've always wanted to know." He shook his head. "No, Lori, I don't think you can be nearly as eager as I am to speak with him."

"Hurry, then," I urged him. "Don't wait for me. I'll catch up."

Kit was too saintly to leave me flounder-ing in the dark, however, so he adjusted his stride to mine, and we entered Gypsy Hol-low side by side. The motor home was still there, and although the night sky was strewn with stars, the patched awning had been reerected on its telescoping poles. Leo sat beneath the awning on the rickety camp chair, with his tin cup in one hand and a long stick in the other, gazing into the campfire that blazed within the ring of stones.

He was wearing the same clothes he'd worn when he'd shared his stew with us — brown rain jacket, blue sweater, brown corduroy trousers tucked into black Wellington boots — and he'd leaned his bicycle against the side of the motor home. His bright blue eyes were somber, almost melancholy, when we emerged from the gap in the trees, but when he spotted us, they lit instantly with the same glimmer of amusement they'd held when I'd slithered down the hill into Gypsy Hollow.

"Well, isn't this nice?" he said. "My old mates Lori and Kit, come to welcome me home." He rested the stick against the arm of the chair and got to his feet. "I'll fetch the stools and a couple of cups. We'll make a party of it."

October's chill had returned at sundown, so it felt good to sit near the fire and sip the hot, sweet tea Leo brought for us from the motor home. When he'd used the word "party," I'd remembered the police report and wondered what kind of drinks he'd serve. I'd been faintly relieved to discover that he'd filled our cups with nothing stronger than tea, cream, and sugar. The same notion must have crossed Kit's mind, because I saw him sniff his tea surreptitiously before sampling it.

"Drink up," said Leo. "There's plenty more where that came from." He stirred the fire with the long stick, then leaned back in his chair and surveyed us amiably. "What've you two been up to while I've been away?"

"We've been worrying about you," I replied frankly. "I don't mean to pry into your private business, Leo, but where in the heck have you been for the past two days?"

Leo slapped his thigh and roared with laughter. "A funny way you have of minding your own business, Lori."

"Lori wasn't the only one who was worried," Kit chimed in loyally. "We were both afraid that you might have had an accident. The weather was pretty rough for cycling."

"True enough," Leo acknowledged agreeably. "It was pretty rough for hunkering down in an old tin can, too. The caravan can get a bit gloomy on wet days, so I cycled to the Oxford Road, hitched a lift into town, and spent the weekend in more cheerful surroundings." He jutted his chin toward the bicycle. "Shredded a tire on the way back, though, so I won't be cycling again anytime soon."

I asked myself what kind of accommodation Leo could possibly afford in a pricey place like Oxford and thought immediately of St. Benedict's, a homeless shelter in which Kit had stayed when he'd been down on his luck. I'd volunteered to work at St. Benedict's often enough to know that the place was clean, warm, and safe, but I wouldn't have described it as cheerful. Then again, I admitted silently, I wasn't Leo. St. Benedict's might have seemed like a five-star hotel to him, compared to the "tin can" he'd driven to Gypsy Hollow.

"Sorry if I gave you a fright," he added. "An old bush ranger like me is used to coming and going as he pleases. It never dawned on me that you might miss me — but I'm touched that you did."

"You should have come to the manor house," said Kit. "The Harrises have lots of spare rooms."

"Kind of you, Kit," said Leo, "but your bosses wouldn't want a stranger pottering round their house."

"I don't think you *are* a stranger to Anscombe Manor," Kit said slowly. "I think you stayed there a long time ago, in your younger days, when you got to know Gypsy Hollow and High Point and the Upper

Deeping Fair."

Leo bent forward to stir the fire again. "Been checking up on me, Kit?"

"Not intentionally," Kit replied. "I was looking through some old newspapers when I ran across the name Leo Sutherland."

"You found the police report," Leo said quietly, still toying with the fire.

"Yes," said Kit.

A vagrant raindrop slid from an overhanging branch onto the awning. Ham, Nell's Labrador retriever, barked once in the distance, then fell silent. Leo rested his elbows on his knees and clasped the stick loosely in his hands, but his gaze never left the fire.

"It was the only time my name got into the paper," he said. "Your father buried all the other stories. He had a lot of clout in the county. Well, he was a war hero with a knighthood to his name, and he had a bucket of cash to throw around. It stands to reason that people did what he told them to do. And he told them straight out to bury every stupid, careless thing I did. He didn't want the world to know that his brother-in-law was nothing but trouble."

Kit inhaled sharply. "Then you're my —"

"I knew it the minute I laid eyes on you," Leo broke in, still talking to the fire. "You've got Amy's mouth, her eyes. She called you Kit straight off, said it was less of a mouthful than Christopher. She adored you, Kit, and she was fairly fond of me, though I don't know why. No brother ever gave his sister more hell than I did. Yes, Kit." Leo pursed his lip and nodded. "Your mother was my sister. I'm sorry to say it, but I'm your uncle."

"I'm not sorry," Kit said softly.

"You will be," Leo said with a bitter smile. "I wasn't a very nice young man, you see. I fell in with a bad crowd when I was about sixteen. By seventeen I was a swaggering punk, the sort that breaks windows and drinks too much and slags off coppers just for the fun of it. Mum and Dad had washed their hands of me by the time I was eighteen, but Amy didn't believe I was beyond redemption. She thought a change of scene would straighten me out." Leo gave a grunt of mirthless laughter.

"Is that when she invited you to Anscombe Manor?" Kit asked.

"Amy and I were like night and day," Leo went on, ignoring Kit's question. "She was a good-hearted, hopeful sort of girl. She truly believed that she could help me turn my life around. She had me move into the manor three months after she married Sir

Miles. I kept my nose clean for a few weeks, stayed away from the boozer and minded my manners, but I'd learned too many bad habits to shake them all at once. One night I got into a scrap with a local yobbo, and it found its way into the dear old *Upper Deeping Despatch.* Sir Miles was ready to throw me out on my ear, but Amy talked him into giving me another chance, and another, and another. . . ." Leo took a deep breath and let it out slowly. "And then I met Charlotte."

"Charlotte DuCaral?" I said.

"Amy's best mate," said Leo in a nostalgic, faraway voice. "She was only seventeen when I met her, two years younger than me. She had white-blond hair and soft gray eyes and the sweetest way about her. She was the kind of girl you don't want to disappoint, you know?"

"I know," said Kit.

Leo gave Kit a searching glance, then turned his gaze to the fire again. "She'd led such a sheltered life, and mine had been so wild, that no one could believe it when we fell head over heels for each other. Charlotte woke something up in me." He shrugged. "I can't explain it, but it made me want to be a better man. I stayed away from the boozer for a whole year. I started thinking with my brain instead of my fists. I turned over a new leaf, just to make her proud of me."

"You were transformed by love," I said softly.

"I was," Leo agreed, "but Charlotte's parents didn't buy it. Looking back, I can't really blame them. I'd made a name for myself, and it wasn't a good one. In their eyes I was a snot-nosed young hooligan who was bound to go from bad to worse. They didn't like it one bit when they found out that their precious daughter was in love with the likes of me."

"They might not have liked it," I said, "but what could they do about it?"

"What do you think they did?" Leo stabbed the stick into the flames. "They told us we couldn't see each other anymore. They banned me from the grounds. They told Sir Miles that if I set a toe on their property, they'd have me arrested, and they'd see to it that the story wasn't hushed up this time."

"Did my mother know that you'd fallen in love with Charlotte?" Kit asked.

"Of course she did," said Leo. "She was Charlotte's best mate, wasn't she? And she was on our side. She acted as our go-between when Charlotte and I came up with

314

a plan to run away together. We'd elope at midnight and be married before her parents knew she was gone. Only marriage would do, for a girl like Charlotte."

I gazed into the darkness beyond the fire and imagined the young Charlotte DuCaral making her escape. I saw her packing a small bag, letting herself out the kitchen door, making her way through the shrubbery and into the woods to the appointed meeting place, where she waited until dawn, when her heart told her that Leo had failed her.

"When the big night came, I lost my nerve," said Leo. "I tried to get it back with a few shots of whiskey, then a few more. It was past midnight by the time I staggered out of Anscombe Manor, nearly dawn when I stumbled down the hill, sucking on a flask to keep my courage up. And who should I run into at the bottom of the hill? Charlotte's father. He had a shotgun, and he waved it in my face. Called me all sorts of names. I lost my temper, grabbed the gun, and I . . . I killed him."

"No!" I exclaimed, sitting bolt upright. "It wasn't *you.* Charlotte's *brother* attacked Maurice."

Leo looked as confused as I felt. "Charlotte's brother was setting up a children's clinic in Africa on the night I shot Maurice. He wasn't even on the same continent."

"Does Charlotte have another brother?" I asked.

"No, just the one, and he died in a plane crash two years later," said Leo, glancing at Kit.

"What about sisters?" I inquired hopefully.

"No sisters. Just one older brother." Leo raised his open palms and asked, with a touch of exasperation, "Why are we talking about brothers and sisters when I've just confessed to murder?"

"Sorry," I said, blushing, and motioned for him to continue. "Carry on."

"Thank you," said Leo, a bit tetchily.

"Lori has a point," said Kit. "You couldn't have killed Maurice DuCaral. He died three years ago."

"I don't know where you're getting your information, Kit," said Leo, "but it's wrong. I was there that night. I know what happened. I didn't mean to kill him, but when the gamekeeper ran up, the shotgun was in my hands and Maurice's body was stretched out in the bracken, covered in blood."

"Are you sure he was dead?" Kit asked.

"I'm sure," said Leo. "I dropped the gun and crawled over to him. He wasn't breathing. He didn't have a pulse. He was dead."

"Hmmm," Kit said ruminatively. "What did you do when you realized that he was dead?"

"I was too shocked to do much of anything," Leo admitted, rubbing the back of his neck. "It was Madeline DuCaral who took charge."

"What was Madeline doing there?" I asked.

"She'd heard the gun go off," said Leo. "She came out to find her husband dead and me with his blood on my hands. I expected her to call the police, or to order the gamekeeper to shoot me, or to shoot me herself, but she just stood there, staring down at Maurice's body. Then she made a deal with me."

"She *what?*" I said, certain I'd misheard him.

"She made a deal with me," Leo repeated. "If I agreed to disappear, she and the gamekeeper would make the shooting look like an accident, and she'd never tell anyone what had really happened. She'd allow me to get away with murder, but only if I promised to leave England and never come back. If I stayed, I'd go to prison."

I stared at him in frank bewilderment. "Why on earth would she let you off the hook? You'd *killed* her *husband.*"

"Yes, and can you imagine what it would do to a girl like Charlotte, to learn that the boy she loved and trusted had murdered her father?" Leo demanded. "Charlotte was a naive eighteen-year-old. She was an innocent. Sure, it'd be hard for her to lose her father, but it'd be a double dose of hell for her if she found out that he'd died by my hand. Mrs. DuCaral didn't give a toss about me. She was trying to protect her daughter."

"So you ran away," said Kit, "for Charlotte's sake."

Leo dismissed the comment with a flick of his hand. "Don't make me out to be a hero, Kit. I ran to save my own skin. I didn't want to spend the rest of my life in prison, and with my reputation the courts would have had no mercy on me. So I ran — straight into that mad old woman, Lizzie Black. She was picking berries here, in Gypsy Hollow, when I came bursting through the trees, all spattered with blood. I was in such a panic that I blurted out, 'I've killed him!' God knows what she thought, but it didn't matter, because no one ever believed a word she said. I didn't see anyone else after that. I just ran flat-out until I reached the manor."

"My mother must have been horrified," said Kit.

"She was," said Leo, "but she was my big sister, and she knew Charlotte better than anyone. She thought it'd kill Charlotte to know the truth, so she cleaned me up, gave me money and the keys to her car, and sent me on my way. I went up to Liverpool, got a job on a cargo ship, and disappeared."

"To Australia," I said.

"I ended up in Australia a year later," said Leo. "I wrote to Amy, to let her know I was all right. She wrote to me from time to time, poste restante in Sydney, because I rarely had a fixed address." He glanced shyly at Kit. "She told me all about you, Kit, sent me a picture of you when you were no bigger than a loaf of bread. When her letters stopped, I made some inquiries and found out that she'd been killed in a car wreck. I couldn't believe it. . . ." He ran a hand through his grizzled hair and sighed. "I'm sorry, Kit. I should have been here for you when you were growing up. But things don't always work out the way they should."

"You're here now," said Kit. "Why did you come back?"

"I wanted to see you," Leo answered simply. "I couldn't go to my grave without seeing Amy's boy."

"I wish you'd told me who you are when we first met," said Kit.

"I wasn't going to tell you at all," Leo confessed shamefacedly. "I knew you'd start asking questions if I played it straight with you, and I was afraid of what you'd think of me when you heard the answers. I killed a man, Kit. I broke a young girl's heart. I ran like a coward because I couldn't take the punishment I deserved. I've tried to become a better man since then, but I'll never truly escape my past. I'll understand it if you want nothing to do with me. And if you want to turn me in —"

"I'm not going to turn you in, Uncle Leo," Kit cut in, as if he found the suggestion utterly ridiculous.

"Uncle Leo," Leo echoed, his voice breaking. "You know how to bring a tear to an old villain's eye."

"I'll bring my fist to your eye if you keep putting yourself down," Kit warned. "I'm not being sentimental, Uncle Leo. I simply don't believe that you killed Maurice Du-Caral."

Leo smiled affectionately at his nephew. "You take after your mother, Kit. You want to think the best of people, even when they —"

"I'll have to prove it to you," Kit interrupted thoughtfully. "And to do that, I'll need time." He stood, tossed the dregs of his tea into a convenient puddle, and carried his cup and his stool back to the motor home. When he returned, he stood before Leo and said sternly, "I don't want you to leave the Anscombe estate until I speak with you again. If we have another storm and you want a hot bath or a hot meal, go to the manor house. I mean it, Uncle Leo. I'll be very upset with you if you disappear."

Leo rose from his chair, looking somewhat bemused. "You're not upset with me for murdering Maurice DuCaral, but you will be upset with me if I take off. Have I got that right?"

"Exactly right." Kit clapped a hand on Leo's shoulder, then enveloped him in a bear hug. "Welcome home, Uncle Leo."

Leo hesitated for a moment before returning the hug, then pushed Kit away, saying gruffly, "Get off home, the both of you. I need my beauty sleep."

I put my cup next to Leo's on the flat stone and followed Kit through the gap in the trees. I glanced over my shoulder before the campfire vanished from sight and saw Leo gazing fixedly at Kit, with an inscrutable expression on his face.

"I hope he's still here when we come back," I murmured when we reached the muddy track.

"He will be," Kit said confidently, and patted his pocket. "I stole the keys to his caravan."

TWENTY

"You sneak!" I exclaimed, both shocked and tickled by Kit's bold act of thievery.

"I had to do something," he said, pulling his flashlight from his pocket and switching it on. "Leo's been running scared for nearly forty years. I can't allow him to run again before I clear his name."

Kit was so absorbed in his thoughts that he was walking at a relatively moderate speed, for which I was profoundly thankful. It was easier to avoid the track's boggy spots when the flashlight's beam wasn't bouncing around quite so much.

"You meant it, then," I said, peering up at him. His finely sculpted profile was silhouetted against the starry sky, but it was too dark to read his expression. "You're really going to prove that Leo didn't kill Maurice DuCaral."

"It shouldn't be too difficult," he said. "While you were confusing the issue with irrelevant questions about Charlotte's non-existent siblings, I was counting up the holes in Leo's story."

"I wasn't confusing the issue," I protested. "I was trying to figure out who Rendor might be."

"Let's set your imaginary monster aside for the moment and concentrate on my very real uncle, shall we?" Kit said brusquely, and went on without waiting for a reply. "We don't live in the Middle Ages, Lori. Madeline DuCaral couldn't have simply bunged Maurice's body into the family mausoleum without notifying the proper authorities — a doctor, the police, a coroner. There would have been an inquest in a shooting death, and the inquest would have been covered by the local newspaper. Yet we didn't find one word in the *Despatch* about a fatal shooting accident at Aldercot Hall."

"Not one word," I agreed meekly. Kit had been so even-tempered all day that his sudden curtness had taken me by surprise. It was like being snapped at by a puppy.

"Apart from that," he continued, "everything we've learned over the past four days contradicts Leo's story. We have it from Henrietta Harcourt as well as Ruth and Louise Pym that Maurice DuCaral was an invalid for nearly forty years and that Charlotte nursed him until his death three years ago. Which means that he was still alive when Leo left him lying in the bracken, all covered in blood. The worst that Leo could have done was injure Maurice. He certainly didn't kill him."

"But, Kit," I ventured hesitantly, "Maurice didn't have a pulse when Leo left him. He wasn't breathing. Unless Lizzie Black has been right all along and Maurice Du-Caral *was* a vampire, so he *could* have been dead one day and alive the next, I'm not sure how you're going to get around the part where he doesn't have a pulse and he's not breathing."

"I'll get around that part when I come to it," Kit declared, his jaw hardening. "My uncle committed petty misdemeanors in his youth — scrawling graffiti, brawling, booz-ing — but he wasn't a hardened criminal. It would have been totally out of character for him to commit murder."

"He was drunk at the time," I reminded Kit.

"Precisely," he said in an oddly elated tone of voice. "He was drunk."

I could almost hear the gears clicking in his brain, so I did nothing more to disrupt his concentration until we reached the Mini, when I said, "I assume you're concocting another cunning plan."

"It's a fairly straightforward plan, actually," he said. "Meet me here at nine o'clock tomorrow morning, and be prepared for a hike. We're going back to Aldercot Hall. I need to speak with Henrietta." He smiled down at me so suddenly and so sweetly that it was as if the sun had risen in the night sky. "You had it right from the start, Lori. Leo *is* a nice man. He and I are going to be great friends." He gave me a quick, strong hug, then spun on his heel and headed for the courtyard and his flat.

I leaned against the Mini, to recover from the smile and the hug, then slid behind the wheel and started the engine. As I drove back to the cottage, I marveled at the powerful pull of family ties. A few short hours ago, Kit would have recoiled in horror from the thought of revisiting Aldercot's kitchen for any reason. Now he was so bent on proving his newfound uncle's innocence that he was willing to place himself within Henrietta Harcourt's astonishingly long reach and risk having his pretty chin chucked yet again.

I'd taken a bullet for my children, but my sacrifice seemed trivial compared to the one Kit was making for Leo. Families, as Kit had so wisely noted, were funny things.

It was half past nine when I walked into the cottage, and everyone, including Stanley, was in bed and asleep. I regretted missing the twins' bedtime, but when I went upstairs to look in on them, I reminded myself that, since the odds of a train filled with chlorine gas derailing next to their school yard were microscopic, there would in all likelihood be many more bedtimes to come.

When I went back downstairs, I found a message from Annelise lying on the kitchen table, conveying the wonderful news that Bill would be home on Thursday, barring further cat fights within the Shuttleworth clan. I crumpled the message and tossed it into the wastebasket, then went to the study to fill Aunt Dimity in on the day's events. After giving Reginald's ears an affectionate twiddle, I lit a fire in the hearth and sat in the tall leather armchair with the blue journal in my lap.

Aunt Dimity's handwriting curled across the page as soon as I opened the journal.

Did you and Kit have any luck in Upper Deeping?

"Yes," I said, "but it wasn't the luck we expected. We didn't discover anything new about the DuCarals, but we found out who Leo is."

*The Leo who's camping in Gypsy Hollow?
The cad who toyed with Charlotte DuCaral's
affections?*

"Yes and no," I said. "Leo is camping in
Gypsy Hollow, but he never meant to toy
with Charlotte's affections. You're not going
to believe this, Dimity, but it turns out that
Leo is Kit's uncle. Kit's mother was Leo's
older sister, and she invited Leo to stay at
Anscombe Manor forty years ago. . . ."

I launched into a dramatic recapitulation
of Leo's story, telling Dimity of his misspent
youth, his transformative love for Charlotte,
her parents' staunch opposition to the
match, and the midnight elopement that
had ended in heartbreak and tragedy. When
I finished, several minutes seemed to pass
before Aunt Dimity responded.

Well? What are you going to do about it?

"What am I going to do about what?" I
asked.

*What are you going to do to exonerate Leo
Sutherland?*

"I'm not sure," I said, "but Kit has a plan.
We're returning to Aldercot tomorrow
morning to talk with Charlotte's cook, Henrietta Harcourt. I don't know what Kit
hopes to accomplish, but he seems to think
—" I broke off as Aunt Dimity's fine copperplate sped across the page.

You're being obtuse, Lori. Kit is trying to find out if Leo killed Maurice DuCaral intentionally, accidentally, or at all. Since there's a great deal of difference between murder, manslaughter, and grievous bodily harm, I think you'll agree that it's important to establish the facts. Leo was drunk at the time of the shooting, so his account of the affair is unreliable. Maurice and Madeline DuCaral are dead, so Kit can't turn to them for the truth. There is, however, one other person who was there that night and who might be willing to tell Kit what really happened.

"But Henrietta's only been at Aldercot Hall for a year or so," I said. "She won't be able to —"

Not Henrietta, my dear dunderhead! The gamekeeper!

"Oh. *Oh.*" My eyebrows shot up as the penny finally dropped. "I'd forgotten about the gamekeeper. He was on the scene before Madeline showed up. He may have witnessed the whole encounter between Leo and Maurice."

And Kit wants to speak with Henrietta because . . . ?

"Because he wants to ask her if the gamekeeper is still alive," I said, spurred on by Aunt Dimity's prompting. "If he is, we'll track him down and find out everything he knows about what happened on the night Maurice DuCaral was shot."

Bravo. Honestly, Lori, I thought you'd never cotton on. You're not usually so slow on the uptake, my dear. In truth, you're far more likely to jump over the facts in order to reach your conclusions more rapidly, but you seem rather distracted this evening. Is something bothering you?

"As a matter of fact, something *is* bothering me," I admitted. "Don't get me wrong, Dimity. I want to do right by Leo. But in all the excitement about proving his innocence, we seem to have forgotten about Rendor."

Oh, dear, so we have. Were you able to learn anything about him in Upper Deeping?

"Nothing," I said gloomily. "But I found out from Leo that Charlotte had only one sibling, an older brother, who was setting up a children's clinic in Africa on the night Maurice was shot and who died two years later in a plane crash. He was setting up a *children's clinic,* Dimity. Why would the Pyms describe him as a man with shameful desires that had to be concealed? He sounds more like a saint to me." I frowned unhappily. "Leo isn't Rendor. Charlotte's brother isn't Rendor. There aren't any guests at Aldercot Hall who could be Rendor. My theories are being knocked down faster than pins in a bowling alley."

I suppose we must ask ourselves once again: Who is Rendor?

"I'd begin to suspect Bellamy the butler if he weren't so old," I said. "But he'd never make it from Aldercot Hall to the apple tree and back again without blowing a heart valve. And Henrietta's the exact opposite of thin and pale. So who did I hear in the attic?"

Perhaps you heard a "what" rather than a "who," my dear.

"What do you mean?" I asked.

I mean that you may have heard bats. Not a vampire in bat form, but plain, ordinary, common or garden-variety bats. Their squeaks might easily be mistaken for a creaking floorboard.

"I had my *ear* pressed to a door covered in *bats?*" My toes curled in disgust. *"Gross."*

There's nothing remotely gross about bats, Lori, and I won't have you maligning them. Bats are exceptionally helpful little creatures. If it weren't for bats, the world would be overrun by midges and mosquitoes.

"I'll take your word for it, Dimity," I said, shuddering. "But even if I did hear bats in Charlotte's attic, it doesn't explain who Will and Rob saw on Emma's Hill or who left the boot prints and the scrap of crimson silk there."

No, I'm afraid it doesn't. But take heart. Gamekeepers are trained observers. They know the lie of the land. They know what belongs on their property and what doesn't. I imagine they see many strange things during the course of their careers.

"The DuCarals' old gamekeeper might know who Rendor is," I said, brightening. "Gosh, Dimity, I hope he's still alive."

As do I. And since it sounds as though you have yet another active, outdoor day ahead of you, I suggest that you get some sleep.

I didn't need coaxing. I said good night to Aunt Dimity and to Reginald, put the blue journal back on its shelf, turned out the lights, and went upstairs to bed.

As I nestled my head into my pillow, I tried to focus my mind on how happy Leo would be when Kit proved that he wasn't a murderer, or on how happy I would be when the gamekeeper revealed Rendor's true identity, or on how happy we all would be when Bill came home on Thursday, but the last thought that floated across my consciousness was . . . *Bats? Yecch!*

TWENTY-ONE

The clear skies and balmy breezes of St. Luke's Little Summer returned the following day. The morning air was so gloriously mild that I dressed Will and Rob in their lightweight summer riding gear before sending them off with Annelise to Anscombe Manor, though I took the precaution of stowing sweaters and jackets in the Range Rover, in case they were needed later on.

I shed one layer from my usual hiking attire, but I tucked the fleece pullover into my day pack, along with my rain jacket, because I'd lived in England long enough to know that St. Luke's Little Summer could become St. Frosty's Big Winter in the blink of an eye.

Nell was in the large riding ring when I pulled into Anscombe Manor's parking area. She was dressed more formally than she had been when I'd last seen her, in a midnight-blue velvet riding coat, spotless white breeches, and highly polished black riding boots, presumably because she was demonstrating dressage techniques to a half dozen children who, like the twins, took riding lessons before school hours.

The children sat on the fence, silent and motionless, absorbed in the demonstration, while Nell and her chestnut mare, Rosie, performed the intricate ballet, flowing effortlessly from one difficult movement to the next. Although Nell's gleaming crown of golden curls was hidden beneath her riding helmet, she rode regally nonetheless, with perfect posture, perfect balance, and in perfect harmony with her horse.

The children weren't the only ones observing Nell's performance. The new stable hands had positioned themselves at various vantage points around the stables, and though they each held a shovel, a broom, or a pitchfork, they weren't actually doing any work. I couldn't blame them. I doubted that any male with a pulse would look away when Nell Harris was in the ring.

Kit, of course, was the exception. He must have known what Nell was doing, but he'd elected to wait for me in the courtyard, which afforded him no view of the riding ring whatsoever. I wasn't sure whether it was Nell he wanted to avoid seeing or the drooling young stable hands, but I suspected it was a little of both.

He, too, had dressed for the fine weather, in a faded denim shirt and blue jeans, but I was sure that he'd also put a sweater and his rain jacket in his day pack. Ham, Nell's black Labrador retriever, lay in a pool of sunlight near the wooden bench. The old dog thumped his tail when he saw me, but he was clearly much too comfortable to rise and greet me, so I squatted beside him to scratch his graying ears and say hello.

"Ready?" Kit said, glancing at his watch.

"I'm ready," I said, straightening. "Lead on."

I'd almost forgotten what it was like to climb Emma's Hill on a nice day. I was so pleased that it wasn't raining, blowing, hailing, or snowing on us that I didn't complain about the rapid pace Kit set. He moved like a man possessed. His violet eyes were burning with a fire I'd never seen in them before, and his mouth was set in a thin, determined line. He didn't waste time explaining the day's mission to me or responding to my rapturous comments on the weather, and he took the shortest route to Aldercot Hall.

The shortest route also happened to be the one least visible from Charlotte DuCaral's music room. After coming down Emma's Hill, we skirted the southern edge of the dense grove of trees, passed behind the stately yews that bordered the family cemetery, and approached the kitchen stairs screened by a row of plane trees.

Henrietta's florid face lit up when she saw Kit standing on her doorstep. She opened her mouth to say heaven-knows-what, but Kit cut her off before a single outrageous syllable left her lips.

"You're not going to play silly buggers with me today, Henrietta," he said in a clipped, no-nonsense tone of voice. "I'm going to ask questions, and you're going to answer them. Understood?"

Henrietta's green eyes narrowed, and I braced myself to catch Kit's head, because I was sure she was going to knock it off his neck. Instead she folded her mighty arms across her bosom and regarded him levelly.

"Right, then, ducky," she said. "What do you want to know?"

"A gamekeeper once worked for Maurice and Madeline DuCaral," said Kit. "Is he still alive?"

" 'Course he is," said Henrietta. "His name is Rory Tanner, and he lives not a mile away, in the cottage the DuCarals gave him when he retired."

"Where is Mr. Tanner's cottage?" Kit asked.

"In the woods north of here," she said, hitching a thumb over her shoulder to indicate the direction. "If you follow the lane beyond the gates, you'll see the path on your right. It's got bracken growing all along it, and bluebells in the spring."

"If we go to Mr. Tanner's cottage now," said Kit, "will he be there?"

"Oh, yes," said Henrietta. "Old Rory doesn't get out much anymore. Are you going to see him after you finish up with me?"

"Yes," said Kit.

"In that case" — Henrietta held up a hand — "wait here. I've got something for you."

As soon as she turned her back on us and went into the kitchen, Kit began to drum his fingers on his leg and glance anxiously over his shoulder, like a man about to miss his boarding call.

"What's your hurry?" I murmured. "Leo's not going anywhere. You made sure of that when you stole his keys."

"I don't know what it is, Lori," he said, "but something's telling me that we *have* to hurry."

Henrietta returned in less than ten minutes, carrying two zippered, insulated bags the size of shopping bags, which she handed to Kit.

"Rory's meals," she explained. "I tucked in a little something for the two of you as well."

"Thank you, Henrietta," Kit threw over his shoulder as he dashed up the kitchen stairs.

"Thanks," I added, and ran up the stairs after Kit.

We raced up the drive, through the gates, and down the lane, until we spotted the bracken-lined path Henrietta had described. We followed it through the grove of trees until we came to a clearing.

The little house that stood in the clearing was a classic slate-roofed, stone-walled cottage, similar to many others I'd seen lining the winding lanes in our part of the Cotswolds. The clearing, on the other hand, was unique. It was littered with bird feeders, birdbaths, birdhouses, nesting hutches, small woodpiles, bales of hay, and chipped bowls containing grains, nuts, raw vegetables, and dried fruit. It was also alive with small furry creatures — squirrels, rabbits, shrews, mice — and a mixed flock of twittering birds. The animals scattered when Kit and I entered the clearing, but I could feel hundreds of tiny eyes watching us as we crossed to the cottage's front door.

Since Kit's hands were full, I knocked on the door and called out, "Mr. Tanner?"

"That you, Henrietta?" a quavering voice called back.

"No, sir," I replied, speaking more loudly, in case the old man was hard of hearing. "But we've brought the meals Henrietta prepared for you."

"Come in," the voice called. "Door's not locked."

Kit and I entered a corridor that divided the cottage in two. I was about to call out again for guidance when the sound of a hacking cough led us through a closed door on our right and into a room that had once served as a front parlor.

It was now a sickroom. Its comfortable furnishings had been rearranged to make space for a hospital bed. The bed sat next to an open window overlooking the south end of the clearing, and although it had no side rails or call buttons attached to it, its upper half had been raised to allow the man lying in it to look out the window. I imagined that the day's warmth meant far more to him than it did to me.

The deep windowsill at his elbow held a pair of binoculars, several notebooks, and a coronation mug bristling with pens and pencils, but a bedside table was cluttered with pill bottles, inhalers, tissue boxes, and dirty dishes. A wastebasket beneath the table was overflowing with used tissues.

The bed's occupant was so thin that his legs barely made a bump in the smooth bedclothes. Although the electric fire in the hearth was pumping out a generous amount of heat, he was wearing a navy-blue stocking cap, fingerless gloves, and a bulky, navy-blue woolen sweater that hung loosely on his diminished frame. He had a prominent beak of a nose and a puckered mouth that suggested the absence of teeth, and his eyes were clouded with fatigue and pain. Kit's impulse to get to the gamekeeper's cottage quickly had, I realized, been a canny one. It didn't look — or sound — as though the old man in the bed had much longer to live.

The hacking cough that racked the man's frail body made me wince. I pulled out my cell phone to call for an ambulance, but when the man saw what I was doing, he signaled to me to put the phone away.

"No doctors," he croaked irritably, when he could finally speak. "No hospitals. It's too late for all of that anyway, and I'd sooner die here than on a ward."

"Are you Rory Tanner?" Kit asked.

"No. I'm Winston Churchill." The old

man rolled his rheumy eyes. "Well, *of course* I'm Rory Tanner. Who *else* would be living in Rory Tanner's cottage? And why are you two standing there like a pair of daft badgers? The room's a tip, and I'm hungry."

Kit and I took the heavily dropped hint and got busy. While Kit made tea and dished up a bowl of Henrietta's nourishing gruel in the surprisingly well-appointed kitchen, I washed the dirty dishes, emptied the wastebasket into a garbage bag I found in a kitchen drawer, and tidied the bedside table.

Kit helped himself to a handful of the jammy biscuits Henrietta had packed, but the mere sight of the bleeding cookies still gave me the willies, so I abstained. We were both fascinated to discover that one of the insulated shopping bags held nothing but airtight containers filled with grains, nuts, raw vegetables, dried fruit, and birdseed. Henrietta, it seemed, had found an outlet for her banqueting skills.

I went outside to top up the bowls and the bird feeders, then returned to the parlor to find Kit spoon-feeding Mr. Tanner. The old man's color was a bit better after he'd had some gruel and tea, and his coughing fits came less often after he'd used one of his inhalers. Kit evidently thought the time was ripe to do what he'd come to do, because he pulled two comfortable walnut armchairs to the side of the bed and motioned for me to sit in one while he sat in the other.

"Mr. Tanner," Kit began.

"Rory," the old man corrected. "And what do they call you when you're at home, sonny?"

"My name is Christopher Anscombe-Smith," Kit said. "Smith was added to our name when my father remarried. My father was Sir Miles Anscombe, and his first wife — my mother — was a girl named Amy Sutherland. Leo Sutherland is my uncle."

Rory's rasping breaths seemed to stop. He stretched his neck out like a tortoise, to study Kit's features at close range, then closed his eyes and let his head fall back on his pillow. When he spoke again, his voice had lost its flippant edge.

"I'm glad you've come," he said, sounding old and infinitely tired. "I didn't want the truth to die with me."

"What truth is that, Rory?" Kit asked gently.

Rory opened his eyes and gazed up at the ceiling. "Maurice never did know one end of a gun from the other. Oh, he paid a fortune for a pair of Purdeys, but he never took the trouble to learn how to use them properly. Trembled in my boots every time I took him out for a shoot. Safest place to be was right next to the bird he was aiming at."

A snicker escaped me before I could stop it. Kit gave me a quelling look, but Rory rolled his head toward me and smiled.

"I wanted to laugh at him sometimes," he admitted. "But the man paid me an honest wage and let me manage the grounds as I saw fit, so I treated him with respect. Besides, I felt sorry for the poor sod. He was neither fish nor fowl, you see. He couldn't go back where he came from and didn't belong where he was. He reckoned his kids would figure it out, though. He pinned all his hopes on his kids."

"It must have been hard for him when he realized that his daughter had fallen in love with someone like Leo," said Kit.

"It damn near killed him," Rory acknowledged. "His princess, in love with a scumbag like Leo?" The rheumy eyes swiveled toward Kit. "Sorry, son, but your uncle was a real piece of work in those days."

"You don't have to apologize," said Kit. "Just keep telling me the truth. How did Maurice find out about the elopement?"

"Miss Charlotte's maid grassed on her,"

said Rory. "Miss Charlotte had already sneaked out of the house, so Maurice grabbed a shotgun and went charging off to find her and stop the whole thing. I went after him, to make sure he didn't blow his own daughter to pieces."

Rory paused to catch his breath, and Kit helped him to take another sip of tea. I looked out the open window and noticed that a pair of rabbits had returned to the bowl with the raw vegetables, and small birds were once again clustering around the feeders.

"Maurice couldn't find his way through a forest if all the trees in it were chopped down," Rory said, "so he blundered around in circles half the night. I caught up with him around dawn, near the mouth of the High Point trail. I'd almost convinced him to hand the gun over to me when Leo showed up, staggering down the hill, drunk as a lord."

I could feel tension radiating from Kit. He sat as if he were carved from stone, gripping the arms of his chair as though his uncle's life depended on what the old gamekeeper said next.

"The two of them got into a slanging match," Rory went on, "and Maurice started waving the damned shotgun around. When

Leo passed out, on account of the drink, Maurice aimed the gun right at the boy's head." Rory frowned disapprovingly. "Not sporting. Not the sort of thing a gentleman would do. Be a good lad and hand me the blue whiffer, will you, Kit?"

Kit passed the inhaler to him. Rory took another hit off it, then passed it back and tucked his hands under the blankets.

"I tried to keep Maurice from killing the lad in cold blood," he said, "and in the tussle he managed to shoot himself in the foot. There was blood everywhere, and Maurice never could stand the sight of blood, so *he* passed out, and I was left with a right old mess on my hands."

Kit's grip relaxed, and he released a long-pent breath. "That was when Madeline Du-Caral came along and straightened out the mess."

"She did." Rory closed his eyes again, and his thin chest seemed to wilt. "I'm ashamed to say it, son, but I helped her."

"I'll take it from here," said Kit, patting the old man's arm. "You stop me when I go wrong."

Rory nodded weakly.

"Madeline staged Maurice's death in order to get rid of Leo once and for all," said Kit. "First she planted the shotgun on

Leo and sprinkled her husband's blood on him. When Leo came round, she convinced him that he'd killed Maurice and scared him into leaving England for good. Then she whisked Maurice off to hospital, where they patched him up and sent him home. There was no need to involve the police, because the shooting had been a mishap, not a crime."

"The wound never did heal right," said Rory. "Which was a blessing, in my opinion, because it forced Maurice to give up shooting."

"Hold on," I said. "Back up a little, will you? How did Madeline convince Leo that Maurice was dead?"

"The power of suggestion," Kit replied, looking to Rory for confirmation.

"You're dead right, if you'll pardon the expression," said Rory.

Kit turned to me. "Picture the scene in your mind, Lori. Leo was so soused that he could have lost a leg and never noticed. When he came to, he was spattered with Maurice's blood and scared out of his wits. The last thing he remembered was grabbing at the shotgun in a fit of drunken rage. His temper had gotten him into trouble so often that he was primed to believe it had gotten him into trouble again."

"Only much worse trouble this time," Rory put in. "The kind of trouble that would've got him hanged in the old days."

"Madeline used the power of suggestion to manipulate Leo," said Kit. "She *told* him that Maurice's heart had stopped beating, that he'd stopped breathing. And Leo was so muddled that he believed it. Madeline was like a magician, Lori. She made Leo believe what she wanted him to believe."

"You've got it in one," said Rory.

"The only thing I don't get," said Kit, turning back to the old man, "is why you went along with it. Maurice and Madeline were trying to keep their daughter from marrying a good-for-nothing young punk. They may have gone about it in the wrong way, but at least they were trying to protect their child. What's your excuse, Rory?"

"I wanted the best for Charlotte, too," Rory said. Then he lowered his eyes and gave a short, defeated sigh. "But I also knew it would set me up for life. The DuCarals paid top dollar for my cooperation. When I retired, they gave me a pension and a done-up cottage — all mod cons. What do you think I'd have got if I hadn't gone along with them?"

"A clear conscience," said Kit.

"It's easy for you to say," Rory mumbled

defensively. "But we don't all have the safety net of being Sir Miles Anscombe's son."

Kit flinched and turned away from the bed, but when he looked back at Rory, something inside him seemed to snap. His nostrils flared, and a flame seemed to leap in his eyes.

"Being Sir Miles Anscombe's son isn't a safety net," he said, in a low, dangerous voice. "It's a handicap. It's a fatal disease."

Alarmed, I put a restraining hand on Kit's arm, but he shrugged it off angrily and went on, the words pouring out in a torrent, like a flood bursting from a dam.

"I would give *anything* to die as you're dying, Rory," he said, "with my mind intact, my faculties unimpaired. But I won't get the chance, because I'm my father's son. He hanged himself — did you know? — but he'd lost his mind long before that. He was insane, just as his grandfather was, and his great-grandfather, and so on and so forth, for six generations. I know, I've checked. The Anscombe men don't show it at first — that's why they've been able to breed — but it comes to them all in the end. So don't talk to me about *safety nets,* Rory Tanner, because there's *nothing* between me and the ground. My fall is *inevitable.*"

I stared at Kit openmouthed, shaken by a

lightning bolt of blinding revelation. His refusal to marry Nell, to marry anyone, suddenly made a certain sort of twisted sense. He believed he'd inherited madness from his father's side of the family, and he didn't want to risk passing it on to yet another generation. He was the last of the Anscombe men. He wanted the family curse to end with him.

"But, Kit," I said, in a small voice, "you're not crazy."

"I behaved very oddly for four long years," he said, still breathing hard and fixing his furious gaze on the floor. "I lived on the streets. I checked myself into an asylum."

"The asylum was a hellhole," I countered. "The only reason you went there was to shut it down. And you succeeded."

"Do I need to remind you of how we met, Lori?" Kit asked. "You found me lying in your driveway, half dead from self-imposed starvation."

"You were overwhelmed with grief for your father," I said, more strongly. "You *weren't* crazy."

"Statistics are against you," he retorted bitterly, still refusing to meet my gaze. "As you pointed out to me just the other day, mental illness often runs in families. It's cut rather a large swath through mine. I have no reason to believe that it will miss me."

To my dismay and immense irritation, our pivotal argument was interrupted by a knock on the parlor door. Leave it to Henrietta, I thought, to choose the worst possible moment to deliver a fruit basket or a roast suckling pig.

"I'll get it," I muttered, and hustled across the room.

I flung the door open impatiently, fell back a step, felt horror rise like bile in my throat, and let loose a scream of pure, unmitigated terror.

Rendor, the Destroyer of Souls, swooped into the room.

TWENTY-TWO

"It's all right, Lori," Kit soothed. "Calm down, relax, *breathe.* . . ."

"What bee got up *her* bum?" Rory grumbled.

"Hush, Rory," scolded a third voice. "Can't you see that the poor girl's upset? I'm so sorry, dear. I didn't mean to startle you. It's this ridiculous ointment. It's enough to give anyone a fright."

I was back in my chair and trembling like a leaf. I wasn't sure how I'd gotten there, because I had no clear memory of what had happened after I'd screamed.

Kit was kneeling before me, holding my hand and peering up at me solicitously, but the corners of his mouth were twitching in an all-too-familiar way.

"What's so *funny?*" I snapped, glaring at him.

"Nothing," he said quickly. "You've been very stressed lately, with the twins going off to school for the first time, and you haven't been getting much sleep since your husband's been away, and you and I had been having a heated discussion, so no one blames you for reacting as you did when you saw *Charlotte.*"

"Charlotte?" I repeated as Kit's cue sailed over my head. "But Charlotte can't be Ren—"

"Can't be *angry* with you for opening the door and screaming in her face," Kit filled in hastily. "And she's not. Are you, Charlotte?"

"Certainly not," said someone standing behind me. "I'd be the last person to criticize anyone's behavior, after the show I put on the last time we met."

I turned slowly in my chair and saw the tall, slender figure of Charlotte DuCaral towering over me in a pair of pointy-toed black leather boots. She'd thrown open her voluminous black cloak to reveal a lining of crimson silk that had a small, neatly mended tear near the hem. She was wearing blood-red lipstick, and she'd covered her face with a gooey white substance that made her look deathly pale.

"Your face," I said shakily. "What's on your face?"

"Zinc oxide," she replied. "Dreadful, I

know, but quite necessary, I assure you. It's difficult to tell now, but I was once a flaxen-haired blonde, and my skin still burns quite easily. On a sunny day like today, I won't leave the house without my cloak and my zinc oxide, but since the ointment bothers you, I'll wipe it off. I can always reapply it before I leave — which, by the way, won't be for a while. I have a few things to say to you, Rory."

As she turned to leave the parlor, the cloak billowed around her, and I saw superimposed upon it a vivid mental image of an afghan swirling around Rob as he twirled in a half circle in my living room.

"He *swooped*," I said under my breath.

"What's that?" said Kit, getting to his feet.

"Nothing." I faced the bed again and rested my chin on my hand.

"You didn't ought to scream like that," said Rory. "You scared the birds."

"I'm sorry," I said, staring blankly into the middle distance. I had no idea why Charlotte had been standing beneath the apple tree on Emma's Hill ten days ago, but I also had no doubt that Will and Rob had seen her there. Rendor wasn't a creepy psycho pervert voyeur who was menacing my children. He was a middle-aged woman who sunburned easily and liked to wear red lipstick when she went out. My vampire hunt, which had begun with so much promise, had ended in farce, and Kit would never let me forget it. I felt ten times a fool.

"Charlotte seems quite chipper, don't you think?" Kit said as he carried another chair over to Rory's bedside.

"Does she?" I said. "I didn't notice."

"She's a different woman from the one who played such mournful music in the music room," said Kit. "She looks ten years younger."

"Must be the zinc oxide," I said indifferently.

"I think we could all do with some tea," Kit said, rubbing his palms together vigorously. "I'll be right back."

Rory took up his binoculars and I continued to stare disconsolately at nothing until Kit shoved a cup of tea under my nose and pulled me out of my cheerless reverie. I looked around and noticed for the first time that Charlotte had returned, with a clean face but without her cloak. She was wearing a gray silk blouse with a blue tweed skirt and looked every inch the country matron.

While I'd been contemplating the mortifying depths to which my vivid imagination had dragged me, Kit had set up an informal tea party on the coffee table, using china from Rory's kitchen and the food Henrietta had packed for us. One plate was filled with crustless sandwiches, one held eclairs, lemon tarts, and cream puffs, and still another was piled high with jammy biscuits.

Rory gummed a jammy biscuit happily, but the sight of the raspberry jam on his puckered lips was enough to put me off raspberries for the rest of my life. I helped myself to a watercress sandwich instead and left the repulsive biscuits for the others.

Charlotte refused the cup of tea Kit offered to her, and instead of sitting in the chair he'd drawn up for her, she stood at the foot of Rory's bed. When Kit had resumed his seat and we'd all finished eating, she rested her hands on the foot railing and smiled down at Kit and me.

"I saw you leave Aldercot Hall this morning," she informed us, "and after speaking with Mrs. Harcourt, I learned that you were coming here, to Rory's cottage. I followed you, intending to apologize for my intemperate outburst the other day, but as I approached the front door, a few words drifted through the open window that stopped me in my tracks."

She ducked her head, and a pink flush rose in her fair cheeks.

"I don't eavesdrop, as a rule," she said,

"but I simply couldn't move. I couldn't speak. I couldn't keep myself from listening to the story drifting through the open window." She raised her head and gazed incredulously at the gamekeeper. "Rory, you old fool. Why didn't you tell me the truth long ago?"

"I didn't see what good it'd do," he said. "You'd only think worse of your parents if you knew how we tricked you, and Leo wasn't ever coming back, so I figured, let sleeping dogs —" He broke off as someone knocked on the front door.

Kit and I exchanged perplexed looks.

"Henrietta," I guessed. "With quail's eggs and chilled duck in aspic."

"I'll get it this time," he said, and went to the front door.

I heard only a murmur of muted voices coming from the corridor, but Charlotte must have heard something else, because her hands tightened on the footrail, her lips parted, and her entire face seemed to glow with an inner light as she stared expectantly at the parlor door. When it opened, she drew in a shuddering breath.

"Leo," she said.

I turned my head and saw the expression on Leo's face when he heard her speak his name. He looked like a man uncertain of his welcome.

"Oh, Leo," Charlotte said, and crossed the room to rest her head upon his chest.

Leo put his arms around her, closed his eyes, and laid his weathered cheek against her white hair. He held her to his heart, breathing in her fragrance, and she released a tremulous sigh, as if she'd reached the end of a long journey. In one suspended moment, the past became the present, and the intervening years faded away, as if they'd never been. The decades Charlotte and Leo had lost meant nothing to them, because true love exists outside of time.

Kit stood behind them, beaming like a priest at a wedding.

"Kit," I whispered loudly, waving to get his attention as I stood. "I think maybe you and I should leave."

"I'm not leaving," growled Rory. "It's my house. If those two want to canoodle, they can go somewhere else."

Charlotte and Leo broke apart, and Leo shook a fist at the old gamekeeper.

"You're skating on thin ice, mate," he said. "I wouldn't push it if I were you."

"No one's leaving," Charlotte added. "Leo, may I pour you a cup of tea?"

"That'd be lovely," said Leo.

He didn't have to tell her how he liked his

tea. She remembered.

A short time later, we were seated in a semicircle at Rory's bedside. Kit had already brought Leo up to speed in the corridor, so Leo was explaining to the rest of us why he'd come to the gamekeeper's cottage.

"It was the way Kit looked at me last night, after I told him about the shooting," he said. "He looked at me as if I couldn't possibly have killed a man, not even when I was a young idiot, not even when I was whiskey-drunk. As if I didn't have it in me" — he tapped his chest — "to do something as bad as that. It got me to thinking. And today I decided to look Rory up and talk over old times with him."

"I'm sorry for what I did, Miss Charlotte," Rory said, staring down at his fingerless gloves. "And I'm sorry for what I did to you, too, Leo."

"Never mind," said Charlotte, leaning forward to put a hand on the old man's brow. "It all happened a very long time ago."

"And you did keep Maurice from blowing my brains out," Leo added. "So I guess I can forgive you for everything else."

Charlotte sat back in her chair, laughing. "I've made a pilgrimage every year to look down on Anscombe Manor and curse your name," she said to Leo. "I should have known this year's would be the last."

"Why's that, love?" asked Leo.

"I tore my cloak on the way back," she answered, twinkling up at him. "It was an *omen.*"

The two of them laughed as though she'd told the funniest joke in the world. I supposed they'd do a lot of laughing for a while, if only to release the joy that was bubbling up in them. I, on the other hand, felt like grinding my teeth, because I now knew why Charlotte had been standing beneath the apple tree ten days ago, when Will and Rob had seen her. Her pilgrimage had sent me on my wild-goose chase.

"My poor parents," said Charlotte, her smile fading. "My father's foot never healed properly, and neither he nor my mother ever got over my brother's death. They were so proud of him, you see. They thought he'd have a Nobel Prize before he was thirty. But his clinic was far out in the bush, and the airstrip was quite primitive. The medical-supply plane crashed one day, and my brother was killed. After that my parents withdrew from the world completely. If I hadn't been there to take care of them, they would have forgotten to eat."

I sank lower in my chair. I'd concocted so many lurid stories about Charlotte and her family over the past ten days that I couldn't bear to look her in the eye. She hadn't been a slave to her dastardly parents. She'd been a good daughter, taking care of a heartbroken mother and father who'd lost their only son. And her brother hadn't been a psychopathic pervert. He'd been the kind of man who risked his life to help the poorest of the poor. I was so ashamed of myself that I wanted to crawl under Rory's bed and never come out.

"My dowry isn't what it used to be," Charlotte said, looking up at Leo. "When my brother died, my father stopped keeping track of his investments. I tried to manage them wisely, but the income slowed to a trickle about ten years ago. I had to let most of the staff go and sell the furniture to make ends meet. Luckily, it was worth quite a lot of money. It was fortunate that my mother insisted on hanging blackout drapes throughout the house. Sun-damaged furniture wouldn't have fetched half as much."

"Is that when you boarded up the attic?" Kit asked.

Charlotte turned to him and nodded. "I shut off the central heating and turned off all but the most essential lights as well, to conserve energy and keep the bills low."

"And you sold the fallow deer for the

360

same reason," said Kit.

"She kept the herd as long as she could, because her mother liked them," Rory piped up.

"The deer were among the few things that made my mother smile," Charlotte said. "But after she died, it was a luxury I couldn't afford."

"Could've sold Aldercot," Rory mumbled.

"Yes," Charlotte agreed, "I could have sold the hall. I've been on the verge of doing so many, many times. But my parents and my brother are buried in the cemetery. Who would look after their graves if I left Aldercot?"

"You'll never have to leave Aldercot," said Leo, putting his arm around her, "and you'll never want for luxuries again. We'll buy a herd of elephants, if you like, and we'll fill the place with the finest furnishings to be had. We'll light it up like a Christmas tree and turn the central heating up to sizzle, and we'll hire enough staff so that you'll never have to lift a finger. Whatever you want, you'll have."

Kit's eyebrows rose at the exact same moment as mine. Leo caught our skeptical expressions and chuckled.

"I made a few bob Down Under," he said. "A few million bob, in fact. Your old uncle's filthy, stinking rich, Kit."

"But you live in a . . . a tin can," I managed.

"I like living rough every once in a while," said Leo. "It reminds me of where I started, keeps me from getting too full of myself. But you can have too much of a good thing. When that ruddy storm hit, I hightailed it to Oxford and spent the weekend at the Randolph, being wined and dined by one of my bankers. It made a nice change."

I picked my jaw up from my lap and tried to revise my image of Leo, but it would take more than a few minutes to move him from St. Benedict's Hostel for Transient Men to one of the poshest hotels in all of England. In the meantime Kit carried on tying up loose ends I was too embarrassed to even think about.

"When Lori and I were at Aldercot the other day," Kit said, "we thought we heard someone moving around upstairs. It seemed a bit odd, because Mr. Bellamy and Mrs. Harcourt were downstairs, in the kitchen."

"It must have been Jacqueline," Charlotte said readily. "She's a photographer, you know. She uses the attic as a darkroom, and she locks the door so Bellamy won't walk in on her and ruin whatever she's developing. We leave the lights on in the stairwell so she can find her way there. One must make some accommodations to the staff, and she really is quite talented."

I sank even lower in my chair.

Charlotte smoothed her skirt. "I didn't come here today to talk about myself, though I suppose, under the circumstances, it couldn't be helped — Leo and I have a lot of catching up to do. But I came here to speak of something else. There's something I must tell you, Kit." She took Leo's hand in hers. "Something we both must tell you."

"Are you sure?" asked Leo.

"Yes." Charlotte stroked his hand. "I know that Amy swore us to secrecy, but I can't live with secrets anymore. You and I have paid too high a price for them. We must tell Kit the truth."

Leo kissed her on the side of the head. "I'm with you all the way, love, but Kit" — he turned his bright blue eyes on his nephew — "had better buckle his seat belt, because he's in for a few jolts."

"I'm tougher than I look, Uncle Leo," said Kit.

"You'd better be," said Leo. "Because the truth of it is, your mother made a big mistake when she married Sir Miles. She knew it before they were back from the honeymoon."

"He was quite a bit older than she was," Kit acknowledged.

"Their problems had nothing to do with age," Leo said firmly.

"Sir Miles was a difficult man," Charlotte interjected. "He went into terrible rages, then sank into deep depressions." She hesitated, then said carefully, "He struck your mother on several occasions."

Kit stared at her, aghast.

"It's true," said Leo. "I had to pull him off her a couple of times."

"W-why did she stay?" Kit stammered.

"Your father's troubles weren't his fault," Charlotte explained. "He was ill. Amy hoped that she could help him."

"But my father never raised a hand to me," said Kit. "He showed me nothing but kindness."

"Then remember him that way," Charlotte urged. "But the truth of the matter is that his second wife was able to control him with new and more effective medications, most of the time. She kept you away from him during his bad spells."

"Your mother wasn't alone during the rough times she had with him, Kit," said Leo. "I told you last night, Charlotte was Amy's best mate. Aldercot Hall was a sanctuary for her. She could always find a bit of peace there."

"And one day," said Charlotte, "she found my brother. He was home for a few months from his travels, and he got to know Amy very well."

"They were birds of a feather," said Leo. "Good, kind, gentle souls, both of them. Always trying to help people."

"They were very much alike," Charlotte agreed. "And she was so miserable and he felt so sorry for her that I suppose it was inevitable that they should fall hopelessly in love."

Leo leaned forward in his chair. "The thing is, Kit —"

"No," Charlotte interrupted. "Let me tell him."

"Tell me what?" Kit said tautly.

Charlotte focused her soft gray eyes directly on Kit's face.

"My brother's name was Christopher," she said. "You're his son."

For a moment the only sound I could hear was the slow rasp of Rory's breathing. No one moved. No one spoke. Even the creatures in the clearing had fallen silent. Then a bird chirped, and Kit shifted his gaze to the open window.

"I'm not Sir Miles Anscombe's son?" he said slowly.

"No," said Charlotte. "You are the son of Amy Sutherland and Christopher Du-Caral."

I put a hand to my head as I realized why Ruth and Louise Pym had refused to talk about Christopher's shameful desires. He'd fathered a child by another man's wife — a child, moreover, who'd grown into a man they both knew and loved. They'd thought it would hurt Kit to learn the truth about his parentage. They couldn't have known that the truth would set him free.

Kit stood abruptly and said, "I have to leave."

"Look here, mate," Leo began.

"I have to leave," Kit repeated, more urgently. He snatched his pack from the floor and strode out of the parlor.

"I knew it would be a shock for him," Charlotte said anxiously.

"It just may be the best shock he'll ever have," I said, scrambling to my feet. "Thanks for your hospitality, Rory. I'll visit you again real soon."

"Who's going to clean up this mess?" Rory demanded, waving a hand toward the coffee table.

"Not me," I said, and, grabbing my day pack, I tore after Kit.

I pounded after him all the way to

Anscombe Manor and got to the stable-yard wall just in time to see him drop his pack on the graveled drive, vault over the riding ring's fence, and charge straight through a dressage class Nell was conducting.

He took the reins from her hands and passed them to a student, then lifted her from the saddle and set her lightly on the ground. He removed her helmet, tossed it over his shoulder, and smoothed her golden curls back from her forehead. He ran his fingers along her brow, her cheeks, her jaw-line, her neck, like a blind man reading a face, and then he drew her close, wrapped his arms around her, and bent his head until his lips met hers.

Fireworks exploded, the earth quaked, and fluttering rose petals filled the air. Crowds cheered, peasants danced, and cannons roared in the distance. Church bells rang, angels sang, and a heart-shaped flock of snow-white doves soared above a glimmering rainbow and into the clear blue sky. And he was still kissing her.

I knew I was the only one who could see, hear, and feel the world rejoicing, but I didn't mind. Sometimes it's a good thing to have a vivid imagination.

Epilogue

The wedding took place two weeks before Christmas. St. George's Church was decked out in poinsettias, white roses, and evergreen boughs and lit romantically with beeswax candles. Although many of the pews were unoccupied, those of us who were there made up for the sparse attendance by beaming at the happy couple with extra warmth. It may have taken them thirty-seven years to walk down the aisle, but they got there in the end, and the long journey made the arrival all the sweeter. Charlotte and Leo were the most radiant bride and groom I'd ever seen.

At the reception Leo used every ounce of Aussie charm he'd acquired during his long exile Down Under to persuade me to try a jammy biscuit. It turned out to be so scrumptious that I rewarded him with a sticky smooch on his weathered cheek, then ran down to the kitchen to get the recipe from Henrietta.

It took Leo less than six months to restore Aldercot Hall to its former glory, and though Charlotte wouldn't allow him to waste money on the many outlandish luxuries he wished to heap upon her, she did allow him to refurbish the gardens, reopen the stables, and re-lay the bridle paths connecting Aldercot land to the Anscombe estate. Will and Rob ride there, under Kit's supervision, every chance they get. They haven't spotted any vampires lately, but they're definitely on the lookout for a herd of elephants.

The house and grounds are still tended to by professional cleaning and landscaping crews, but Leo and Charlotte now use companies based in Upper Deeping instead of London, and they patronize local shops as well. Finch's residents stopped thinking of Aldercot as the dark side of the moon when the Sutherlands extended the hand of friendship — as well as their considerable purchasing power — from one valley to the other.

Leo hired three live-in maids in order to make his most ingenious scheme work. Aldercot's corridors have become a lot noisier since students started attending Henrietta's cooking classes, Mr. Bellamy's buttling courses, and Jacqueline's seminars on nature photography. Charlotte jokingly refers to her once-silent home as Aldercot College, but the music she plays is as lively as the young people who dash up and down the hall's well-lit and well-heated marble staircase.

Rory Tanner passed away in February, surrounded by his beloved birds and beasts, but he lived long enough to give Leo a few querulous tips on forest management. His cottage serves as the headquarters for a local conservation group, and Henrietta makes sure they keep the bowls, baths, and feeders properly filled.

Kit has done a lot of quiet thinking since Charlotte told him the truth about both of his fathers — the one who gave him life and the one who raised him — and he's slowly adjusting to his new reality. He speaks of Sir Miles more freely now, without a trace of bitterness, but with sincere and heartfelt pity for a man driven by mental illness to abuse his own wife.

It's helped Kit to have his newly discovered aunt and uncle living just over the hill. He's learned a great deal about Christopher DuCaral from Charlotte and Leo, and so have I. I'll leave it to the experts to decide if insanity can be passed down from father to son, but there's no denying that Kit takes after the good, greathearted man Amy Sutherland loved.

When Kit becomes too introspective, Nell's there to rescue him. Their understanding is so flawless that they seldom need to speak. A look, a touch is all she needs to bring him out of the shadows. I have no doubt that her love will heal every wound he's ever suffered, but I wish she'd hurry up. My heart's set on a June wedding, and I can hardly wait to see what their children will look like.

Nell was beautiful before Kit kissed her, but she's gone so far beyond beautiful since then that I don't know how to describe her. To compare her to Botticelli's Venus now would be like comparing the Grand Canyon to a crack in the sidewalk. Her love for Kit surrounds her like a nimbus, and the coolness that once protected her has been replaced by a warmth that springs straight from her heart. No one can pass her without smiling, because she doesn't hoard her happiness, she radiates it for all the world to see.

Nell's happiness came at a price, however. A few days after the long-awaited kiss took place — in full view of everyone at the stables — Emma had to advertise for an entirely new crew of stable hands. Thankfully, it's worked out for the best. The new boys work ten times harder than the old ones, because they are under no illusions about Nell's availability.

I wish I could be proud of the fact that the new stable hands spend more time watching me than they spend ogling Nell, but the only reason they watch me is that they've never seen anyone ride as badly as I do. Old Toby is as patient as Kit, however, and with their help, and *lots* of practice, I may one day be able to ride from one end of the ring to the other without hearing snorts of laughter in the distance.

Little Matilda Lawrence's nightmares have stopped, as have Clive Pickle's excursions into his brother's bedroom, and I've had an easier time dealing with Miss Archer since she came back from spring break with a blond perm and a tan. The twins liked her old look better, but on parent-teacher days I'd rather face a surfer chick than the bride of Dracula. I've developed a strong aversion to anything that reminds me of Rendor.

On the night before Bill came home from London, I sat down in the study for a chat with Aunt Dimity. I expected to dazzle her and Reginald with a dozen revelations, but most of them fizzled pathetically.

Aunt Dimity had, of course, figured out what was troubling Kit long before I had.

I'm sorry to disappoint you, Lori, but after everything you'd told me, I couldn't help but conclude that Kit thought he was, or would soon be, mad. He declared himself unfit for marriage, described himself as deeply flawed, agreed that mental illness runs in families, and reacted badly when you mentioned the years he'd spent living on the streets. I didn't know that he'd discovered a history of instability in the Anscombe family, but I knew what had happened to Sir Miles. It didn't take much effort to fit the pieces of the puzzle together.

"Did you know that Christopher DuCaral was Kit's father?" I asked.

I had my suspicions. Amy had spent a lot of time at Aldercot Hall, and she'd named the baby Christopher instead of Miles. I'm afraid it comes as no surprise to me to learn that her child was Christopher's son.

"I suppose you already knew about Charlotte and Leo, too," I said.

Everyone knew about Charlotte and Leo. It was the worst-kept secret in the county. I did not, however, know what had really happened on the night of their ill-starred elopement. When Lizzie Black told me that Leo had killed Maurice, I realized that something strange was afoot, because although Leo had vanished — as would a man guilty of murder — Maurice was very much alive. I've waited for nearly forty years to hear the truth, and I'm immensely grateful to you and Kit for unearthing it at last.

"I'm glad it worked out in the end for Leo and Charlotte," I said. "It kept my ridiculous vampire hunt from being entirely pointless."

Your vampire hunt may have been a bit ridiculous, Lori, but it certainly wasn't pointless. It worked exactly as Bill and I hoped it would.

I reread the last line several times before asking Aunt Dimity to explain herself, which she did, in excruciating detail.

Bill didn't believe you for one moment when you told him that you wouldn't worry about Rendor. He knew that as soon as he left for London, you'd go looking for the figure Will and Rob had seen, and he decided to put your vampire hunt to good use.

"He set me up?" I said in disbelief.

He wasn't alone. He enlisted my help, as well as Kit's and Emma's. I did what I could to encourage you — I told you what I know about vampires, I sent you to see Lizzie Black, and every time you started to come to your senses, I inserted a note of doubt that would reawaken your concerns. Emma took over Kit's duties at the stables so that Kit could accompany you. Bill was afraid that you might drive a stake through an innocent bird-watcher, and he counted on Kit to rein you in.

I glanced at Reginald, who seemed to be avoiding my eyes, and realized instantly that he, too, had been part of the cabal.

"You *all* set me up?" I said incredulously.

We had to do something to get through to you. You were taking the twins' temperatures, peering down their throats, and palpating their glands so often that if they weren't fundamentally levelheaded, they would have become hypochondriacs. You were calling the school nurse every morning to inquire about student illnesses and combing the news daily for reports on disasters and plagues. You were so drained by fear and worry that you never left the cottage. You neglected your neighbors, your volunteer activities, and your friends, because you had no energy to spare for them. We had to find a way to snap you out of your malaise.

"And you chose a *vampire hunt?*" I said, outraged.

No, Lori. You chose a vampire hunt. I simply went along with your choice in order to get you out of the cottage and focused on something other than nits and measles. I had no idea your search would lead you to a real mystery, one of far greater importance than the one you'd manufactured. If it hadn't been for your vampire hunt, Charlotte and Leo might never have been reunited.

"But . . . *you set me up!*" I exclaimed indignantly.

Yes, I did. Consider it the bucket of cold water you needed to release you from your hysteria.

I wanted to sulk and be snippy, but I let those impulses go. My darling husband, my two dearest friends, and my most trusted confidante *had* set me up, but they'd done so in order to help me, and their under-handed, conniving, and thoroughly loving plan had worked. I hadn't palpated the twins' glands once since I'd started looking for Rendor, and I was sure that the school nurse had marked her calendar with big smiley-faces to celebrate each day that had gone by without a frantic call from me.

"You know, Dimity," I said, "the vicar told me that I hadn't been myself since the twins started school, but I wouldn't have heard him if you and Bill and Emma and Kit hadn't lured me out of the cottage. So I guess I won't be angry with you. In a month or two, I might even thank you."

Be sure to thank Bill when he comes home.

He loves you very much, Lori.

"I don't know why," I said. "He must think I'm the world's biggest goofball."

He thinks that there hasn't been a dull moment in his life since you came into it. And I can safely say that the same holds true for me.

I hoped Charlotte would never learn that she'd been mistaken for a vampire, but the twins gave the game away the next time they saw her daubed with zinc oxide. Instead of being offended, she was so amused that she and Leo gave the boys a bat box for Christmas, along with memberships in the Bat Conservation Trust and two adorable plush bats with shiny black eyes.

The bat box hangs on a tree down in the meadow, and though I'll never let a bat sleep on my pillow, I've learned to appreciate the helpful little creatures. Sometimes we have to look deeply into a thing to see its beauty. Charlotte looked into the bright blue eyes of a dissolute, swaggering punk and saw the better man he could become. Nell looked into violet eyes shadowed with grief and despair and saw the saint Kit had always been.

When my husband looks deeply into my eyes, he sees a goofball, but according to him she's a passionate, caring goofball whose ridiculous vampire hunt brought four loving souls together and restored a sense of balance to her own.

I'll never buy a copy of *Rendor, the Destroyer of Souls,* but I just might write a thank-you note to the author — after I finish thanking Bill, who knows, better than anyone, how to heal mine.

CHARLOTTE'S
JAMMY BISCUITS

Makes 5 dozen

1 cup shortening
1 cup granulated sugar
1 cup packed brown sugar
2 eggs
1/4 cup sour milk *or* buttermilk
1 teaspoon vanilla
3 1/2 cups all-purpose flour
1 teaspoon baking powder
1 teaspoon baking soda
1 teaspoon salt
1 teaspoon ground nutmeg
Blackberry, raspberry, or strawberry jam

Preheat oven to 350 degrees Fahrenheit.

In a large bowl, cream the shortening and the sugars. Add the eggs, milk, and vanilla; mix till smooth. Stir together the flour, baking powder, baking soda, salt, and nutmeg;

stir into the creamed mixture. Cover and chill.

On a floured surface, roll the dough to an 1/8-inch thickness. Use a cookie cutter to cut the dough into 1 1/2-inch rounds. Place 1 teaspoon of jam each on *half* the rounds; use the remaining rounds to top the jam-topped rounds. Lightly seal the edges with a fork. With a sharp knife, cut shallow criss-cross slits in the tops of the cookies, to allow the steam to vent during baking.

Bake until golden, 10 to 15 minutes.

ABOUT THE AUTHOR

Nancy Atherton is the bestselling author of twelve other Aunt Dimity mysteries. The first book in the series, *Aunt Dimity's Death,* was voted "One of the Century's 100 Favorite Mysteries" by the Independent Mystery Booksellers Association. She lives in Colorado Springs, Colorado.

We hope you have enjoyed this Large Print book. Other Thorndike, Wheeler, and Chivers Press Large Print books are available at your library or directly from the publishers.

For information about current and upcoming titles, please call or write, without obligation, to:

Publisher
Thorndike Press
295 Kennedy Memorial Drive
Waterville, ME 04901
Tel. (800) 223-1244

or visit our Web site at:

http://gale.cengage.com/thorndike

OR

Chivers Large Print
published by BBC Audiobooks Ltd
St James House, The Square
Lower Bristol Road
Bath BA2 3SB
England
Tel. +44(0) 800 136919
email: bbcaudiobooks@bbc.co.uk
www.bbcaudiobooks.co.uk

All our Large Print titles are designed for easy reading, and all our books are made to last.